CW01270659

JOLLY FESTIVE, JEEVES

*Seasonal Stories from
the World of Wodehouse*

Also by P. G. Wodehouse

Jeeves and Wooster

The Inimitable Jeeves
Carry On, Jeeves
Very Good, Jeeves
Thank You, Jeeves
Right Ho, Jeeves
The Code of the Woosters
Joy in the Morning
The Mating Season
Ring for Jeeves
Jeeves and the Feudal Spirit
Jeeves in the Offing
Stiff Upper Lip, Jeeves
Much Obliged, Jeeves
Aunts Aren't Gentlemen

Blandings Castle

Something Fresh
Leave it to Psmith
Summer Lightning
Full Moon
Pigs Have Wings
A Pelican at Blandings
Sunset at Blandings

Uncle Fred

Uncle Fred in the Springtime
Uncle Dynamite
Cocktail Time
Service with a Smile

Monty Bodkin

The Luck of the Bodkins

Standalone novels

The Pothunters
Piccadilly Jim
A Damsel in Distress
The Adventures of Sally
The Small Bachelor
Money for Nothing
Big Money
Hot Water
Laughing Gas
Summer Moonshine
The Girl in Blue

JOLLY FESTIVE, JEEVES

*Seasonal Stories from
the World of Wodehouse*

P. G. Wodehouse

HUTCHINSON
HEINEMANN

3 5 7 9 10 8 6 4

Hutchinson Heinemann
20 Vauxhall Bridge Road
London SW1V 2SA

Hutchinson Heinemann is part of the Penguin Random House group of companies whose addresses can be found at global.penguinrandomhouse.com.

Penguin Random House UK

Copyright © The Trustees of the Wodehouse Estate 2023
Introduction copyright © Cathy Rentzenbrink 2023

The Trustees of the Wodehouse Estate have asserted
P. G. Wodehouse's right under the Copyright, Designs and
Patents Act, 1988, to be identified as the author of this work.

This collection first published by Hutchinson Heinemann in 2023

www.penguin.co.uk

A CIP catalogue record for this book is available from the British Library.

ISBN: 978–1–529–15356–9

Please be aware that the stories in this collection were originally published in the 1910s, 1920s and 1930s and contain language, themes or characterisations which you may find outdated.

Typeset in 12.5 pt/14.75 pt Garamond MT Std by Jouve (UK), Milton Keynes
Printed and bound in Great Britain by Clays Ltd, Elcograf S.p.A.

The authorised representative in the EEA is Penguin Random House Ireland, Morrison Chambers, 32 Nassau Street, Dublin D02 YH68

Penguin Random House is committed to a sustainable future for our business, our readers and our planet. This book is made from Forest Stewardship Council® certified paper.

MIX
Paper | Supporting responsible forestry
FSC® C018179

Contents

Introduction by Cathy Rentzenbrink   vii

December
'Jeeves and the Yule-tide Spirit'
(from *Very Good, Jeeves*)   1

January
'Sundered Hearts'
(from *The Clicking of Cuthbert*)   27

February
'The Passing of Ambrose'
(from *Mr Mulliner Speaking*)   50

March
'The Heel of Achilles'
(from *The Clicking of Cuthbert*)   76

April
'The Story of William'
(from *Meet Mr Mulliner*)   96

May
'Jeeves Exerts the Old Cerebellum'
(from *The Inimitable Jeeves*)   117

June
'Mr Potter Takes a Rest Cure'
(from *Blandings Castle and Elsewhere*)   129

July
'Pig-Hoo-o-o-o-ey'
(from *The World of Blandings*) 157

August
'Lord Emsworth and the Girl Friend'
(from *Blandings Castle and Elsewhere*) 186

September
'The Début of Battling Billson'
(from *Ukridge*) 212

October
'The Metropolitan Touch'
(from *The Inimitable Jeeves*) 243

November
'The Magic Plus Fours'
(from *The Heart of a Goof*) 270

December
'The Knightly Quest of Mervyn'
(from *Mulliner Nights*) 295

Introduction

'As Shakespeare says, if you're going to do a thing you might just as well pop right at it and get it over.' So thinks Bertie Wooster as he fortifies himself with coffee and kippers before confessing to his valet, Jeeves, that they are no longer going to Monte Carlo for Christmas. Bertie anticipates that Jeeves will be disappointed – he has a 'keen sporting streak' and enjoys the tables – but after several days of strained relations and 'frigid detachment', Bertie is exhausted and decides the only thing to do is to put Jeeves in possession of the facts behind the change of plan:

'In the first place, does one get the Yule-tide spirit at a spot like Monte Carlo?'

'Does one desire the Yule-tide spirit, sir?'

'Certainly one does. I am all for it.'

It turns out that Bertie has angled for an invitation from Lady Wickham because of a desire to revenge himself on that 'fiend in human shape', Tuppy Glossop. But that's not all:

'And now, Jeeves, we come to the most important reason why I had to spend Christmas at Skeldings. Jeeves,' I said, diving into the old cup once more for a moment and bringing myself out wreathed in blushes, 'the fact of the matter is, I'm in love.'

The object of Bertie's desire is Bobbie Wickham, the

daughter of the house. Jeeves says she is a charming young lady, agrees that '*espièglerie*' is exactly the right word, but throws doubt on her as a suitable mate: 'In my opinion Miss Wickham lacks seriousness, sir. She is too volatile and frivolous. To qualify as Miss Wickham's husband, a gentleman would need to possess a commanding personality and considerable strength of character.'

Bertie, of course, fails to immediately see that he lacks the requisite qualities and a sequence of humiliating and potentially dangerous events unfolds.

P. G. Wodehouse has been providing entertainment and consolation for over a century. Seán O'Casey referred to him as English literature's 'performing flea', which Wodehouse later used as a title for a collection of letters, giving us all a lesson in how to deal gracefully with disdain. But the more I think about this, the more I think, and so what? What's wrong with wanting to entertain? Wodehouse created both Jeeves and Wooster and Blandings Castle during the First World War. Did soldiers or nurses have much time to read? Inasmuch as I can imagine myself into the trenches, can grasp towards what it would be like to kill, or to watch my friends get blown up, or to tend dying men in a makeshift field hospital, and then be unable to escape the squalor of mud and lice, the smell of blood and death, I think I might have been grateful for a performing flea.

Many years ago I worked at Hatchards, the oldest bookshop in London, and was at my happiest down in the basement among the paperback fiction. Being a bookseller is a great privilege, and never more so when customers share their troubles, ask for something to get them through the night, or seek advice as to what they should buy for a friend in hospital. P. G. Wodehouse was my recommendation of choice.

'They are light and easy,' I'd say, 'not demanding but not trashy. They feel nourishing. The language, the wit, the humour, the recurring characters, the idyllic settings full of impostors . . .'

One customer came back to tell me how grateful her friend was that escaping to Blandings Castle had helped her through chemotherapy. I remembered this when my mother was rendered sleepless but unable to concentrate on reading during her cancer treatment. I bought her Wodehouse on audio. She had never read any before, and assumed they were too 'posh' for her. She was worried she wouldn't be able to follow the plots.

'That doesn't really matter,' I said. 'There will be misunderstandings that get sorted out. Nothing horrible happens. It's the language that makes them so enjoyable; you can just relax and listen.'

Reader, she joined the long list of people who now understand the Wodehouse hand-hold. Because while I might visit Blandings or hang out with Jeeves and Wooster to pleasantly pass a happy afternoon, I am most in need of a Wodehouse prescription when I am down and troubled, when I am sick in mind or body, and must seek refuge in the stretch of my bookcase that offers distraction and comfort. That's when I most want to read about Bobbie Wickham's adventures − snakes! Burst hot-water bottles! Suitors getting shot in the leg! − and how anyone who falls for her 'finds himself sooner or later up to the Adam's apple in some ghastly mess.' And I want to see Lord Emsworth repeatedly getting the wrong end of the stick, which he does so deliciously in this collection. When other people want to talk about Angela's broken engagement, all Lord Emsworth cares about is why his black Berkshire sow, the Empress of Blandings, has gone off her food just days before the Fat Pigs class at the eighty-seventh annual Shropshire Agricultural Show. And we have the romantic difficulties of Bingo Little, the nervous breakdowns of publishers, the autocratic behaviour of lady novelists, the pursuit of strawberries in winter, and how the San Francisco earthquake wins a young man his bride.

I do hope you enjoy these stories. I wonder will you have read them all by New Year's Eve, or will you be able to ration them out month by month? Perhaps, like Bertie finding that Sir Roderick Glossop is on the guest list for Skeldings, you too may have to keep company you'd rather not: 'It seemed to me that even at Christmas time, with all the peace on earth and goodwill towards men that there is knocking about at that season, a reunion with this bloke was likely to be tough going.'

I will make a Christmas wish that Wodehouse aids you in finding rest and respite. And, hopefully, whatever your own festive challenges may be, you won't end up like Bertie, declaring that 'love is dead' and fleeing across the fields needing to hire a car to escape the consequences of following Bobbie Wickham's advice. Though, of course, because Jeeves is always right and gets what he wants, and because order must be restored in the world of Wodehouse, we know that Jeeves will soon be free to indulge himself at the tables in Monte Carlo, as Bertie strolls around happily, ready to fall in love again.

Cathy Rentzenbrink, 2023

December

Jeeves and the Yule-Tide Spirit

The letter arrived on the morning of the sixteenth. I was pushing a bit of breakfast into the Wooster face at the moment and, feeling fairly well fortified with coffee and kippers, I decided to break the news to Jeeves without delay. As Shakespeare says, if you're going to do a thing you might just as well pop right at it and get it over. The man would be disappointed, of course, and possibly even chagrined: but, dash it all, a splash of disappointment here and there does a fellow good. Makes him realise that life is stern and life is earnest.

'Oh, Jeeves,' I said.

'Sir?'

'We have here a communication from Lady Wickham. She has written inviting me to Skeldings for the festives. So you will see about bunging the necessaries together. We repair thither on the twenty-third. Plenty of white ties, Jeeves, also a few hearty country suits for use in the daytime. We shall be there some little time, I expect.'

There was a pause. I could feel he was directing a frosty gaze at me, but I dug into the marmalade and refused to meet it.

'I thought I understood you to say, sir, that you proposed to visit Monte Carlo immediately after Christmas.'

'I know. But that's all off. Plans changed.'

'Very good, sir.'

At this point the telephone bell rang, tiding over very nicely what had threatened to be an awkward moment. Jeeves unhooked the receiver.

'Yes? ... Yes, madam ... Very good, madam. Here is Mr Wooster.' He handed me the instrument. 'Mrs Spenser Gregson, sir.'

You know, every now and then I can't help feeling that Jeeves is losing his grip. In his prime it would have been with him the work of a moment to have told Aunt Agatha that I was not at home. I gave him one of those reproachful glances, and took the machine.

'Hullo?' I said. 'Yes? Hullo? Hullo? Bertie speaking. Hullo? Hullo? Hullo?'

'Don't keep on saying Hullo,' yipped the old relative in her customary curt manner. 'You're not a parrot. Sometimes I wish you were, because then you might have a little sense.'

Quite the wrong sort of tone to adopt towards a fellow in the early morning, of course, but what can one do?

'Bertie, Lady Wickham tells me she has invited you to Skeldings for Christmas. Are you going?'

'Rather!'

'Well, mind you behave yourself. Lady Wickham is an old friend of mine.'

I was in no mood for this sort of thing over the telephone. Face to face, I'm not saying, but at the end of a wire, no.

'I shall naturally endeavour, Aunt Agatha,' I replied

stiffly, 'to conduct myself in a manner befitting an English gentleman paying a visit—'

'What did you say? Speak up. I can't hear.'

'I said, Right ho.'

'Oh? Well, mind you do. And there's another reason why I particularly wish you to be as little of an imbecile as you can manage while at Skeldings. Sir Roderick Glossop will be there.'

'What!'

'Don't bellow like that. You nearly deafened me.'

'Did you say Sir Roderick Glossop?'

'I did.'

'You don't mean Tuppy Glossop?'

'I mean Sir Roderick Glossop. Which was my reason for saying Sir Roderick Glossop. Now, Bertie, I want you to listen to me attentively. Are you there?'

'Yes. Still here.'

'Well, then, listen. I have at last succeeded, after incredible difficulty, and in face of all the evidence, in almost persuading Sir Roderick that you are not actually insane. He is prepared to suspend judgement until he has seen you once more. On your behaviour at Skeldings, therefore—'

But I had hung up the receiver. Shaken. That's what I was. S to the core.

Stop me if I've told you this before: but, in case you don't know, let me just mention the facts in the matter of this Glossop. He was a formidable old bird with a bald head and outsize eyebrows, by profession a loony-doctor. How it happened, I couldn't tell you to this day, but I once got engaged to his daughter, Honoria, a ghastly dynamic exhibit who read Nietzsche and had a laugh like waves breaking on a stern and rock-bound coast. The fixture was scratched owing to events occurring which convinced the old boy that I was off my napper; and since then he has always had my name at the top of his list of 'Loonies I have Lunched With'.

It seemed to me that even at Christmas time, with all the peace on earth and goodwill towards men that there is knocking about at that season, a reunion with this bloke was likely to be tough going. If I hadn't had more than one particularly good reason for wanting to go to Skeldings, I'd have called the thing off.

'Jeeves,' I said, all of a twitter, 'do you know what? Sir Roderick Glossop is going to be at Lady Wickham's.'

'Very good, sir. If you have finished breakfast, I will clear away.'

Cold and haughty. No symp. None of the rallying-round spirit which one likes to see. As I had anticipated, the information that we were not going to Monte Carlo had got in amongst him. There is a keen sporting streak in Jeeves, and I knew he had been looking forward to a little flutter at the tables.

We Woosters can wear the mask. I ignored his lack of decent feeling.

'Do so, Jeeves,' I said proudly, 'and with all convenient speed.'

Relations continued pretty fairly strained all through the rest of the week. There was a frigid detachment in the way the man brought me my dollop of tea in the mornings.

Going down to Skeldings in the car on the afternoon of the twenty-third, he was aloof and reserved. And before dinner on the first night of my visit he put the studs in my dress shirt in what I can only call a marked manner. The whole thing was extremely painful, and it seemed to me, as I lay in bed on the morning of the twenty-fourth, that the only step to take was to put the whole facts of the case before him and trust to his native good sense to effect an understanding.

I was feeling considerably in the pink that morning. Everything had gone like a breeze. My hostess, Lady Wickham, was a beaky female built far too closely on the lines of my Aunt Agatha for comfort, but she had seemed matey enough on my arrival. Her daughter, Roberta, had welcomed me with a warmth which, I'm bound to say, had set the old heart-strings fluttering a bit. And Sir Roderick, in the brief moment we had had together, appeared to have let the Yule-tide spirit soak into him to the most amazing extent. When he saw me, his mouth sort of flickered at one corner, which I took to be his idea of smiling, and he said, 'Ha, young man!' Not particularly chummily, but he said it: and my view was that it practically amounted to the lion lying down with the lamb.

So, all in all, life at this juncture seemed pretty well all to the mustard, and I decided to tell Jeeves exactly how matters stood.

'Jeeves,' I said, as he appeared with the steaming.
'Sir?'
'Touching on this business of our being here, I would like to say a few words of explanation. I consider that you have a right to the facts.'

'Sir?'

'I'm afraid scratching that Monte Carlo trip has been a bit of a jar for you, Jeeves.'

'Not at all, sir.'

'Oh, yes, it has. The heart was set on wintering in the world's good old Plague Spot, I know. I saw your eye light up when I said we were due for a visit there. You snorted a bit and your fingers twitched. I know, I know. And now that there has been a change of programme the iron has entered into your soul.'

'Not at all, sir.'

'Oh, yes, it has. I've seen it. Very well, then, what I wish to impress upon you, Jeeves, is that I have not been actuated in this matter by any mere idle whim. It was through no light and airy caprice that I accepted this invitation to Lady Wickham's. I have been angling for it for weeks, prompted by many considerations. In the first place, does one get the Yule-tide spirit at a spot like Monte Carlo?'

'Does one desire the Yule-tide spirit, sir?'

'Certainly one does. I am all for it. Well, that's one thing. Now here's another. It was imperative that I should come to Skeldings for Christmas, Jeeves, because I knew that young Tuppy Glossop was going to be here.'

'Sir Roderick Glossop, sir?'

'His nephew. You may have observed hanging about the place a fellow with light hair and a Cheshire-cat grin. That is Tuppy, and I have been anxious for some time to get to grips with him. I have it in for that man of wrath. Listen to the facts, Jeeves, and tell me if I am not justified in planning a hideous vengeance.' I took a sip of tea, for the mere memory of my wrongs had shaken me. 'In spite of the fact that young Tuppy is the nephew of Sir Roderick Glossop, at whose hands, Jeeves, as you are aware, I have suffered much, I fraternised with him freely, both at the Drones Club and elsewhere. I said to myself that a man is not to be blamed for his relations, and that I would hate to have my pals hold my Aunt Agatha, for instance, against me. Broad-minded, Jeeves, I think?'

'Extremely, sir.'

'Well, then, as I say, I sought this Tuppy out, Jeeves, and hobnobbed, and what do you think he did?'

'I could not say, sir.'

'I will tell you. One night after dinner at the Drones he betted me I wouldn't swing myself across the swimming bath by the ropes and rings. I took him on and was buzzing along in great style until I came to the last ring. And then I found that this fiend in human shape had looped it back against the rail, thus leaving me hanging in the void with no means of getting ashore to my home and loved ones. There was nothing for it but to drop into the water. He told me that he had often caught fellows that way: and what I maintain, Jeeves, is that, if I can't get back at him somehow at Skeldings – with all the vast resources which a country house affords at my disposal – I am not the man I was.'

'I see, sir.'

There was still something in his manner which told me that even now he lacked complete sympathy and understanding, so, delicate though the subject was, I decided to put all my cards on the table.

'And now, Jeeves, we come to the most important reason why I had to spend Christmas at Skeldings. Jeeves,' I said, diving into the old cup once more for a moment and bringing myself out wreathed in blushes, 'the fact of the matter is, I'm in love.'

'Indeed, sir?'

'You've seen Miss Roberta Wickham?'

'Yes, sir.'

'Very well, then.'

There was a pause, while I let it sink in.

'During your stay here, Jeeves,' I said, 'you will, no doubt, be thrown a good deal together with Miss Wickham's maid. On such occasions, pitch it strong.'

'Sir?'

'You know what I mean. Tell her I'm rather a good chap. Mention my hidden depths. These things get round. Dwell on the fact that I have a kind heart and was runner-up in the Squash Handicap at the Drones this year. A boost is never wasted, Jeeves.'

'Very good, sir. But—'

'But what?'

'Well, sir—'

'I wish you wouldn't say "Well, sir" in that soupy tone of voice. I have had to speak of this before. The habit is one that is growing upon you. Check it. What's on your mind?'

'I hardly like to take the liberty—'

'Carry on, Jeeves. We are always glad to hear from you, always.'

'What I was about to remark, if you will excuse me, sir, was that I would scarcely have thought Miss Wickham a suitable—'

'Jeeves,' I said coldly, 'if you have anything to say against that lady, it had better not be said in my presence.'

'Very good, sir.'

'Or anywhere else, for that matter. What is your kick against Miss Wickham?'

'Oh, really, sir!'

'Jeeves, I insist. This is a time for plain speaking. You have beefed about Miss Wickham. I wish to know why.'

'It merely crossed my mind, sir, that for a gentleman of your description Miss Wickham is not a suitable mate.'

'What do you mean by a gentleman of my description?'

'Well, sir—'

'Jeeves!'

'I beg your pardon, sir. The expression escaped me inadvertently. I was about to observe that I can only asseverate—'

'Only what?'

'I can only say that, as you have invited my opinion—'

'But I didn't.'

'I was under the impression that you desired to canvass my views on the matter, sir.'

'Oh? Well, let's have them, anyway.'

'Very good, sir. Then briefly, if I may say so, sir, though Miss Wickham is a charming young lady—'

'There, Jeeves, you spoke an imperial quart. What eyes!'

'Yes, sir.'

'What hair!'

'Very true, sir.'

'And what *espièglerie*, if that's the word I want.'

'The exact word, sir.'

'All right, then. Carry on.'

'I grant Miss Wickham the possession of all these desirable qualities, sir. Nevertheless, considered as a matrimonial prospect for a gentleman of your description, I cannot look upon her as suitable. In my opinion Miss Wickham lacks seriousness, sir. She is too volatile and frivolous. To qualify as Miss Wickham's husband, a gentleman would need to possess a commanding personality and considerable strength of character.'

'Exactly!'

'I would always hesitate to recommend as a life's companion a young lady with quite such a vivid shade of red hair. Red hair, sir, in my opinion, is dangerous.'

I eyed the blighter squarely.

'Jeeves,' I said, 'you're talking rot.'

'Very good, sir.'

'Absolute drivel.'

'Very good, sir.'

'Pure mashed potatoes.'

'Very good, sir.'

'Very good, sir – I mean very good, Jeeves, that will be all,' I said.

And I drank a modicum of tea, with a good deal of hauteur.

It isn't often that I find myself able to prove Jeeves in the wrong, but by dinnertime that night I was in a position to do so, and I did it without delay.

'Touching on that matter we were touching on, Jeeves,' I said, coming in from the bath and tackling him as he studied the shirt, 'I should be glad if you would give me your careful attention for a moment. I warn you that what I am about to say is going to make you look pretty silly.'

'Indeed, sir?'

'Yes, Jeeves. Pretty dashed silly it's going to make you look. It may lead you to be rather more careful in future about broadcasting these estimates of yours of people's characters. This morning, if I remember rightly, you stated that Miss Wickham was volatile, frivolous and lacking in seriousness. Am I correct?'

'Quite correct, sir.'

'Then what I have to tell you may cause you to alter that opinion. I went for a walk with Miss Wickham this afternoon: and, as we walked, I told her about what young Tuppy Glossop did to me in the swimming bath at the Drones. She hung upon my words, Jeeves, and was full of sympathy.'

'Indeed, sir?'

'Dripping with it. And that's not all. Almost before I had finished, she was suggesting the ripest, fruitiest, brainiest scheme for bringing young Tuppy's grey hairs in sorrow to the grave that anyone could possibly imagine.'

'That is very gratifying, sir.'

'Gratifying is the word. It appears that at the girls' school where Miss Wickham was educated, Jeeves, it used to become necessary from time to time for the right-thinking element of the community to slip it across certain of the baser sort. Do you know what they did, Jeeves?'

'No, sir.'

'They took a long stick, Jeeves, and – follow me closely here – they tied a darning needle to the end of it. Then at dead of night, it appears, they sneaked privily into the party of the second part's cubicle and shoved the needle through the bedclothes and punctured her hot-water bottle. Girls are much subtler in these matters than boys,

Jeeves. At my old school one would occasionally heave a jug of water over another bloke during the night-watches, but we never thought of effecting the same result in this particularly neat and scientific manner. Well, Jeeves, that was the scheme which Miss Wickham suggested I should work on young Tuppy, and that is the girl you call frivolous and lacking in seriousness. Any girl who can think up a wheeze like that is my idea of a helpmeet. I shall be glad, Jeeves, if by the time I come to bed tonight you have waiting for me in this room a stout stick with a good sharp darning needle attached.'

'Well, sir—'

I raised my hand.

'Jeeves,' I said. 'Not another word. Stick, one, and needle, darning, good, sharp, one, without fail in this room at eleven-thirty tonight.'

'Very good, sir.'

'Have you any idea where young Tuppy sleeps?'

'I could ascertain, sir.'

'Do so, Jeeves.'

In a few minutes he was back with the necessary informash.

'Mr Glossop is established in the Moat Room, sir.'

'Where's that?'

'The second door on the floor below this, sir.'

'Right ho, Jeeves. Are the studs in my shirt?'

'Yes, sir.'

'And the links also?'

'Yes, sir.'

'Then push me into it.'

*

The more I thought about this enterprise which a sense of duty and good citizenship had thrust upon me, the better it seemed to me. I am not a vindictive man, but I felt, as anybody would have felt in my place, that if fellows like young Tuppy are allowed to get away with it the whole fabric of Society and Civilisation must inevitably crumble. The task to which I had set myself was one that involved hardship and discomfort, for it meant sitting up till well into the small hours and then padding down a cold corridor, but I did not shrink from it. After all, there is a lot to be said for family tradition. We Woosters did our bit in the Crusades.

It being Christmas Eve, there was, as I had foreseen, a good deal of revelry and what not. First, the village choir surged round and sang carols outside the front door, and then somebody suggested a dance, and after that we hung around chatting of this and that, so that it wasn't till past one that I got to my room. Allowing for everything, it didn't seem that it was going to be safe to start my little expedition till half-past two at the earliest: and I'm bound to say that it was only the utmost resolution that kept me from snuggling into the sheets and calling it a day. I'm not much of a lad now for late hours.

However, by half-past two everything appeared to be quiet. I shook off the mists of sleep, grabbed the good old stick-and-needle and toddled off along the corridor. And presently, pausing outside the Moat Room, I turned the handle, found the door wasn't locked, and went in.

I suppose a burglar – I mean a real professional who works at the job six nights a week all the year round – gets so that finding himself standing in the dark in somebody else's bedroom means absolutely nothing to him. But for a bird like me, who has had no previous experience, there's a lot to be said in favour of washing the whole thing out and closing the door gently and popping back to bed again. It was only by summoning up all the old bulldog courage of the Woosters, and reminding myself that, if I let this opportunity slip another might never occur, that I managed to stick out what you might call the initial minute of the binge. Then the weakness passed, and Bertram was himself again.

At first when I beetled in, the room had seemed as black as a coal-cellar: but after a bit things began to lighten. The curtains weren't quite drawn over the window and I could see a trifle of the scenery here and there. The bed was opposite the window, with the head against the wall and the end where the feet were jutting out towards where I stood, thus rendering it possible after one had sown the seed, so to speak, to make a quick getaway. There only remained now the rather tricky problem of locating the old hot-water bottle. I mean to say, the one thing you can't do if you want to carry a job like this through with secrecy and dispatch is to stand at the end of a fellow's bed, jabbing the blankets at random with a darning needle. Before proceeding to anything in the nature of definite steps, it is imperative that you locate the bot.

I was a good deal cheered at this juncture to hear a fruity snore from the direction of the pillows. Reason told me that a bloke who could snore like that wasn't going to be awakened by a trifle. I edged forward and ran a hand in a gingerly sort of way over the coverlet. A moment later I had found the bulge. I steered the good old darning needle on to it, gripped the stick, and shoved. Then, pulling out the weapon, I sidled towards the door, and in another moment would have been outside, buzzing for home and the good night's rest, when suddenly there was a crash that sent my spine shooting up through the top of my head and the contents of the bed sat up like a jack-in-the-box and said:

'Who's that?'

It just shows how your most careful strategic moves can be the very ones that dish your campaign. In order to facilitate the orderly retreat according to plan I had left the door open, and the beastly thing had slammed like a bomb.

But I wasn't giving much thought to the causes of the explosion, having other things to occupy my mind. What was disturbing me was the discovery that, whoever else the bloke in the bed might be, he was not young Tuppy. Tuppy has one of those high, squeaky voices that sound like the tenor of the village choir failing to hit a high note. This one was something in between the last Trump and a tiger calling for breakfast after being on a diet for a day or two. It was the sort of nasty, rasping voice you hear shouting 'Fore!' when you're one of a slow foursome on the links and are holding up a couple of retired colonels. Among the qualities it lacked were kindliness, suavity and that sort of dove-like cooing note which makes a fellow feel he has found a friend.

I did not linger. Getting swiftly off the mark, I dived for the door-handle and was off and away, banging the door behind me. I may be a chump in many ways, as my Aunt Agatha will freely attest, but I know when and when not to be among those present.

And I was just about to do the stretch of corridor leading to the stairs in a split second under the record time for the course, when something brought me up with a sudden jerk. One moment, I was all dash and fire and speed; the next, an irresistible force had checked me in my stride and was holding me straining at the leash, as it were.

You know, sometimes it seems to me as if Fate were going out of its way to such an extent to snooter you that you wonder if it's worth while continuing to struggle. The night being a trifle chillier than the dickens, I had donned for this expedition a dressing gown. It was the tail of this infernal garment that had caught in the door and pipped me at the eleventh hour.

The next moment the door had opened, light was streaming through it, and the bloke with the voice had grabbed me by the arm.

It was Sir Roderick Glossop.

The next thing that happened was a bit of a lull in the proceedings. For about three and a quarter seconds or possibly more we just stood there, drinking each other in, so to speak, the old boy still attached with a limpet-like grip to my elbow. If I hadn't been in a dressing gown and he in pink pyjamas with a blue stripe, and if he hadn't been glaring quite so much as if he were shortly going to commit a murder, the tableau would have looked rather like one of those advertisements you see in the magazines, where the experienced elder is patting the young man's arm, and saying to him, 'My boy, if you subscribe to the Mutt-Jeff Correspondence School of Oswego, Kan., as I did, you may some day, like me, become Third

Assistant Vice President of the Schenectady Consolidated Nail-File and Eyebrow Tweezer Corporation.'

'You!' said Sir Roderick finally. And in this connection I want to state that it's all rot to say you can't hiss a word that hasn't an 's' in it. The way he pushed out that 'You!' sounded like an angry cobra, and I am betraying no secrets when I mention that it did me no good whatsoever.

By rights, I suppose, at this point I ought to have said something. The best I could manage, however, was a faint, soft bleating sound. Even on ordinary social occasions, when meeting this bloke as man to man and with a clear conscience, I could never be completely at my ease: and now those eyebrows seemed to pierce me like a knife.

'Come in here,' he said, lugging me into the room. 'We don't want to wake the whole house. Now,' he said, depositing me on the carpet and closing the door and doing a bit of eyebrow work, 'kindly inform me what is this latest manifestation of insanity?'

It seemed to me that a light and cheery laugh might help the thing along. So I had a pop at one.

'Don't gibber!' said my genial host. And I'm bound to admit that the light and cheery hadn't come out quite as I'd intended.

I pulled myself together with a strong effort.

'Awfully sorry about all this,' I said in a hearty sort of voice. 'The fact is, I thought you were Tuppy.'

'Kindly refrain from inflicting your idiotic slang on me. What do you mean by the adjective "tuppy"?'

'It isn't so much an adjective, don't you know. More of a noun, I should think, if you examine it squarely. What I mean to say is, I thought you were your nephew.'

'You thought I was my nephew? Why should I be my nephew?'

'What I'm driving at is, I thought this was his room.'

'My nephew and I changed rooms. I have a great dislike for sleeping on an upper floor. I am nervous about fire.'

For the first time since this interview had started, I braced up a trifle. The injustice of the whole thing stirred me to such an extent that for a moment I lost that sense of being a toad under the harrow which had been cramping my style up till now. I even went so far as to eye this pink-pyjamaed poltroon with a good deal of contempt and loathing. Just because he had this craven fear of fire and this selfish preference for letting Tuppy be cooked instead of himself should the emergency occur, my nicely reasoned plans had gone up the spout. I gave him a look, and I think I may even have snorted a bit.

'I should have thought that your man servant would have informed you,' said Sir Roderick, 'that we contemplated making this change. I met him shortly before luncheon and told him to tell you.'

I reeled. Yes, it is not too much to say that I reeled. This extraordinary statement had taken me amidships without any preparation, and it staggered me. That Jeeves had been aware all along that this old crumb would be the occupant of the bed which I was proposing to prod with darning needles and had let me rush upon my doom without a word of warning was almost beyond belief. You might say I was aghast. Yes, practically aghast.

'You told Jeeves that you were going to sleep in this room?' I gasped.

'I did. I was aware that you and my nephew were on terms of intimacy, and I wished to spare myself the possibility of a visit from you. I confess that it never occurred to me that such a visit was to be anticipated at three o'clock in the morning. What the devil do you mean,' he barked, suddenly hotting up, 'by prowling about the house at this hour? And what is that thing in your hand?'

I looked down, and found that I was still grasping the stick. I give you my honest word that, what with the maelstrom of emotions into which his revelation about Jeeves had cast me, the discovery came as an absolute surprise.

'This?' I said. 'Oh, yes.'

'What do you mean, "Oh, yes"? What is it?'

'Well, it's a long story—'

'We have the night before us.'

'It's this way. I will ask you to picture me some weeks ago, perfectly peaceful and inoffensive, after dinner at the Drones, smoking a thoughtful cigarette and—'

I broke off. The man wasn't listening. He was goggling in a rapt sort of way at the end of the bed, from which there had now begun to drip on to the carpet a series of drops.

'Good heavens!'

'—thoughtful cigarette and chatting pleasantly of this and that—'

I broke off again. He had lifted the sheets and was gazing at the corpse of the hot-water bottle.

'Did you do this?' he said in a low, strangled sort of voice.

'Er – yes. As a matter of fact, yes. I was just going to tell you—'

'And your aunt tried to persuade me that you were not insane!'

'I'm not. Absolutely not. If you'll just let me explain.'

'I will do nothing of the kind.'

'It all began—'

'Silence!'

'Right ho.'

He did some deep-breathing exercises through the nose.

'My bed is drenched!'

'The way it all began—'

'Be quiet!' He heaved somewhat for a while. 'You wretched, miserable idiot,' he said, 'kindly inform me which bedroom you are supposed to be occupying?'

'It's on the floor above. The Clock Room.'

'Thank you. I will find it.'

He gave me the eyebrow.

'I propose,' he said, 'to pass the remainder of the night in your room, where, I presume, there is a bed in a condition to be slept in. You may bestow yourself as comfortably as you can here. I will wish you good night.'

He buzzed off, leaving me flat.

Well, we Woosters are old campaigners. We can take the rough with the smooth. But to say that I liked the prospect now before me would be paltering with the truth. One glance at the bed told me that any idea of sleeping there was out. A goldfish could have done it, but not Bertram. After a bit of a look round, I decided that the best chance of getting a sort of night's rest was to doss as well as I could in the armchair. I pinched a couple of pillows off the bed, shoved the hearthrug over my knees, and sat down and started counting sheep.

But it wasn't any good. The old lemon was sizzling much too much to admit of anything in the nature of slumber. This hideous revelation of the blackness of Jeeves's treachery kept coming back to me every time I nearly succeeded in dropping off: and, what's more, it seemed to get colder and colder as the long night wore on. I was just wondering if I would ever get to sleep again in this world when a voice at my elbow said, 'Good morning, sir,' and I sat up with a jerk.

I could have sworn I hadn't so much as dozed off for even a minute, but apparently I had. For the curtains were drawn back and daylight was coming in through the window and there was Jeeves standing beside me with a cup of tea on a tray.

'Merry Christmas, sir!'

I reached out a feeble hand for the restoring brew. I swallowed a mouthful or two, and felt a little better. I was aching in every limb and the dome felt like lead, but I was now able to think with a certain amount of clearness, and I fixed the man with a stony eye and prepared to let him have it.

'You think so, do you?' I said. 'Much, let me tell you, depends on what you mean by the adjective "merry". If, moreover, you suppose that it is going to be merry for you, correct that impression. Jeeves,' I said, taking another half-oz of tea and speaking in a cold, measured voice, 'I wish to ask you one question. Did you or did you not know that Sir Roderick Glossop was sleeping in this room last night?'

'Yes, sir.'

'You admit it!'

'Yes, sir.'

'And you didn't tell me!'

'No, sir. I thought it would be more judicious not to do so.'

'Jeeves—'

'If you will allow me to explain, sir.'

'Explain!'

'I was aware that my silence might lead to something in the nature of an embarrassing contretemps, sir—'

'You thought that, did you?'

'Yes, sir.'

'You were a good guesser,' I said, sucking down further Bohea.

'But it seemed to me, sir, that whatever might occur was all for the best.'

I would have put in a crisp word or two here, but he carried on without giving me the opp.

'I thought that possibly, on reflection, sir, your views being what they are, you would prefer your relations with Sir Roderick Glossop and his family to be distant rather than cordial.'

'My views? What do you mean, my views?'

'As regards a matrimonial alliance with Miss Honoria Glossop, sir.'

Something like an electric shock seemed to zip through me. The man had opened up a new line of thought. I suddenly saw what he was driving at, and realised all in a flash that I had been wronging this faithful fellow. All the while I supposed he had been landing me in the soup, he had really been steering me away from it. It was like those stories one used to read as a kid about the traveller going along on a dark night and his dog grabs him by the leg of his trousers and he says, 'Down, sir! What are you doing, Rover?' and the dog hangs on and he gets rather hot under the collar and curses a bit but the dog won't let him go and then suddenly the moon shines through the clouds and he finds he's been standing on the edge of a precipice and one more step would have— Well, anyway, you get the idea: and what I'm driving at is that much the same sort of thing seemed to have been happening now.

It's perfectly amazing how a fellow will let himself get off his guard and ignore the perils which surround him. I give you my honest word, it had never struck me till this moment that my Aunt Agatha had been scheming to get me in right with Sir Roderick so that I should eventually be received back into the fold, if you see what I mean, and subsequently pushed off on Honoria.

'My God, Jeeves!' I said, paling.

'Precisely, sir.'

'You think there was a risk?'

'I do, sir. A very grave risk.'

A disturbing thought struck me.

'But, Jeeves, on calm reflection won't Sir Roderick have gathered by now that my objective was young Tuppy and that puncturing his hot-water bottle was just one of those things that occur when the Yule-tide spirit is abroad – one of those things that have to be overlooked and taken with the indulgent smile and the fatherly shake of the head? I mean to say, Young Blood and all that sort of thing? What I mean is he'll realise that I wasn't trying to snooter him, and then all the good work will have been wasted.'

'No, sir. I fancy not. That might possibly have been Sir Roderick's mental reaction, had it not been for the second incident.'

'The second incident?'

'During the night, sir, while Sir Roderick was occupying your bed, somebody entered the room, pierced his hot-water bottle with some sharp instrument, and vanished in the darkness.'

I could make nothing of this.

'What! Do you think I walked in my sleep?'

'No, sir. It was young Mr Glossop who did it. I encountered him this morning, sir, shortly before I came here. He was in cheerful spirits and enquired of me how you were feeling about the incident. Not being aware that his victim had been Sir Roderick.'

'But, Jeeves, what an amazing coincidence!'

'Sir?'

'Why, young Tuppy getting exactly the same idea as I did. Or, rather, as Miss Wickham did. You can't say that's not rummy. A miracle, I call it.'

'Not altogether, sir. It appears that he received the suggestion from the young lady.'

'From Miss Wickham?'

'Yes, sir.'

'You mean to say that, after she had put me up to the scheme of puncturing Tuppy's hot-water bottle, she went away and tipped Tuppy off to puncturing mine?'

'Precisely, sir. She is a young lady with a keen sense of humour, sir.'

I sat there, you might say stunned. When I thought how near I had come to offering the heart and hand to a girl capable of double-crossing a strong man's honest love like that, I shivered.

'Are you cold, sir?'

'No, Jeeves. Just shuddering.'

'The occurrence, if I may take the liberty of saying so, sir, will perhaps lend colour to the view which I put forward yesterday that Miss Wickham, though in many respects a charming young lady—'

I raised the hand.

'Say no more, Jeeves,' I replied. 'Love is dead.'

'Very good, sir.'

I brooded for a while.

'You've seen Sir Roderick this morning, then?'

'Yes, sir.'

'How did he seem?'

'A trifle feverish, sir.'

'Feverish?'

'A little emotional, sir. He expressed a strong desire to meet you, sir.'

'What would you advise?'

'If you were to slip out by the back entrance as soon as you are dressed, sir, it would be possible for you to make your way across the field without being observed and reach the village, where you could hire an automobile to take you to London. I could bring on your effects later in your own car.'

'But London, Jeeves? Is any man safe? My Aunt Agatha is in London.'

'Yes, sir.'

'Well, then?'

He regarded me for a moment with a fathomless eye.

'I think the best plan, sir, would be for you to leave England, which is not pleasant at this time of the year, for some little while. I would not take the liberty of dictating your movements, sir, but as you already have accommodation engaged on the Blue Train for Monte Carlo for the day after tomorrow—'

'But you cancelled the booking?'

'No, sir.'

'I thought you had.'

'No, sir.'

'I told you to.'

'Yes, sir. It was remiss of me, but the matter slipped my mind.'

'Oh?'

'Yes, sir.'

'All right, Jeeves. Monte Carlo ho, then.'

'Very good, sir.'

'It's lucky, as things have turned out, that you forgot to cancel that booking.'

'Very fortunate indeed, sir. If you will wait here, sir, I will return to your room and procure a suit of clothes.'

January

Sundered Hearts

In the smoking room of the clubhouse a cheerful fire was burning, and the Oldest Member glanced from time to time out of the window into the gathering dusk. Snow was falling lightly on the links. From where he sat, the Oldest Member had a good view of the ninth green; and presently, out of the greyness of the December evening, there appeared over the brow of the hill a golf-ball. It trickled across the green, and stopped within a yard of the hole. The Oldest Member nodded approvingly. A good approach-shot.

A young man in a tweed suit clambered on to the green, holed out with easy confidence, and, shouldering his bag, made his way to the clubhouse. A few moments later he entered the smoking room, and uttered an exclamation of rapture at the sight of the fire.

'I'm frozen stiff!'

He rang for a waiter and ordered a hot drink. The Oldest Member gave a gracious assent to the suggestion that he should join him.

'I like playing in winter,' said the young man. 'You get the course to yourself, for the world is full of slackers who only turn out when the weather suits them. I cannot understand where they get the nerve to call themselves golfers.'

'Not everyone is as keen as you are, my boy,' said the Sage, dipping gratefully into his hot drink. 'If they were, the world would be a better place, and we should hear less of all this modern unrest.'

'I *am* pretty keen,' admitted the young man.

'I have only encountered one man whom I could describe as keener. I allude to Mortimer Sturgis.'

'The fellow who took up golf at thirty-eight and let the girl he was engaged to marry go off with someone else because he hadn't the time to combine golf with courtship? I remember. You were telling me about him the other day.'

'There is a sequel to that story, if you would care to hear it,' said the Oldest Member.

'You have the honour,' said the young man. 'Go ahead!'

Some people (began the Oldest Member) considered that Mortimer Sturgis was too wrapped up in golf, and blamed him for it. I could never see eye to eye with them. In the days of King Arthur nobody thought the worse of a young knight if he suspended all his social and business engagements in favour of a search for the Holy Grail. In the Middle Ages a man could devote his whole life to the Crusades, and the public fawned upon him. Why, then, blame the man of today for a zealous attention to the modern equivalent, the Quest of Scratch? Mortimer Sturgis never became a scratch player, but he did eventually get his handicap down to nine, and I honour him for it.

The story which I am about to tell begins in what might be called the middle period of Sturgis's career. He had reached the stage when his handicap was a wobbly twelve;

and, as you are no doubt aware, it is then that a man really begins to golf in the true sense of the word. Mortimer's fondness for the game until then had been merely tepid compared with what it now became. He had played a little before, but now he really buckled to and got down to it. It was at this point, too, that he began once more to entertain thoughts of marriage. A profound statistician in this one department, he had discovered that practically all the finest exponents of the art are married men; and the thought that there might be something in the holy state which improved a man's game, and that he was missing a good thing, troubled him a great deal. Moreover, the paternal instinct had awakened in him. As he justly pointed out, whether marriage improved your game or not, it was to Old Tom Morris's marriage that the existence of young Tommy Morris, winner of the British Open Championship four times in succession, could be directly traced. In fact, at the age of forty-two, Mortimer Sturgis was in just the frame of mind to take some nice girl aside and ask her to become a stepmother to his eleven drivers, his baffy, his twenty-eight putters, and the rest of the ninety-four clubs which he had accumulated in the course of his golfing career. The sole stipulation, of course, which he made when dreaming his daydreams was that the future Mrs Sturgis must be a golfer. I can still recall the horror in his face when one girl, admirable in other respects, said that she had never heard of Harry Vardon, and didn't he mean Dolly Varden? She has since proved an excellent wife and mother, but Mortimer Sturgis never spoke to her again.

With the coming of January, it was Mortimer's practice to leave England and go to the South of France, where there was sunshine and crisp dry turf. He pursued his usual custom this year. With his suitcase and his ninety-four clubs he went off to Saint Brüle, staying as he always did at the Hotel Superbe, where they knew him, and treated with an amiable tolerance his habit of practising chip-shots in his bedroom. On the first evening, after breaking a statuette of the Infant Samuel in Prayer, he dressed and went down to dinner. And the first thing he saw was Her.

Mortimer Sturgis, as you know, had been engaged before, but Betty Weston had never inspired the tumultuous rush of emotion which the mere sight of this girl had set loose in him. He told me later that just to watch her holing out her soup gave him a sort of feeling you get when your drive collides with a rock in the middle of a tangle of rough and kicks back into the middle of the fairway. If golf had come late in life to Mortimer Sturgis, love came later still, and just as the golf, attacking him in middle life, had been some golf, so was the love considerable love. Mortimer finished his dinner in a trance, which is the best way to do it at some hotels, and then scoured the place for someone who would introduce him. He found such a person eventually and the meeting took place.

She was a small and rather fragile-looking girl, with big blue eyes and a cloud of golden hair. She had a sweet expression, and her left wrist was in a sling. She looked up at Mortimer as if she had at last found something that amounted to something. I am inclined to think it was a case of love at first sight on both sides.

'Fine weather we're having,' said Mortimer, who was a capital conversationalist.

'Yes,' said the girl.

'I like fine weather.'

'So do I.'

'There's something about fine weather!'

'Yes.'

'It's – it's – well, fine weather's so much finer than weather that isn't fine,' said Mortimer.

He looked at the girl a little anxiously, fearing he might be taking her out of her depth, but she seemed to have followed his train of thought perfectly.

'Yes, isn't it?' she said. 'It's so – so fine.'

'That's just what I meant,' said Mortimer. 'So fine. You've just hit it.'

He was charmed. The combination of beauty with intelligence is so rare.

'I see you've hurt your wrist,' he went on, pointing to the sling.

'Yes. I strained it a little playing in the championship.'

'The championship?' Mortimer was interested. 'It's awfully rude of me,' he said, apologetically, 'but I didn't catch your name just now.'

'My name is Somerset.'

Mortimer had been bending forward solicitously. He overbalanced and nearly fell off his chair. The shock had been stunning. Even before he had met and spoken to her, he had told himself that he loved this girl with the stored-up love of a lifetime. And she was Mary Somerset! The hotel lobby danced before Mortimer's eyes.

The name will, of course, be familiar to you. In the early rounds of the Ladies' Open Golf Championship of that year nobody had paid much attention to Mary Somerset.

She had survived her first two matches, but her opponents had been nonentities like herself. And then, in the third round, she had met and defeated the champion. From that point on, her name was on everybody's lips. She became favourite. And she had justified the public confidence by sailing into the final and winning easily. And here she was, talking to him like an ordinary person, and, if he could read the message in her eyes, not altogether indifferent to his charms, if you could call them that.

'Golly!' said Mortimer, awed.

Their friendship ripened rapidly, as friendships do in the South of France. In that favoured clime, you find the girl and Nature does the rest. On the second morning of their acquaintance Mortimer invited her to walk round the links with him and watch him play. He did it a little diffidently, for his golf was not of the calibre that would be likely to extort admiration from a champion. On the other hand, one should never let slip the opportunity of acquiring wrinkles on the game, and he thought that Miss Somerset, if she watched one or two of his shots, might tell him just what he ought to do. And sure enough, the opening arrived on the fourth hole, where Mortimer, after a drive which surprised even himself, found his ball in a nasty cuppy lie.

He turned to the girl.

'What ought I to do here?' he asked.

Miss Somerset looked at the ball. She seemed to be weighing the matter in her mind.

'Give it a good hard knock,' she said.

Mortimer knew what she meant. She was advocating

a full iron. The only trouble was that, when he tried anything more ambitious than a half-swing, except off the tee, he almost invariably topped. However, he could not fail this wonderful girl, so he swung well back and took a chance. His enterprise was rewarded. The ball flew out of the indentation in the turf as cleanly as though John Henry Taylor had been behind it, and rolled, looking neither to left nor to right, straight for the pin. A few moments later Mortimer Sturgis had holed out one under bogey, and it was only the fear that, having known him for so short a time, she might be startled and refuse him that kept him from proposing then and there. This exhibition of golfing generalship on her part had removed his last doubts. He knew that, if he lived for ever, there could be no other girl in the world for him. With her at his side, what might he not do? He might get his handicap down to six – to three – to scratch – to plus something! Good heavens, why, even the Amateur Championship was not outside the range of possibility. Mortimer Sturgis shook his putter solemnly in the air, and vowed a silent vow that he would win this pearl among women.

Now, when a man feels like that, it is impossible to restrain him long. For a week Mortimer Sturgis's soul sizzled within him: then he could contain himself no longer. One night, at one of the informal dances at the hotel, he drew the girl out on to the moonlit terrace.

'Miss Somerset—' he began, stuttering with emotion like an imperfectly corked bottle of ginger beer. 'Miss Somerset – may I call you Mary?'

The girl looked at him with eyes that shone softly in the dim light.

'Mary?' she repeated. 'Why, of course, if you like—'

'If I like!' cried Mortimer. 'Don't you know that it is my dearest wish? Don't you know that I would rather be permitted to call you Mary than do the first hole at Muirfield in two? Oh, Mary, how I have longed for this moment! I love you! I love you! Ever since I met you I have known that you were the one girl in this vast world whom I would die to win! Mary, will you be mine? Shall we go round together? Will you fix up a match with me on the links of life which shall end only when the Grim Reaper lays us both a stymie?'

She drooped towards him.

'Mortimer!' she murmured.

He held out his arms, then drew back. His face had grown suddenly tense, and there were lines of pain about his mouth.

'Wait!' he said, in a strained voice. 'Mary, I love you dearly, and because I love you so dearly I cannot let you trust your sweet life to me blindly. I have a confession to make. I am not – I have not always been' – he paused – 'a good man,' he said, in a low voice.

She started indignantly.

'How can you say that? You are the best, the kindest, the bravest man I have ever met! Who but a good man would have risked his life to save me from drowning?'

'Drowning?' Mortimer's voice seemed perplexed. 'You? What do you mean?'

'Have you forgotten the time when I fell in the sea last week, and you jumped in with all your clothes on—'

'Of course, yes,' said Mortimer. 'I remember now. It was the day I did the long seventh in five. I got off a good tee-shot straight down the fairway, took a baffy for my second, and— But that is not the point. It is sweet and generous of you to think so highly of what was the merest commonplace act of ordinary politeness, but I must repeat that, judged by the standards of your snowy purity, I am not a good man. I do not come to you clean and spotless as a young girl should expect her husband to come to her. Once, playing in a foursome, my ball fell in some long grass. Nobody was near me. We had no caddies, and the others were on the fairway. God knows—' His voice shook. 'God knows I struggled against the temptation. But I fell. I kicked the ball on to a little bare mound, from which it was an easy task with a nice half-mashie to reach the green for a snappy seven. Mary, there have been times when, going round by myself, I have allowed myself ten-foot putts on three holes in succession, simply in order to be able to say I had done the course in under a hundred. Ah! you shrink from me! You are disgusted!'

'I'm not disgusted! And I don't shrink! I only shivered because it is rather cold.'

'Then you can love me in spite of my past?'

'Mortimer!'

She fell into his arms.

'My dearest,' he said, presently, 'what a happy life ours will be. That is, if you do not find that you have made a mistake.'

'A mistake!' she cried, scornfully.

'Well, my handicap is twelve, you know, and not so darned twelve at that. There are days when I play my second from the fairway of the next hole but one, days when I couldn't putt into a coal-hole with "Welcome!"

written over it. And you are a Ladies' Open Champion. Still, if you think it's all right— Oh, Mary, you little know how I have dreamed of some day marrying a really first-class golfer! Yes, that was my vision – of walking up the aisle with some sweet plus-two girl on my arm. You shivered again. You are catching cold.'

'It is a little cold,' said the girl. She spoke in a small voice.

'Let me take you in, sweetheart,' said Mortimer. 'I'll just put you in a comfortable chair with a nice cup of coffee, and then I think I really must come out again and tramp about and think how perfectly splendid everything is.'

They were married a few weeks later, very quietly, in the little village church of Saint Brüle. The secretary of the local golf-club acted as best man for Mortimer, and a girl from the hotel was the only bridesmaid. The whole business was rather a disappointment to Mortimer, who had planned out a somewhat florid ceremony at St George's, Hanover Square, with the Vicar of Tooting (a scratch player excellent at short approach-shots) officiating, and 'The Voice That Breathed O'er St Andrews' booming from the organ. He had even had the idea of copying the military wedding and escorting his bride out of the church under an arch of crossed cleeks. But she would have none of this pomp. She insisted on a quiet wedding, and for the honeymoon trip preferred a tour through Italy. Mortimer, who had wanted to go to Scotland to visit the birthplace of James Braid, yielded amiably, for he loved her dearly. But he did not think much of Italy. In Rome, the great monuments of the past left him cold. Of the Temple of

Vespasian, all he thought was that it would be a devil of a place to be bunkered behind. The Colosseum aroused a faint spark of interest in him, as he speculated whether Abe Mitchell would use a full brassey to carry it. In Florence, the view over the Tuscan Hills from the Torre Rossa, Fiesole, over which his bride waxed enthusiastic, seemed to him merely a nasty bit of rough which would take a deal of getting out of.

And so, in the fullness of time, they came home to Mortimer's cosy little house adjoining the links.

Mortimer was so busy polishing his ninety-four clubs on the evening of their arrival that he failed to notice that his wife was preoccupied. A less busy man would have perceived at a glance that she was distinctly nervous. She started at sudden noises, and once, when he tried the newest of his mashie-niblicks and broke one of the drawing room windows, she screamed sharply. In short her manner was strange, and, if Edgar Allan Poe had put her into 'The Fall of the House of Usher', she would have fitted it like the paper on the wall. She had the air of one waiting tensely for the approach of some imminent doom. Mortimer, humming gaily to himself as he sandpapered the blade of his twenty-second putter, observed nothing of this. He was thinking of the morrow's play.

'Your wrist's quite well again now, darling, isn't it?' he said.

'Yes. Yes, quite well.'

'Fine!' said Mortimer. 'We'll breakfast early – say at half-past seven – and then we'll be able to get in a couple of rounds before lunch. A couple more in the afternoon will about see us through. One doesn't want to over-golf oneself the first day.' He swung the putter joyfully. 'How had we better play do you think? We might start with you giving me a half.'

She did not speak. She was very pale. She clutched the arm of her chair tightly till the knuckles showed white under the skin.

To anybody but Mortimer her nervousness would have been even more obvious on the following morning, as they reached the first tee. Her eyes were dull and heavy, and she started when a grasshopper chirruped. But Mortimer was too occupied with thinking how jolly it was having the course to themselves to notice anything.

He scooped some sand out of the box, and took a ball out of her bag. His wedding present to her had been a brand-new golf-bag, six dozen balls, and a full set of the most expensive clubs, all born in Scotland.

'Do you like a high tee?' he asked.

'Oh, no,' she replied, coming with a start out of her thoughts. 'Doctors say it's indigestible.'

Mortimer laughed merrily.

'Deuced good!' he chuckled. 'Is that your own or did you read it in a comic paper? There you are!' He placed the ball on a little hill of sand, and got up. 'Now let's see some of that championship form of yours!'

She burst into tears.

'My darling!'

Mortimer ran to her and put his arms round her. She tried weakly to push him away.

'My angel! What is it?'

She sobbed brokenly. Then, with an effort, she spoke.

'Mortimer, I have deceived you!'

'Deceived me?'

'I have never played golf in my life! I don't even know how to hold the caddie!'

Mortimer's heart stood still. This sounded like the gibberings of an unbalanced mind, and no man likes his wife to begin gibbering immediately after the honeymoon.

'My precious! You are not yourself!'

'I am! That's the whole trouble! I'm myself and not the girl you thought I was!'

Mortimer stared at her, puzzled. He was thinking that it was a little difficult and that, to work it out properly, he would need a pencil and a bit of paper.

'My name is not Mary!'

'But you said it was.'

'I didn't. You asked if you could call me Mary, and I said you might, because I loved you too much to deny your smallest whim. I was going on to say that it wasn't my name, but you interrupted me.'

'Not Mary!' The horrid truth was coming home to Mortimer. 'You were not Mary Somerset?'

'Mary is my cousin. My name is Mabel.'

'But you said you had sprained your wrist playing in the championship.'

'So I had. The mallet slipped in my hand.'

'The mallet!' Mortimer clutched at his forehead. 'You didn't say "the mallet"?'

'Yes, Mortimer! The mallet!'

A faint blush of shame mantled her cheek, and into her blue eyes there came a look of pain, but she faced him bravely.

'I am the Ladies' Open Croquet Champion!' she whispered.

Mortimer Sturgis cried aloud, a cry that was like the shriek of some wounded animal.

'Croquet!' He gulped, and stared at her with unseeing eyes. He was no prude, but he had those decent prejudices of which no self-respecting man can wholly rid himself, however broad-minded he may try to be. 'Croquet!'

There was a long silence. The light breeze sang in the pines above them. The grasshoppers chirruped at their feet.

She began to speak again in a low, monotonous voice.

'I blame myself! I should have told you before, while there was yet time for you to withdraw. I should have confessed this to you that night on the terrace in the moonlight. But you swept me off my feet, and I was in your arms before I realised what you would think of me. It was only then that I understood what my supposed skill at golf meant to you, and then it was too late. I loved you too much to let you go! I could not bear the thought of you recoiling from me. Oh, I was mad – mad! I knew that I could not keep up the deception for ever, that you must find me out in time. But I had a wild hope that by then we should be so close to one another that you might find it in your heart to forgive. But I was wrong. I see it now. There are some things that no man can forgive. Some things,' she repeated, dully, 'which no man can forgive.'

She turned away. Mortimer awoke from his trance.

'Stop!' he cried. 'Don't go!'

'I must go.'

'I want to talk this over.'

She shook her head sadly and started to walk slowly

across the sunlit grass. Mortimer watched her, his brain in a whirl of chaotic thoughts. She disappeared through the trees.

Mortimer sat down on the tee-box, and buried his face in his hands. For a time he could think of nothing but the cruel blow he had received. This was the end of those rainbow visions of himself and her going through life side by side, she lovingly criticising his stance and his back-swing, he learning wisdom from her. A croquet player! He was married to a woman who hit coloured balls through hoops. Mortimer Sturgis writhed in torment. A strong man's agony.

The mood passed. How long it had lasted, he did not know. But suddenly, as he sat there, he became once more aware of the glow of the sunshine and the singing of the birds. It was as if a shadow had lifted. Hope and optimism crept into his heart.

He loved her. He loved her still. She was part of him, and nothing that she could do had power to alter that. She had deceived him, yes. But why had she deceived him? Because she loved him so much that she could not bear to lose him. Dash it all, it was a bit of a compliment.

And, after all, poor girl, was it her fault? Was it not rather the fault of her upbringing? Probably she had been taught to play croquet when a mere child, hardly able to distinguish right from wrong. No steps had been taken to eradicate the virus from her system, and the thing had become chronic. Could she be blamed? Was she not more to be pitied than censured?

Mortimer rose to his feet, his heart swelling with generous forgiveness. The black horror had passed from him.

The future seemed once more bright. It was not too late. She was still young, many years younger than he himself had been when he took up golf, and surely, if she put herself into the hands of a good specialist and practised every day, she might still hope to become a fair player. He reached the house and ran in, calling her name.

No answer came. He sped from room to room, but all were empty.

She had gone. The house was there. The furniture was there. The canary sang in its cage, the cook in the kitchen. The pictures still hung on the walls. But she had gone. Everything was at home except his wife.

Finally, propped up against the cup he had once won in a handicap competition, he saw a letter. With a sinking heart he tore open the envelope.

It was a pathetic, a tragic letter, the letter of a woman endeavouring to express all the anguish of a torn heart with one of those fountain pens which suspend the flow of ink about twice in every three words. The gist of it was that she felt she had wronged him; that, though he might forgive, he could never forget; and that she was going away, away out into the world alone.

Mortimer sank into a chair, and stared blankly before him. She had scratched the match.

I am not a married man myself, so have had no experience of how it feels to have one's wife whizz off silently into the unknown; but I should imagine that it must be something like taking a full swing with a brassey and missing the ball. Something, I take it, of the same sense of mingled shock, chagrin, and the feeling that nobody loves one, which attacks a man in such circumstances, must come to the bereaved husband. And one can readily understand how terribly the incident must have shaken Mortimer Sturgis. I was away at the time, but I am told by those who saw him that his game went all to pieces.

He had never shown much indication of becoming anything in the nature of a first-class golfer, but he had managed to acquire one or two decent shots. His work with the light iron was not at all bad, and he was a fairly steady putter. But now, under the shadow of this tragedy, he dropped right back to the form of his earliest period. It was a pitiful sight to see this gaunt, haggard man with the look of dumb anguish behind his spectacles taking as many as three shots sometimes to get past the ladies' tee. His slice, of which he had almost cured himself, returned with such virulence that in the list of ordinary hazards he had now to include the tee-box. And, when he was not slicing, he was pulling. I have heard that he was known, when driving at the sixth, to get bunkered in his own caddie, who had taken up his position directly behind him. As for the deep sand-trap in front of the seventh green, he spent so much of his time in it that there was some informal talk among the members of the committee of charging him a small weekly rent.

A man of comfortable independent means, he lived during these days on next to nothing. Golf-balls cost him a certain amount, but the bulk of his income he spent in efforts to discover his wife's whereabouts. He advertised in all the papers. He employed private detectives. He even, much as it revolted his finer instincts, took to travelling about the country, watching croquet matches. But she was never among the players. I am not sure that he did not find a melancholy comfort in this, for it seemed to show that, whatever his wife might be and whatever she might be doing, she had not gone right under.

Summer passed. Autumn came and went. Winter arrived. The days grew bleak and chill, and an early fall of snow, heavier than had been known at that time of the year for a long while, put an end to golf. Mortimer spent his days indoors, staring gloomily through the window at the white mantle that covered the earth.

It was Christmas Eve.

The young man shifted uneasily on his seat. His face was long and sombre.

'All this is very depressing,' he said.

'These soul tragedies,' agreed the Oldest Member, 'are never very cheery.'

'Look here,' said the young man, firmly, 'tell me one thing frankly, as man to man. Did Mortimer find her dead in the snow, covered except for her face, on which still lingered that faint, sweet smile which he remembered so well? Because, if he did, I'm going home.'

'No, no,' protested the Oldest Member. 'Nothing of that kind.'

'You're sure? You aren't going to spring it on me suddenly?'

'No, no!'

The young man breathed a relieved sigh.

'It was your saying that about the white mantle covering the earth that made me suspicious.'

The Sage resumed.

*

It was Christmas Eve. All day the snow had been falling, and now it lay thick and deep over the countryside. Mortimer Sturgis, his frugal dinner concluded – what with losing his wife and not being able to get any golf, he had little appetite these days – was sitting in his drawing room, moodily polishing the blade of his jigger. Soon wearying of this once congenial task, he laid down the club and went to the front door, to see if there was any chance of a thaw. But no. It was freezing. The snow, as he tested it with his shoe, crackled crisply. The sky above was black and full of cold stars. It seemed to Mortimer that the sooner he packed up and went to the South of France, the better. He was just about to close the door, when suddenly he thought he heard his own name called.

'Mortimer!'

Had he been mistaken? The voice had sounded faint and far away.

'Mortimer!'

He thrilled from head to foot. This time there could be no mistake. It was the voice he knew so well, his wife's voice, and it had come from somewhere down near the garden gate. It is difficult to judge distance where sounds are concerned, but Mortimer estimated that the voice had spoken about a short mashie-niblick and an easy putt from where he stood.

The next moment he was racing down the snow-covered path. And then his heart stood still. What was that dark something on the ground just inside the gate? He leaped towards it. He passed his hands over it. It was a human body. Quivering, he struck a match. It went out. He struck another. That went out, too. He struck a third, and it burned with a steady flame; and, stooping, he saw that it was his wife who lay there, cold and stiff. Her eyes were closed, and on her face still lingered that faint, sweet smile which he remembered so well.

The young man rose with a set face. He reached for his golf-bag.

'I call that a dirty trick,' he said, 'after you promised—'
The Sage waved him back to his seat.

'Have no fear! She had only fainted.'

'You said she was cold.'

'Wouldn't you be cold if you were lying in the snow?'

'And stiff.'

'Mrs Sturgis was stiff because the train service was bad, it being the holiday season, and she had had to walk all the way from the junction, a distance of eight miles. Sit down and allow me to proceed.'

Tenderly, reverently Mortimer Sturgis picked her up and began to bear her into the house. Halfway there, his foot slipped on a piece of ice and he fell heavily, barking his shin and shooting his lovely burden out on to the snow.

The fall brought her to. She opened her eyes.

'Mortimer, darling!' she said.

Mortimer had just been going to say something else, but he checked himself.

'Are you alive?' he asked.

'Yes,' she replied.

'Thank God!' said Mortimer, scooping some of the snow out of the back of his collar.

Together they went into the house, and into the

drawing room. Wife gazed at husband, husband at wife. There was a silence.

'Rotten weather!' said Mortimer.

'Yes, isn't it!'

The spell was broken. They fell into each other's arms. And presently they were sitting side by side on the sofa, holding hands, just as if that awful parting had been but a dream.

It was Mortimer who made the first reference to it.

'I say, you know,' he said, 'you oughtn't to have nipped away like that!'

'I thought you hated me!'

'Hated *you*! I love you better than life itself! I would sooner have smashed my pet driver than have had you leave me!'

She thrilled at the words.

'Darling!'

Mortimer fondled her hand.

'I was just coming back to tell you that I loved you still. I was going to suggest that you took lessons from some good professional. And I found you gone!'

'I wasn't worthy of you, Mortimer!'

'My angel!' He pressed his lips to her hair, and spoke solemnly. 'All this has taught me a lesson, dearest. I knew all along, and I know it more than ever now, that it is you – you that I want. Just you! I don't care if you don't play golf. I don't care—' He hesitated, then went on manfully. 'I don't care even if you play croquet, so long as you are with me!'

For a moment her face showed a rapture that made it almost angelic. She uttered a low moan of ecstasy. She kissed him. Then she rose.

'Mortimer, look!'

'What at?'

'Me. Just look!'

The jigger which he had been polishing lay on a chair close by. She took it up. From the bowl of golf-balls on the mantelpiece she selected a brand-new one. She placed it on the carpet. She addressed it. Then, with a merry cry of 'Fore!' she drove it hard and straight through the glass of the china-cupboard.

'Good God!' cried Mortimer, astounded. It had been a bird of a shot.

She turned to him, her whole face alight with that beautiful smile.

'When I left you, Mortie,' she said, 'I had but one aim in life, somehow to make myself worthy of you. I saw your advertisements in the papers, and I longed to answer them, but I was not ready. All this long, weary while I have been in the village of Auchtermuchtie, in Scotland, studying under Tammas McMickle.'

'Not the Tammas McMickle who finished fourth in the Open Championship of 1911, and had the best ball in the foursome in 1912 with Jock McHaggis, Andy McHeather, and Sandy McHoots!'

'Yes, Mortimer, the very same. Oh, it was difficult at first. I missed my mallet, and longed to steady the ball with my foot and use the toe of the club. Wherever there was a direction post I aimed at it automatically. But I conquered my weakness. I practised steadily. And now Mr McMickle says my handicap would be a good twenty-four on any links.' She smiled apologetically. 'Of course, that doesn't sound much to you! You were a twelve when

I left you, and now I suppose you are down to eight or something.'

Mortimer shook his head.

'Alas, no!' he replied, gravely. 'My game went right off for some reason or other, and I'm twenty-four, too.'

'For some reason or other!' She uttered a cry. 'Oh, I know what the reason was! How can I ever forgive myself! I have ruined your game!'

The brightness came back to Mortimer's eyes. He embraced her fondly.

'Do not reproach yourself, dearest,' he murmured. 'It is the best thing that could have happened. From now on, we start level, two hearts that beat as one, two drivers that drive as one. I could not wish it otherwise. By George! It's just like that thing of Tennyson's.'

He recited the lines softly:

'My bride,
My wife, my life. Oh, we will walk the links
Yoked in all exercise of noble end,
And so thro' those dark bunkers off the course
That no man knows. Indeed, I love thee: come,
Yield thyself up: our handicaps are one;
Accomplish thou my manhood and thyself;
Lay thy sweet hands in mine and trust to me.'

She laid her hands in his.

'And now, Mortie, darling,' she said, 'I want to tell you all about how I did the long twelfth at Auchtermuchtie in one under bogey.'

February

The Passing of Ambrose

'Right ho,' said Algy Crufts. 'Then I shall go alone.'
'Right ho,' said Ambrose Wiffin. 'Go alone.'
'Right ho,' said Algy Crufts. 'I will.'
'Right ho,' said Ambrose Wiffin. 'Do.'
'Right ho, then,' said Algy Crufts.
'Right ho,' said Ambrose Wiffin.
'Right ho,' said Algy Crufts.

Few things (said Mr Mulliner) are more painful than an altercation between two boyhood friends. Nevertheless, when these occur, the conscientious narrator must record them.

It is also, no doubt, the duty of such a narrator to be impartial. In the present instance, however, it would be impossible to avoid bias. To realise that Algy Crufts was perfectly justified in taking an even stronger tone, one has only to learn the facts. It was the season of the year when there comes upon all right-thinking young men the urge to go off to Monte Carlo: and the plan had been that he and Ambrose should catch the ten o'clock boat-train on the morning of the sixteenth of February. All the arrangements had been made – the tickets bought; the trunks packed; the 'One Hundred Systems of Winning at

Roulette' studied from end to end: and here was Ambrose, on the afternoon of February the fourteenth, calmly saying that he proposed to remain in London for another fortnight.

Algy Crufts eyed him narrowly. Ambrose Wiffin was always a nattily dressed young man, but today there had crept into his outer crust a sort of sinister effulgence which could have but one meaning. It shouted from his white carnation: it shrieked from his trouser-crease: and Algy read it in a flash.

'You're messing about after some beastly female,' he said.

Ambrose Wiffin reddened and brushed his top hat the wrong way.

'And I know who it is. It's that Wickham girl.'

Ambrose reddened again, and brushed his top hat once more – this time the right way, restoring the *status quo*.

'Well,' he said, 'you introduced me to her.'

'I know I did. And, if you recollect, I drew you aside immediately afterwards and warned you to watch your step.'

'If you have anything to say against Miss Wickham . . .'

'I haven't anything to say against her. She's one of my best pals. I've known young Bobbie Wickham since she was a kid in arms, and I'm what you might call immune where she's concerned. But you can take it from me that every other fellow who comes in contact with Bobbie finds himself sooner or later up to the Adam's apple in some ghastly mess. She lets them down with a dull, sickening thud. Look at Roland Attwater. He went to stay at her place, and he had a snake with him . . .'

'Why?'

'I don't know. He just happened to have a snake with him, and Bobbie put it in a fellow's bed and let everyone think it was Attwater who had done it. He had to leave by the milk-train at three in the morning.'

'Attwater had no business lugging snakes about with him to country houses,' said Ambrose primly. 'One can readily understand how a high-spirited girl would feel tempted...'

'And then there was Dudley Finch. She asked him down for the night and forgot to tell her mother he was coming, with the result that he was taken for a Society burglar and got shot in the leg by the butler as he was leaving to catch the milk-train.'

A look such as Sir Galahad might have worn on hearing gossip about Queen Guinevere lent a noble dignity to Ambrose Wiffin's pink young face.

'I don't care,' he said stoutly. 'She's the sweetest girl on earth, and I'm taking her to the Dog Show on Saturday.'

'Eh? What about our Monte Carlo binge?'

'That'll have to be postponed. Not for long. She's up in London, staying with an aunt of sorts, for another couple of weeks. I could come after that.'

'Do you mean to say you have the immortal crust to expect me to hang about for two weeks, waiting for you?'

'I don't see why not.'

'Oh, don't you? Well, I'm jolly well not going to.'

'Right ho. Just as you like.'

'Right ho. Then I shall go alone.'

'Right ho. Go alone.'

'Right ho. I will.'

'Right ho. Do.'
'Right ho, then.'
'Right ho,' said Ambrose Wiffin.
'Right ho,' said Algy Crufts.

At almost exactly the moment when this very distressing scene was taking place at the Drones Club in Dover Street, Roberta Wickham, in the drawing room of her aunt Marcia's house in Eaton Square, was endeavouring to reason with her mother, and finding the going a bit heavy. Lady Wickham was notoriously a difficult person to reason with. She was a woman who knew her mind.

'But, Mother!'

Lady Wickham advanced her forceful chin another inch.

'It's no use arguing, Roberta . . .'

'But, Mother! I keep telling you! Jane Falconer has just rung up and wants me to go round and help her choose the cushions for her new flat.'

'And I keep telling you that a promise is a promise. You voluntarily offered after breakfast this morning to take your cousin Wilfred and his little friend, Esmond Bates, to the moving-pictures today, and you cannot disappoint them now.'

'But if Jane's left to herself she'll choose the most awful things.'

'I cannot help that.'

'She's relying on me. She said so. And I swore I'd go.'

'I cannot help that.'

'I'd forgotten all about Wilfred.'

'I cannot help that. You should not have forgotten.

You must ring your friend up and tell her that you are unable to see her this afternoon. I think you ought to be glad of the chance of giving pleasure to these two boys. One ought not always to be thinking of oneself. One ought to try to bring a little sunshine into the lives of others. I will go and tell Wilfred you are waiting for him.'

Left alone, Roberta wandered morosely to the window and stood looking down into the Square. From this vantage-point she was able to observe a small boy in an Eton suit sedulously hopping from the pavement to the bottom step of the house and back again. This was Esmond Bates, next door's son and heir, and the effect the sight of him had on Bobbie was to drive her from the window and send her slumping onto the sofa, where for a space she sat, gazing before her and disliking life. It may not seem to everybody the summit of human pleasure to go about London choosing cushions, but Bobbie had set her heart on it: and the iron was entering deeply into her soul when the door opened and the butler appeared.

'Mr Wiffin,' announced the butler. And Ambrose walked in, glowing with that holy reverential emotion which always surged over him at the sight of Bobbie.

Usually, there was blended with this a certain diffidence, unavoidable in one visiting the shrine of a goddess: but today the girl seemed so unaffectedly glad to see him that diffidence vanished. He was amazed to note how glad she was to see him. She had bounded from the sofa on his entry, and now was looking at him with shining eyes like a shipwrecked mariner who sights a sail.

'Oh, Ambrose!' said Bobbie. 'I'm so glad you came.'

Ambrose thrilled from his quiet but effective sock-clocks to his Stacombed hair. How wise, he felt, he had been to spend that long hour perfecting the minutest details of his toilet. As a glance in the mirror on the landing had just assured him, his hat was right, his coat was right, his trousers were right, his shoes were right, his buttonhole was right, and his tie was right. He was one hundred per cent, and girls appreciate such things.

'Just thought I'd look in,' he said, speaking in the guttural tones which agitated vocal cords always forced upon him when addressing the queen of her species, 'and see if you were doing anything this afternoon. If,' he added, 'you see what I mean.'

'I'm taking my cousin Wilfred and a little friend of his to the movies. Would you like to come?'

'I say! Thanks awfully! May I?'

'Yes, do.'

'I say! Thanks awfully!' He gazed at her with worshipping admiration. 'But I say, how frightfully kind of you to mess up an afternoon taking a couple of kids to the movies. Awfully kind. I mean kind. I mean I call it dashed kind of you.'

'Oh, well!' said Bobbie modestly. 'I feel I ought to be glad of the chance of giving pleasure to these two boys. One ought not always to be thinking of oneself. One ought to try to bring a little sunshine into the lives of others.'

'You're an angel!'

'No, no.'

'An absolute angel,' insisted Ambrose, quivering fervently. 'Doing a thing like this is ... well, absolutely angelic. If you follow me. I wish Algy Crufts had been here to see it.'

'Why Algy?'

'Because he was saying some very unpleasant things about you this afternoon. Most unpleasant things.'

'What did he say?'

'He said . . .' Ambrose winced. The vile words were choking him. 'He said you let people down.'

'Did he! Did he, forsooth! I'll have to have a word with young Algernon P. Crufts. He's getting above himself. He seems to forget,' said Bobbie, a dreamy look coming into her beautiful eyes, 'that we live next to each other in the country and that I know which his room is. What young Algy wants is a frog in his bed.'

'Two frogs,' amended Ambrose.

'Two frogs,' agreed Bobbie.

The door opened and there appeared on the mat a small boy. He wore an Eton suit, spectacles, and, low down over his prominent ears, a bowler hat: and Ambrose thought he had seldom seen anything fouler. He would have looked askance at Royalty itself, had Royalty interrupted a *tête-à-tête* with Miss Wickham.

'I'm ready,' said the boy.

'This is Aunt Marcia's son Wilfred,' said Bobbie.

'Oh?' said Ambrose coldly.

Like so many young men, Ambrose Wiffin was accustomed to regard small boys with a slightly jaundiced eye. It was his simple creed that they wanted their heads smacked. When not having their heads smacked, they should be out of the picture altogether. He stared disparagingly at this specimen. A half-formed resolve to love him for Bobbie's sake perished at birth. Only the thought that Bobbie would be of the company enabled him to endure the prospect of being seen in public with this outstanding piece of cheese.

'Let's go,' said the boy.

'All right,' said Bobbie. 'I'm ready.'

'We'll find Old Stinker on the steps,' the boy assured her, as one promising a deserving person some delightful treat.

Old Stinker, discovered as predicted, seemed to Ambrose just the sort of boy who would be a friend of Bobbie's cousin Wilfred. He was goggle-eyed and freckled and also, as it was speedily to appear, an officious little devil who needed six of the best with a fives-bat.

'The cab's waiting,' said Old Stinker.

'How clever of you to have found a cab, Esmond,' said Bobbie indulgently.

'I didn't find it. It's his cab. I told it to wait.'

A stifled exclamation escaped Ambrose, and he shot a fevered glance at the taxi's clock. The sight of the figures on it caused him a sharp pang. Not six with a fives-bat, he felt. Ten. And of the juiciest.

'Splendid,' said Bobbie. 'Hop in. Tell him to drive to the Tivoli.'

Ambrose suppressed the words he had been about to utter; and, climbing into the cab, settled himself down and devoted his attention to trying to avoid the feet of Bobbie's cousin Wilfred, who sat opposite him. The boy seemed as liberally equipped with these as a centipede, and there was scarcely a moment when his boots were not rubbing the polish off Ambrose's glittering shoes. It was with something of the emotions of the Ten Thousand Greeks on beholding the sea that at long last he sighted the familiar architecture of the Strand. Soon he would be sitting next to Bobbie in a dimly lighted auditorium, and a man with that in prospect could afford to rough it a bit on the journey. He alighted from the cab and plunged into the queue before the box office.

Wedged in among the crowd of pleasure-seekers, Ambrose, though physically uncomfortable, felt somehow a sort of spiritual refreshment. There is nothing a young man in love finds more delightful than the doing of some knightly service for the loved one: and, though to describe as a knightly service the act of standing in a queue and buying tickets for a motion-picture entertainment may seem straining the facts a little, to one in Ambrose's condition a service is a service. He would have preferred to be called upon to save Bobbie's life: but, this not being at the moment feasible, it was something to be jostling in a queue for her sake.

Nor was the action so free from peril as might appear at first sight. Sheer, black disaster was lying in wait for Ambrose Wiffin. He had just forced his way to the pay-box and was turning to leave after buying the tickets when the thing happened. From somewhere behind him an arm shot out, there was an instant's sickening suspense, and then the top hat which he loved nearly as much as life itself was rolling across the lobby with a stout man in the uniform of a Czeko-Slovakian Rear Admiral in pursuit.

In the sharp agony of this happening, it had seemed to Ambrose that he had experienced the worst moment of his career. Then he discovered that it was in reality merely the worst but one. The sorrow's crown of sorrow was achieved an instant later when the Admiral returned, bearing in his hand a battered something which for a space he was unable to recognise.

The Admiral was sympathetic. There was a bluff, sailorly sympathy in his voice as he spoke.

'Here you are, sir,' he said. 'Here's your rat. A little the worse for wear, this sat is, I'm afraid, sir. A gentleman happened to step on it. You can't step on a nat,' he said sententiously, 'not without hurting it. That tat is not the yat it was.'

Although he spoke in the easy manner of one making genial conversation, his voice had in it a certain purposeful note. He seemed like a Rear Admiral who was waiting for something: and Ambrose, as if urged by some hypnotic spell, produced half a crown and pressed it into his hand. Then, placing the remains on his head, he tottered across the lobby to join the girl he loved.

That she could ever, after seeing him in a hat like that, come to love him in return seemed to him at first unbelievable. Then Hope began to steal shyly back. After all, it was in her cause that he had suffered this great blow. She would take that into account. Furthermore, girls of Roberta Wickham's fine fibre do not love a man entirely for his hat. The trousers count, so do the spats. It was in a spirit almost optimistic that he forced his way through the crowd to the spot where he had left the girl. And as he reached it the squeaky voice of Old Stinker smote his ear.

'Golly!' said Old Stinker. 'What have you done to your hat?'

Another squeaky voice spoke. Aunt Marcia's son Wilfred

was regarding him with the offensive interest of a biologist examining some lower organism under the microscope.

'I say,' said Wilfred, 'I don't know if you know it, but somebody's been sitting on your hat or something. Did you ever see a hat like that, Stinker?'

'Never in my puff,' replied his friend.

Ambrose gritted his teeth.

'Never mind my hat! Where's Miss Wickham?'

'Oh, she had to go,' said Old Stinker.

It was not for a moment that the hideous meaning of the words really penetrated Ambrose's consciousness. Then his jaw fell and he stared aghast.

'Go? Go where?'

'I don't know where. She went.'

'She said she had just remembered an appointment,' explained Wilfred. 'She said . . .'

'. . . that you were to take us in and she would join us later if she could.'

'She rather thought she wouldn't be able to, but she said leave her ticket at the box office in case.'

'She said she knew we would be all right with you,' concluded Old Stinker. 'Come on, let's beef in or we'll be missing the educational two-reel comic.'

Ambrose eyed them wanly. All his instincts urged him to smack these two heads as heads should be smacked, to curse a good deal, to wash his hands of the whole business and stride away. But Love conquers all. Reason told him that here were two small boys, a good deal ghastlier than any small boy he had yet encountered. In short, mere smack-fodder. But Love, stronger than reason, whispered that they were a sacred trust. Roberta

Wickham expected him to take them to the movies and he must do it.

And such was his love that not yet had he begun to feel any resentment at this desertion of hers. No doubt, he told himself, she had had some good reason. In anyone a shade less divine, the act of sneaking off and landing him with these two disease-germs might have seemed culpable: but what he felt at the moment was that the Queen could do no wrong.

'Oh, all right,' he said dully. 'Push in.'

Old Stinker had not yet exhausted the theme of the hat.

'I say,' he observed, 'that hat looks pretty rummy, you know.'

'Absolutely weird,' assented Wilfred.

Ambrose regarded them intently for a moment, and his gloved hand twitched a little. But the iron self-control of the Wiffins stood him in good stead.

'Push in,' he said in a strained voice. 'Push in.'

In the last analysis, however many highly salaried stars its cast may contain and however superb and luxurious the settings of its orgy scenes, the success of a super-film's appeal to an audience must always depend on what company each unit of that audience is in when he sees it. Start wrong in the vestibule, and entertainment in the true sense is out of the question.

For the picture which the management of the Tivoli was now presenting to its patrons Hollywood had done all that Art and Money could effect. Based on Wordsworth's well-known poem 'We are Seven', it was entitled 'Where

Passion Lurks', and offered such notable favourites of the silver screen as Laurette Byng, G. Cecil Terwilliger, Baby Bella, Oscar the Wonder-Poodle, and Professor Pond's Educated Sea-Lions. And yet it left Ambrose cold.

If only Bobbie had been at his side, how different it all would have been. As it was, the beauty of the story had no power to soothe him, nor could he get the slightest thrill out of the Babylonian Banquet scene which had cost five hundred thousand dollars. From start to finish he sat in a dull apathy: then, at last, the ordeal over, he stumbled out into daylight and the open air. Like G. Cecil Terwilliger at a poignant crisis in the fourth reel, he was as one on whom Life has forced its bitter cup, and who has drained it to the lees.

And it was this moment, when a strong man stood face to face with his soul, that Old Stinker with the rashness of Youth selected for beginning again about the hat.

'I say,' said Old Stinker, as they came out into the bustling Strand, 'you've no idea what a blister you look in that lid.'

'Priceless,' agreed Wilfred cordially.

'All you want is a banjo and you could make a fortune singing comic songs outside the pubs.'

On his first introduction to these little fellows it had seemed to Ambrose that they had touched the lowest possible level to which Humanity can descend. It now became apparent that there were hitherto unimagined depths which it was in their power to plumb. There is a point beyond which even a Wiffin's self-control fails to function. The next moment, above the roar of London's traffic there sounded the crisp note of a well-smacked head.

It was Wilfred who, being nearest, had received the treatment: and it was at Wilfred that an elderly lady, pausing, pointed with indignant horror in every waggle of her fingertip.

'Why did you strike that little boy?' demanded the elderly lady.

Ambrose made no answer. He was in no mood for conundrums. Besides, to reply fully to the question, he would have been obliged to trace the whole history of his love, to dilate on the agony it had caused him to discover that his goddess had feet of clay, to explain how little by little through the recent entertainment there had grown a fever in his blood, caused by this boy sucking peppermints, shuffling his feet, giggling and reading out the subtitles. Lastly, he would have had to discuss at length the matter of the hat.

Unequal to these things, he merely glowered: and such was the calibre of his scowl that the other supposed that here was the authentic Abysmal Brute.

'I've a good mind to call a policeman,' she said.

It is a peculiar phenomenon of life in London that the magic word 'policeman' has only to be whispered in any of its thoroughfares to attract a crowd of substantial dimensions: and Ambrose, gazing about him, now discovered that their little group had been augmented by some thirty citizens, each of whom was regarding him in much the same way that he would have regarded the accused in a big murder trial at the Old Bailey.

A passionate desire to be elsewhere came upon the young man. Of all things in this life he disliked most a scene: and this was plainly working up into a scene of the worst kind. Seizing his sacred trusts by the elbow he ran them across the street. The crowd continued to stand and stare at the spot where the incident had occurred.

For some little time, safe on the opposite pavement, Ambrose was too busily occupied in reassembling his disintegrated nervous system to give any attention to the world about him. He was recalled to mundane matters by a piercing squeal of ecstasy from his young companions.

'Oo! Oysters!'

'Golly! Oysters!'

And he became aware that they were standing outside a restaurant whose window was deeply paved with these shellfish. On these the two lads were gloating with bulging eyes.

'I could do with an oyster!' said Old Stinker.

'So could I jolly well do with an oyster,' said Wilfred.

'I bet I could eat more oysters than you.'

'I bet you couldn't.'

'I bet I could.'

'I bet you couldn't.'

'I bet you a million pounds I could.'

'I bet you a million trillion pounds you couldn't.'

Ambrose had had no intention of presiding over the hideous sporting contest which they appeared to be planning. Apart from the nauseous idea of devouring oysters at half-past four in the afternoon, he resented the notion of spending any more of his money on these gargoyles. But at this juncture he observed, threading her way nimbly through the traffic, the elderly lady who had made the Scene. A Number 33 omnibus could quite easily have got her, but through sheer carelessness and over-confidence failed to do so: and now she was on the pavement and heading in their direction. There was not an instant to be lost.

'Push in,' he said hoarsely. 'Push in.'

A moment later, they were seated at a table and a waiter, who looked like one of the executive staff of the Black Hand, was hovering beside them with pencil and pad.

Ambrose made one last appeal to his guests' better feelings.

'You can't really want oysters at this time of day,' he said almost pleadingly.

'I bet you we can,' said Old Stinker.

'I bet you a billion pounds we can,' said Wilfred.

'Oh, all right,' said Ambrose. 'Oysters.'

He sank back in his chair and endeavoured to avert his eyes from the grim proceedings. Aeons passed, and he was aware that the golluping noises at his side had ceased. All things end in time. Even the weariest river winds somewhere to the sea. Wilfred and Old Stinker had stopped eating oysters.

'Finished?' he asked in a cold voice.

There was a moment's pause. The boys seemed hesitant.

'Yes, if there aren't any more.'

'There aren't,' said Ambrose. He beckoned to the waiter, who was leaning against the wall dreaming of old, happy murders of his distant youth. 'Ladishion,' he said curtly.

'Sare?'

'The bill.'

'The pill? Oh yes, sare.'

Shrill and jovial laughter greeted the word.

'He said "pill"!' gurgled Old Stinker.

'"Pill"!' echoed Wilfred.

They punched each other delightedly to signify their appreciation of this excellent comedy. The waiter flushed darkly, muttered something in his native tongue and seemed about to reach for his stiletto. Ambrose reddened to the eyebrows. Laughing at waiters was simply one of the things that aren't done, and he felt his position acutely. It was a relief when the Black Hander returned with his change.

There was only a solitary sixpence on the plate, and Ambrose hastened to dip in his pocket for further coins to supplement this. A handsome tip would, he reasoned, show the waiter that, though circumstances had forced these two giggling outcasts upon him, spiritually he had no affiliation with them. It would be a gesture which would put him at once on an altogether different plane. The man would understand that, dubious though the company might be in which he had met him, Ambrose Wiffin himself was all right and had a heart of gold. 'Simpatico', he believed these Italians called it.

And then he sat up, tingling as from an electric shock. From pocket to pocket his fingers flew, and in each found only emptiness. The awful truth was clear. An afternoon spent in paying huge taxi-fares, buying seats for motion-picture performances, pressing half-crowns into the palms of Czeko-Slovakian Rear Admirals and filling small boys with oysters had left him a financial ruin. That sixpence was all he had to get these two blighted boys back to Eaton Square.

Ambrose Wiffin paused at the crossroads. In all his life he had never left a waiter untipped. He had not supposed it could be done. He had looked upon the tipping of waiters as a natural process, impossible to evade, like breathing or leaving the bottom button of your waistcoat unfastened. Ghosts of bygone Wiffins – Wiffins who had scattered largesse to the multitude in the Middle Ages, Wiffins who in Regency days had flung landlords purses of gold – seemed to crowd at his elbow, imploring the last of their line not to disgrace the family name. On the other hand, sixpence would just pay for bus fares and remove from him the necessity of walking two miles through the streets of London in a squashed top hat and in the society of Wilfred and Old Stinker . . .

If it had been Wilfred alone . . . Or even Old Stinker alone . . . Or if that hat did not look so extraordinarily like something off the stage of a low-class music-hall . . .

Ambrose Wiffin hesitated no longer. Pocketing the sixpence with one swift motion of the hand and breathing heavily through his nose, he sprang to his feet.

'Come on!' he growled.

He could have betted on his little friends. They acted just as he had expected they would. No tact. No reticence. Not an effort towards handling the situation. Just two bright young children of Nature, who said the first thing that came into their heads, and who, he hoped, would wake up tomorrow morning with ptomaine-poisoning.

'I say!' It was Wilfred who gave tongue first of the pair, and his clear voice rang through the restaurant like a bugle. 'You haven't tipped him!'

'I say!' Old Stinker chiming in, extraordinarily bell-like. 'Dash it all, aren't you going to tip him?'

'You haven't tipped the waiter,' said Wilfred, making his meaning clearer.

'The waiter,' explained Old Stinker, clarifying the situation of its last trace of ambiguity. 'You haven't tipped him!'

'Come on!' moaned Ambrose. 'Push out! Push out!'

A hundred dead Wiffins shrieked a ghostly shriek and covered their faces with their winding sheets. A stunned waiter clutched his napkin to his breast. And Ambrose, with bowed head, shot out of the door like a conscience-stricken rabbit. In that supreme moment he even forgot that he was wearing a top hat like a concertina. So true is it that the greater emotion swallows up the less.

A heaven-sent omnibus stopped before him in a traffic block. He pushed his little charges in, and, as they charged in their gay, boyish way to the further end of the vehicle, seated himself next to the door, as far away from them as possible. Then, removing the hat, he sat back and closed his eyes.

Hitherto, when sitting back with closed eyes, it had always been the custom of Ambrose Wiffin to give himself up to holy thoughts about Bobbie. But now they refused to come. Plenty of thoughts, but not holy ones. It was as though the supply had petered out.

Too dashed bad of the girl, he meant, letting him in for a thing like this. Absolutely too dashed bad of her. And, mark you, she had intended from the very beginning, mind you, to let him in for it. Oh yes, she had. All that about suddenly remembering an appointment, he meant to say. Perfect rot. Wouldn't hold water for a second. She had never had the least intention of coming into that bally moving-picture place. Right from the start she had planned to lure him into the thing and then ooze off and land him with these septic kids, and what he meant was that it was too dashed bad of her.

Yes, he declined to mince his words. Too dashed bad. Not playing the game. A bit thick. In short – well, to put it in a nutshell, too dashed bad.

The omnibus rolled on. Ambrose opened his eyes in order to note progress. He was delighted to observe that they were already nearing Hyde Park Corner. At last he permitted himself to breathe freely. His martyrdom was practically over. Only a little longer now, only a few short minutes, and he would be able to deliver the two pestilences F.O.B. at their dens in Eaton Square, wash them out of his life for ever, return to the comfort and safety of his cosy rooms, and there begin life anew.

The thought was heartening: and Ambrose, greatly restored, turned to sketching out in his mind the details of the drink which his man, under his own personal supervision, should mix for him immediately upon his return. As to this he was quite clear. Many fellows in his position – practically, you might say, saved at last from worse than death – would make it a stiff whisky-and-soda. But Ambrose, though he had no prejudice against whisky-and-soda, felt otherwise. It must be a cocktail. The cocktail of a lifetime. A cocktail that would ring down the ages, in which gin blended smoothly with Italian vermouth and the spot of old brandy nestled like a trusting child against the dash of absinthe . . .

He sat up sharply. He stared. No, his eyes had not deceived him. At the far end of the omnibus Trouble was rearing its ugly head.

On occasions of great disaster it is seldom that the spectator perceives instantly every detail of what is toward. The thing creeps upon him gradually, impinging itself upon his consciousness in progressive stages. All that the inhabitants of Pompeii, for example, observed in the early stages of that city's doom was probably a mere puff of smoke. 'Ah,' they said, 'a puff of smoke!' and let it go at that. So with Ambrose Wiffin in the case of which we are treating.

The first thing that attracted Ambrose's attention was the face of a man who had come in at the last stop and seated himself immediately opposite Old Stinker. It was an extraordinarily solemn face, spotty in parts and bathed in a rather remarkable crimson flush. The eyes, which were prominent, wore a fixed far-away look. Ambrose had noted them as they passed him. They were round, glassy eyes. They were, briefly, the eyes of a man who has lunched.

In the casual way in which one examines one's fellow-passengers on an omnibus, Ambrose had allowed his gaze to flit from time to time to this person's face. For some minutes its expression had remained unaltered. The man might have been sitting for his photograph. But now into the eyes there was creeping a look almost of animation. The flush had begun to deepen. For some reason or other, it was plain, the machinery of the brain was starting to move once more.

Ambrose watched him idly. No premonition of doom came to him. He was simply mildly interested. And then, little by little, there crept upon him a faint sensation of discomfort.

The man's behaviour had now begun to be definitely peculiar. There was only one adjective to describe his manner, and that was the adjective odd. Slowly he had heaved himself up into a more rigid posture, and with his hands on his knees was bending slightly forward. His eyes had taken on a still glassier expression, and now with the glassiness was blended horror. Unmistakable horror. He was staring fixedly at some object directly in front of him.

It was a white mouse. Or, rather, at present merely the head of a white mouse. This head, protruding from the breast-pocket of Old Stinker's jacket, was moving slowly from side to side. Then, tiring of confinement, the entire mouse left the pocket, climbed down its proprietor's person until it reached his knee, and, having done a little washing and brushing-up, twitched its whiskers and looked across with benevolent pink eyes at the man opposite. The latter drew a sharp breath, swallowed, and moved his lips for a moment. It seemed to Ambrose that he was praying.

The glassy-eyed passenger was a man of resource. Possibly this sort of thing had happened to him before and he knew the procedure. He now closed his eyes, kept them closed for perhaps half a minute, then opened them again.

The mouse was still there.

It is at moments such as this that the best comes out in a man. You may impair it with a series of injudicious lunches, but you can never wholly destroy the spirit that has made Englishmen what they are. When the hour strikes, the old bulldog strain will show itself. Shakespeare noticed the same thing. His back against the wall, an Englishman, no matter how well he has lunched, will always sell his life dearly.

The glassy-eyed man, as he would have been the first to admit, had had just that couple over the eight which make all the difference, but he was a Briton. Whipping off his hat and uttering a hoarse cry – possibly, though the words could not be distinguished, that old, heart-stirring appeal to St George which rang out over the fields of Agincourt and Crécy – he leaned forward and smacked at the mouse.

The mouse, who had seen it coming, did the only possible thing. It sidestepped and, slipping to the floor, went into retreat there. And instantaneously from every side there arose the stricken cries of women in peril.

History, dealing with the affair, will raise its eyebrows at the conductor of the omnibus. He was patently inadequate. He pulled a cord, stopped the vehicle, and, advancing into the interior, said "Ere!' Napoleon might just as well have said "Ere!' at the battle of Waterloo. Forces far beyond the control of mere words had been unchained. Old Stinker was kicking the glassy-eyed passenger's shin. The glassy-eyed man was protesting that he was a gentleman. Three women were endeavouring to get through an exit planned by the omnibus's architect to accommodate but one traveller alone.

And then a massive, uniformed figure was in their midst.

'Wot's this?'

Ambrose waited no longer. He had had sufficient. Edging round the newcomer, he dropped from the omnibus and with swift strides vanished into the darkness.

The morning of February the fifteenth came murkily to London in a mantle of fog. It found Ambrose Wiffin breakfasting in bed. On the tray before him was a letter. The handwriting was the handwriting that once he had loved, but now it left him cold. His heart was dead, he regarded the opposite sex as a washout, and letters from Bobbie Wickham could stir no chord.

He had already perused this letter, but now he took it up once more and, his lips curved in a bitter smile, ran his eyes over it again, noting some of its high spots.

'... very disappointed in you ... cannot understand how you could have behaved in such an extraordinary way ...'

Ha!

'... did think I could have trusted you to look after ... And then you go and leave the poor little fellows alone in the middle of London ...'

Oh, ha, ha!

'... Wilfred arrived home in charge of a policeman, and mother is furious. I don't think I have ever seen her so pre-War ...'

Ambrose Wiffin threw the letter down and picked up the telephone.

'Hullo.'

'Hullo.'

'Algy?'

'Yes. Who's that?'

'Ambrose Wiffin.'

'Oh? What ho!'

'What ho!'

'What ho!'

'What ho!'

'I say,' said Algy Crufts. 'What became of you yesterday afternoon? I kept trying to get you on the phone and you were out.'

'Sorry,' said Ambrose Wiffin. 'I was taking a couple of kids to the movies.'

'What on earth for?'

'Oh, well, one likes to get the chance of giving a little pleasure to people, don't you know. One ought not always to be thinking of oneself. One ought to try to bring a little sunshine into the lives of others.'

'I suppose,' said Algy sceptically, 'that as a matter of fact, young Bobbie Wickham was with you, too, and you held her bally hand all the time.'

'Nothing of the kind,' replied Ambrose Wiffin with dignity. 'Miss Wickham was not among those present. What were you trying to get me on the phone about yesterday?'

'To ask you not to be a chump and stay hanging around London in this beastly weather. Ambrose, old bird, you simply must come tomorrow.'

'Algy, old cork, I was just going to ring you up to say I would.'

'You were?'

'Absolutely.'

'Great work! Sound egg! Right ho, then, I'll meet you under the clock at Charing Cross at half-past nine.'

'Right ho. I'll be there.'

'Right ho. Under the clock.'

'Right ho. The good old clock.'

'Right ho,' said Algy Crufts.

'Right ho,' said Ambrose Wiffin.

March

The Heel of Achilles

On the young man's face, as he sat sipping his ginger ale in the clubhouse smoking room, there was a look of disillusionment. 'Never again!' he said.

The Oldest Member glanced up from his paper.

'You are proposing to give up golf once more?' he queried.

'Not golf. Betting on golf.' The Young Man frowned. 'I've just been let down badly. Wouldn't you have thought I had a good thing, laying seven to one on McTavish against Robinson?'

'Undoubtedly,' said the Sage. 'The odds, indeed, generous as they are, scarcely indicate the former's superiority. Do you mean to tell me that the thing came unstitched?'

'Robinson won in a walk, after being three down at the turn.'

'Strange! What happened?'

'Why, they looked in at the bar to have a refresher before starting for the tenth,' said the young man, his voice quivering, 'and McTavish suddenly discovered that there was a hole in his trouser-pocket and sixpence had dropped out. He worried so frightfully about it that on the second nine he couldn't do a thing right. Went completely off his game and didn't win a hole.'

The Sage shook his head gravely.

'If this is really going to be a lesson to you, my boy, never to bet on the result of a golf match, it will be a blessing in disguise. There is no such thing as a certainty in golf. I wonder if I ever told you a rather curious episode in the career of Vincent Jopp?'

'*The* Vincent Jopp? The American multi-millionaire?'

'The same. You never knew he once came within an ace of winning the American Amateur Championship, did you?'

'I never heard of his playing golf.'

'He played for one season. After that he gave it up and has not touched a club since. Ring the bell and get me a small lime juice, and I will tell you all.'

It was long before your time (said the Oldest Member) that the events which I am about to relate took place. I had just come down from Cambridge, and was feeling particularly pleased with myself because I had secured the job of private and confidential secretary to Vincent Jopp, then a man in the early thirties, busy in laying the foundations of his present remarkable fortune. He engaged me, and took me with him to Chicago.

Jopp was, I think, the most extraordinary personality I have encountered in a long and many-sided life. He was admirably equipped for success in finance, having the steely eye and square jaw without which it is hopeless for a man to enter that line of business. He possessed also an overwhelming confidence in himself, and the ability to switch a cigar from one corner of his mouth to the other without wiggling his ears, which, as you know, is the stamp of the true Monarch of the Money Market. He was the nearest approach to the financier on the films, the fellow who makes his jaw muscles jump when he is telephoning, that I have ever seen.

Like all successful men, he was a man of method. He kept a pad on his desk on which he would scribble down his appointments, and it was my duty on entering the office each morning to take this pad and type its contents neatly in a loose-leaved ledger. Usually, of course, these entries referred to business appointments and deals which he was contemplating, but one day I was interested to note, against the date May 3rd, the entry:

Propose to Amelia.

I was interested, as I say, but not surprised. Though a man of steel and iron, there was nothing of the celibate about Vincent Jopp. He was one of those men who marry early and often. On three separate occasions before I joined his service he had jumped off the dock, to scramble back to shore again later by means of the Divorce Court lifebelt. Scattered here and there about the country there were three ex-Mrs Jopps, drawing their monthly envelope, and now, it seemed, he contemplated the addition of a fourth to the platoon.

I was not surprised, I say, at this resolve of his. What did seem a little remarkable to me was the thorough way in which he had thought the thing out. This iron-willed man recked nothing of possible obstacles. Under the date of June 1st was the entry:

Marry Amelia;

while in March of the following year he had arranged to have his first-born christened Thomas Reginald. Later on, the short-coating of Thomas Reginald was arranged for, and there was a note about sending him to school. Many hard things have been said of Vincent Jopp, but nobody has ever accused him of not being a man who looked ahead.

On the morning of May 4th Jopp came into the office, looking, I fancied, a little thoughtful. He sat for some moments staring before him with his brow a trifle furrowed; then he seemed to come to himself. He rapped his desk.

'Hi! You!' he said. It was thus that he habitually addressed me.

'Mr Jopp?' I replied.

'What's golf?'

I had at that time just succeeded in getting my handicap down into single figures, and I welcomed the opportunity of dilating on the noblest of pastimes. But I had barely begun my eulogy when he stopped me.

'It's a game, is it?'

'I suppose you could call it that,' I said, 'but it is an off-hand way of describing the holiest—'

'How do you play it?'

'Pretty well,' I said. 'At the beginning of the season I didn't seem able to keep 'em straight at all, but lately I've been doing fine. Getting better every day. Whether it was that I was moving my head or gripping too tightly with the right hand—'

'Keep the reminiscences for your grandchildren during the long winter evenings,' he interrupted, abruptly, as was his habit. 'What I want to know is what a fellow does when he plays golf. Tell me in as few words as you can just what it's all about.'

'You hit a ball with a stick till it falls into a hole.'

'Easy!' he snapped. 'Take dictation.'

I produced my pad.

'May the fifth, take up golf. What's an Amateur Championship?'

'It is the annual competition to decide which is the best player among the amateurs. There is also a Professional Championship, and an Open event.'

'Oh, there are golf professionals, are there? What do they do?'

'They teach golf.'

'Which is the best of them?'

'Sandy McHoots won both British and American Open events last year.'

'Wire him to come here at once.'

'But McHoots is in Inverlochty, in Scotland.'

'Never mind. Get him; tell him to name his own terms. When is the Amateur Championship?'

'I think it is on September the twelfth this year.'

'All right, take dictation. September twelfth, win Amateur Championship.'

I stared at him in amazement, but he was not looking at me.

'Got that?' he said. 'September thir— Oh, I was forgetting! Add September twelfth, corner wheat. September thirteenth, marry Amelia.'

'Marry Amelia,' I echoed, moistening my pencil.

'Where do you play this – what's-its-name – golf?'

'There are clubs all over the country. I belong to the Wissahicky Glen.'

'That a good place?'

'Very good.'

'Arrange today for my becoming a member.'

Sandy McHoots arrived in due course, and was shown into the private office.

'Mr McHoots?' said Vincent Jopp.

'Mphm!' said the Open Champion.

'I have sent for you, Mr McHoots, because I hear that you are the greatest living exponent of this game of golf.'

'Aye,' said the champion, cordially. 'I am that.'

'I wish you to teach me the game. I am already somewhat behind schedule owing to the delay incident upon your long journey, so let us start at once. Name a few of the most important points in connection with the game. My secretary will make notes of them, and I will memorise them. In this way we shall save time. Now, what is the most important thing to remember when playing golf?'

'Keep your heid still.'

'A simple task.'

'Na sae simple as it soonds.'

'Nonsense!' said Vincent Jopp, curtly. 'If I decide to keep my head still, I shall keep it still. What next?'

'Keep yer ee on the ba'.'

'It shall be attended to. And the next?'

'Dinna press.'

'I won't. And to resume.'

Mr McHoots ran through a dozen of the basic rules, and I took them down in shorthand. Vincent Jopp studied the list.

'Very good. Easier than I had supposed. On the first tee at Wissahicky Glen at eleven sharp tomorrow, Mr McHoots. Hi! You!'

'Sir?' I said.

'Go out and buy me a set of clubs, a red jacket, a cloth cap, a pair of spiked shoes, and a ball.'

'One ball?'

'Certainly. What need is there of more?'

'It sometimes happens,' I explained, 'that a player who is learning the game fails to hit his ball straight, and then he often loses it in the rough at the side of the fairway.'

'Absurd!' said Vincent Jopp. 'If I set out to drive my ball straight, I shall drive it straight. Good morning, Mr McHoots. You will excuse me now. I am busy cornering Woven Textiles.'

Golf is in its essence a simple game. You laugh in a sharp, bitter, barking manner when I say this, but nevertheless it is true. Where the average man goes wrong is in making the game difficult for himself. Observe the non-player, the man who walks round with you for the sake of the fresh air. He will hole out with a single carefree flick of his umbrella the twenty-foot putt over which you would ponder and hesitate for a full minute before sending it right off the line. Put a driver in his hands, and he pastes the ball into the next county without a thought. It is only when he takes to the game in earnest that he becomes self-conscious and anxious, and tops his shots even as you and I. A man who could retain through his golfing career the almost scornful confidence of the non-player would be unbeatable. Fortunately such an attitude of mind is beyond the scope of human nature.

It was not, however, beyond the scope of Vincent Jopp, the superman. Vincent Jopp was, I am inclined to think, the only golfer who ever approached the game in a spirit of Pure Reason. I have read of men who, never having swum in their lives, studied a textbook on their way down to the swimming bath, mastered its contents, and dived in and won the big race. In just such a spirit did Vincent Jopp start to play golf. He committed McHoots's hints to memory, and then went out on the links and put them into practice. He came to the tee with a clear picture in his mind of what he had to do, and he did it. He was not intimidated, like the average novice, by the thought that if he pulled in his hands he would slice, or if he gripped too tightly with the right he would pull. Pulling in the hands was an error, so he did not pull in his hands. Gripping too tightly was a defect, so he did not grip too tightly. With that weird concentration which had served him so well in business he did precisely what he had set out to do – no less and no more. Golf with Vincent Jopp was an exact science.

The annals of the game are studded with the names of those who have made rapid progress in their first season. Colonel Quill, we read in our Vardon, took up golf at the age of fifty-six, and by devising an ingenious machine consisting of a fishing line and a sawn-down bedpost was enabled to keep his head so still that he became a scratch player before the end of the year. But no one, I imagine, except Vincent Jopp, has ever achieved scratch on his first morning on the links.

The main difference, we are told, between the amateur and the professional golfer is the fact that the latter is always aiming at the pin, while the former has in his mind a vague picture of getting somewhere reasonably near it. Vincent Jopp invariably went for the pin. He tried to hole out from anywhere inside two hundred and twenty yards. The only occasion on which I ever heard him express any chagrin or disappointment was during the afternoon round on his first day out, when from the tee on the two-hundred-and-eighty-yard seventh he laid his ball within six inches of the hole.

'A marvellous shot!' I cried, genuinely stirred.

'Too much to the right,' said Vincent Jopp, frowning.

He went on from triumph to triumph. He won the monthly medal in May, June, July, August, and September. Towards the end of May he was heard to complain that Wissahicky Glen was not a sporting course. The Greens Committee sat up night after night trying to adjust his handicap so as to give other members an outside chance against him. The golf experts of the daily papers wrote columns about his play. And it was pretty generally considered throughout the country that it would be a pure formality for anyone else to enter against him in the Amateur Championship – an opinion which was borne out when he got through into the final without losing a hole. A safe man to have betted on, you would have said. But mark the sequel.

*

The American Amateur Championship was held that year in Detroit. I had accompanied my employer there; for, though engaged on this nerve-wearing contest, he refused to allow his business to be interfered with. As he had indicated in his schedule, he was busy at the time cornering wheat; and it was my task to combine the duties of caddie and secretary. Each day I accompanied him round the links with my notebook and his bag of clubs, and the progress of his various matches was somewhat complicated by the arrival of a stream of telegraph boys bearing important messages. He would read these between the strokes and dictate replies to me, never, however, taking more than the five minutes allowed by the rules for an interval between strokes. I am inclined to think that it was this that put the finishing touch on his opponents' discomfiture. It is not soothing for a nervous man to have the game hung up on the green while his adversary dictates to his caddie a letter beginning 'Yours of the eleventh inst. received and contents noted. In reply would state—' This sort of thing puts a man off his game.

I was resting in the lobby of our hotel after a strenuous day's work, when I found that I was being paged. I answered the summons, and was informed that a lady wished to see me. Her card bore the name 'Miss Amelia Merridew'. Amelia! The name seemed familiar. Then I remembered. Amelia was the name of the girl Vincent Jopp intended to marry, the fourth of the long line of Mrs Jopps. I hurried to present myself, and found a tall, slim girl, who was plainly labouring under a considerable agitation.

'Miss Merridew?' I said.

'Yes,' she murmured. 'My name will be strange to you.'

'Am I right,' I queried, 'in supposing that you are the lady to whom Mr Jopp—'

'I am! I am!' she replied. 'And, oh, what shall I do?'

'Kindly give me particulars,' I said, taking out my pad from force of habit.

She hesitated a moment, as if afraid to speak.

'You are caddying for Mr Jopp in the final tomorrow?' she said at last.

'I am.'

'Then could you – would you mind – would it be giving you too much trouble if I asked you to shout "Boo!" at him when he is making his stroke, if he looks like winning?'

I was perplexed.

'I don't understand.'

'I see that I must tell you all. I am sure you will treat what I say as absolutely confidential.'

'Certainly.'

'I am provisionally engaged to Mr Jopp.'

'Provisionally?'

She gulped.

'Let me tell you my story. Mr Jopp asked me to marry him, and I would rather do anything on earth than marry him. But how could I say "No!" with those awful eyes of his boring me through? I knew that if I said "No," he would argue me out of it in two minutes. I had an idea. I gathered that he had never played golf, so I told him that I would marry him if he won the Amateur Championship this year. And now I find that he has been a golfer all along, and, what is more, a plus man! It isn't fair!'

'He was not a golfer when you made that condition,' I said. 'He took up the game on the following day.'

'Impossible! How could he have become as good as he is in this short time?'

'Because he is Vincent Jopp! In his lexicon there is no such word as impossible.'

She shuddered.

'What a man! But I can't marry him,' she cried. 'I want to marry somebody else. Oh, won't you help me? Do shout "Boo!" at him when he is starting his down-swing!'

I shook my head.

'It would take more than a single "boo" to put Vincent Jopp off his stroke.'

'But won't you try it?'

'I cannot. My duty is to my employer.'

'Oh, do!'

'No, no. Duty is duty, and paramount with me. Besides, I have a bet on him to win.'

The stricken girl uttered a faint moan, and tottered away.

I was in our suite shortly after dinner that night, going over some of the notes I had made that day, when the telephone rang. Jopp was out at the time, taking a short stroll with his after-dinner cigar. I unhooked the receiver, and a female voice spoke.

'Is that Mr Jopp?'

'Mr Jopp's secretary speaking. Mr Jopp is out.'

'Oh, it's nothing important. Will you say that Mrs Luella Mainprice Jopp called up to wish him luck? I shall be on the course tomorrow to see him win the final.'

I returned to my notes. Soon afterwards the telephone rang again.

'Vincent, dear?'

'Mr Jopp's secretary speaking.'

'Oh, will you say that Mrs Jane Jukes Jopp called up to wish him luck? I shall be there tomorrow to see him play.'

I resumed my work. I had hardly started when the telephone rang for the thrid time.

'Mr Jopp?'

'Mr Jopp's secretary speaking.'

'This is Mrs Agnes Parsons Jopp. I just called up to wish him luck. I shall be looking on tomorrow.'

I shifted my work nearer to the telephone table so as to be ready for the next call. I had heard that Vincent Jopp had only been married three times, but you never knew.

Presently Jopp came in.

'Anybody called up?' he asked.

'Nobody on business. An assortment of your wives were on the wire wishing you luck. They asked me to say that they will be on the course tomorrow.'

For a moment it seemed to me that the man's iron repose was shaken.

'Luella?' he asked.

'She was the first.'

'Jane?'

'And Jane.'

'And Agnes?'

'Agnes,' I said, 'is right.'

'H'm!' said Vincent Jopp. And for the first time since I had known him I thought that he was ill at ease.

*

The day of the final dawned bright and clear. At least, I was not awake at the time to see, but I suppose it did; for at nine o'clock, when I came down to breakfast, the sun was shining brightly. The first eighteen holes were to be played before lunch, starting at eleven. Until twenty minutes before the hour Vincent Jopp kept me busy taking dictation, partly on matters connected with his wheat deal and partly on a signed article dealing with the final, entitled 'How I Won'. At eleven sharp we were out on the first tee.

Jopp's opponent was a nice-looking young man, but obviously nervous. He giggled in a distraught sort of way as he shook hands with my employer.

'Well, may the best man win,' he said.

'I have arranged to do so,' replied Jopp, curtly, and started to address his ball.

There was a large crowd at the tee, and, as Jopp started his down-swing, from somewhere on the outskirts of this crowd there came suddenly a musical 'Boo!' It rang out in the clear morning air like a bugle.

I had been right in my estimate of Vincent Jopp. His forceful stroke never wavered. The head of his club struck the ball, dispatching it a good two hundred yards down the middle of the fairway. As we left the tee I saw Amelia Merridew being led away with bowed head by two members of the Greens Committee. Poor girl! My heart bled for her. And yet, after all, Fate had been kind in removing her from the scene, even in custody, for she could hardly have borne to watch the proceedings. Vincent Jopp made rings round his antagonist. Hole after hole he won in his remorseless, machine-like way, until when lunchtime came at the end of the eighteenth he was ten up. All the other holes had been halved.

It was after lunch, as we made our way to the first tee, that the advance guard of the Mrs Jopps appeared in the person of Luella Mainprice Jopp, a kittenish little woman with blonde hair and a Pekingese dog. I remembered reading in the papers that she had divorced my employer for persistent and aggravated mental cruelty, calling witnesses to bear out her statement that he had said he did not like her in pink, and that on two separate occasions had insisted on her dog eating the leg of a chicken instead of the breast; but Time, the great healer, seemed to have removed all bitterness, and she greeted him affectionately.

'Wassums going to win great big championship against nasty rough strong man?' she said.

'Such,' said Vincent Jopp, 'is my intention. It was kind of you, Luella, to trouble to come and watch me. I wonder if you know Mrs Agnes Parsons Jopp?' he said, courteously, indicating a kind-looking, motherly woman who had just come up. 'How are you, Agnes?'

'If you had asked me that question this morning, Vincent,' replied Mrs Agnes Parsons Jopp, 'I should have been obliged to say that I felt far from well. I had an odd throbbing feeling in the left elbow, and I am sure my temperature was above the normal. But this afternoon I am a little better. How are you, Vincent?'

Although she had, as I recalled from the reports of the case, been compelled some years earlier to request the Court to sever her marital relations with Vincent Jopp on the ground of calculated and inhuman brutality, in that he had callously refused, in spite of her pleadings, to take old Dr Bennett's Tonic Swamp-Juice three times a day, her voice, as she spoke, was kind and even anxious. Badly as this man had treated her – and I remember hearing that several of the jury had been unable to restrain their tears when she was in the witness box giving her evidence – there still seemed to linger some remnants of the old affection.

'I am quite well, thank you, Agnes,' said Vincent Jopp.

'Are you wearing your liver-pad?'

A frown flitted across my employer's strong face.

'I am not wearing my liver-pad,' he replied, brusquely.

'Oh, Vincent, how rash of you!'

He was about to speak, when a sudden exclamation from his rear checked him. A genial-looking woman in a sports coat was standing there, eyeing him with a sort of humorous horror.

'Well, Jane,' he said.

I gathered that this was Mrs Jane Jukes Jopp, the wife who had divorced him for systematic and ingrowing fiendishness on the ground that he had repeatedly outraged her feelings by wearing a white waistcoat with a dinner jacket. She continued to look at him dumbly, and then uttered a sort of strangled, hysterical laugh.

'Those legs!' she cried. 'Those legs!'

Vincent Jopp flushed darkly. Even the strongest and most silent of us have our weaknesses, and my employer's was the rooted idea that he looked well in knickerbockers. It was not my place to try to dissuade him, but there was no doubt that they did not suit him. Nature, in bestowing upon him a massive head and a jutting chin, had forgotten to finish him off at the other end. Vincent Jopp's legs were skinny.

'You poor dear man!' went on Mrs Jane Jukes Jopp. 'What practical joker ever lured you into appearing in public in knickerbockers?'

'I don't object to the knickerbockers,' said Mrs Agnes Parsons Jopp, 'but when he foolishly comes out in quite a strong east wind without his liver-pad—'

'Little Tinky-Ting don't need no liver-pad, he don't,' said Mrs Luella Mainprice Jopp, addressing the animal in her arms, 'because he was his muzzer's pet, he was.'

I was standing quite near to Vincent Jopp, and at this moment I saw a bead of perspiration spring out on his forehead, and into his steely eyes there came a positively hunted look. I could understand and sympathise. Napoleon himself would have wilted if he had found himself in the midst of a trio of females, one talking baby talk, another fussing about his health, and the third making derogatory observations on his lower limbs. Vincent Jopp was becoming unstrung.

'May as well be starting, shall we?'

It was Jopp's opponent who spoke. There was a strange, set look on his face – the look of a man whose back is against the wall. Ten down on the morning's round, he had drawn on his reserves of courage and was determined to meet the inevitable bravely.

Vincent Jopp nodded absently, then turned to me.

'Keep those women away from me,' he whispered tensely. 'They'll put me off my stroke!'

'Put *you* off your stroke!' I exclaimed, incredulously.

'Yes, me! How the deuce can I concentrate, with people babbling about liver-pads, and – and knickerbockers all round me? Keep them away!'

He started to address his ball, and there was a weak uncertainty in the way he did it that prepared me for what was to come. His club rose, wavered, fell; and the ball, badly topped, trickled two feet and sank into a cuppy lie.

'Is that good or bad?' inquired Mrs Luella Mainprice Jopp.

A sort of desperate hope gleamed in the eye of the other competitor in the final. He swung with renewed vigour. His ball sang through the air, and lay within chip-shot distance of the green.

'At the very least,' said Mrs Agnes Parsons Jopp, 'I hope, Vincent, that you are wearing flannel next your skin.'

I heard Jopp give a stifled groan as he took his spoon from the bag. He made a gallant effort to retrieve the lost ground, but the ball struck a stone and bounded away into the long grass to the side of the green. His opponent won the hole.

We moved to the second tee.

'Now, *that* young man,' said Mrs Jane Jukes Jopp, indicating her late husband's blushing antagonist, 'is quite right to wear knickerbockers. He can carry them off. But a glance in the mirror must have shown you that you—'

'I'm sure you're feverish, Vincent,' said Mrs Agnes Parsons Jopp, solicitously. 'You are quite flushed. There is a wild gleam in your eyes.'

'Muzzer's pet's got little buttons of eyes, that don't never have no wild gleam in zem because he's muzzer's own darling, he was!' said Mrs Luella Mainprice Jopp.

A hollow groan escaped Vincent Jopp's ashen lips.

I need not recount the play hole by hole, I think. There are some subjects that are too painful. It was pitiful to watch Vincent Jopp in his downfall. By the end of the first nine his lead had been reduced to one, and his antagonist, rendered a new man by success, was playing magnificent golf. On the next hole he drew level. Then with a superhuman effort Jopp contrived to halve the eleventh, twelfth, and thirteenth. It seemed as though his iron will might still assert itself, but on the fourteenth the end came.

He had driven a superb ball, outdistancing his opponent by a full fifty yards. The latter played a good second to within a few feet of the green. And then, as Vincent Jopp was shaping for his stroke, Luella Mainprice gave tongue.

'Vincent!'

'Well?'

'Vincent, that other man – bad man – not playing fair. When your back was turned just now, he gave his ball a great bang. *I* was watching him.'

'At any rate,' said Mrs Agnes Parsons Jopp, 'I do hope, when the game is over, Vincent, that you will remember to cool slowly.'

'Flesho!' cried Mrs Jane Jukes Jopp triumphantly. 'I've been trying to remember the name all the afternoon. I saw about it in one of the papers. The advertisements speak most highly of it. You take it before breakfast and again before retiring, and they guarantee it to produce firm, healthy flesh on the most sparsely covered limbs in next to no time. Now, *will* you remember to get a bottle tonight? It comes in two sizes, the five-shilling (or large size) and the smaller at half a crown. G. K. Chesterton writes that he used it regularly for years.'

Vincent Jopp uttered a quavering moan, and his hand, as he took the mashie from his bag, was trembling like an aspen.

Ten minutes later, he was on his way back to the club-house, a beaten man.

And so (concluded the Oldest Member) you see that in golf there is no such thing as a soft snap. You can never be certain of the finest player. Anything may happen to the greatest expert at any stage of the game. In a recent competition George Duncan took eleven shots over a hole which eighteen-handicap men generally do in five. No! Back horses or go down to Throgmorton Street and try to take it away from the Rothschilds, and I will applaud you as a shrewd and cautious financier. But to bet at golf is pure gambling.

April

The Story of William

Miss Postlethwaite, our able and vigilant barmaid, had whispered to us that the gentleman sitting over there in the corner was an American gentleman.

'Comes from America,' added Miss Postlethwaite, making her meaning clearer.

'From America?' echoed we.

'From America,' said Miss Postlethwaite. 'He's an American.'

Mr Mulliner rose with an old-world grace. We do not often get Americans in the bar-parlour of the Angler's Rest. When we do, we welcome them. We make them realise that Hands Across the Sea is no mere phrase.

'Good evening, sir,' said Mr Mulliner. 'I wonder if you would care to join my friend and myself in a little refreshment?'

'Very kind of you, sir.'

'Miss Postlethwaite, the usual. I understand you are from the other side, sir. Do you find our English countryside pleasant?'

'Delightful. Though, of course, if I may say so, scarcely to be compared with the scenery of my home State.'

'What State is that?'

'California,' replied the other, baring his head.

'California, the Jewel State of the Union. With its azure sea, its noble hills, its eternal sunshine, and its fragrant flowers, California stands alone. Peopled by stalwart men and womanly women . . .'

'California would be all right,' said Mr Mulliner, 'if it wasn't for the earthquakes.'

Our guest started as though some venomous snake had bitten him.

'Earthquakes are absolutely unknown in California,' he said, hoarsely.

'What about the one in 1906?'

'That was not an earthquake. It was a fire.'

'An earthquake, I always understood,' said Mr Mulliner. 'My Uncle William was out there during it, and many a time has he said to me, "My boy, it was the San Francisco earthquake that won me a bride."'

'Couldn't have been the earthquake. May have been the fire.'

'Well, I will tell you the story, and you shall judge for yourself.'

'I shall be glad to hear your story about the San Francisco fire,' said the Californian, courteously.

My Uncle William (said Mr Mulliner) was returning from the East at the time. The commercial interests of the Mulliners have always been far-flung: and he had been over in China looking into the workings of a tea-exporting business in which he held a number of shares. It was his intention to get off the boat at San Francisco and cross the continent by rail. He particularly wanted to see the Grand Canyon of Arizona. And when he found that

Myrtle Banks had for years cherished the same desire, it seemed to him so plain a proof that they were twin souls that he decided to offer her his hand and heart without delay.

This Miss Banks had been a fellow-traveller on the boat all the way from Hong Kong; and day by day William Mulliner had fallen more and more deeply in love with her. So on the last day of the voyage, as they were steaming in at the Golden Gate, he proposed.

I have never been informed of the exact words which he employed, but no doubt they were eloquent. All the Mulliners have been able speakers, and on such an occasion, he would, of course, have extended himself. When at length he finished, it seemed to him that the girl's attitude was distinctly promising. She stood gazing over the rail into the water below in a sort of rapt way. Then she turned.

'Mr Mulliner,' she said, 'I am greatly flattered and honoured by what you have just told me.' These things happened, you will remember, in the days when girls talked like that. 'You have paid me the greatest compliment a man can bestow on a woman. And yet...'

William Mulliner's heart stood still. He did not like that 'And yet...'

'Is there another?' he muttered.

'Well, yes, there is. Mr Franklyn proposed to me this morning. I told him I would think it over.'

There was a silence. William was telling himself that he had been afraid of that bounder Franklyn all along. He might have known, he felt, that Desmond Franklyn would be a menace. The man was one of those lean, keen, hawk-faced, Empire-building sort of chaps you find out East – the kind of fellow who stands on deck chewing his moustache with a far-away look in his eyes, and then, when the girl asks him what he is thinking about, draws a short, quick breath and says he is sorry to be so absent-minded, but a sunset like that always reminds him of the day when he killed the four pirates with his bare hands and saved dear old Tuppy Smithers in the nick of time.

'There is a great glamour about Mr Franklyn,' said Myrtle Banks. 'We women admire men who do things. A girl cannot help but respect a man who once killed three sharks with a Boy Scout pocket knife.'

'So he says,' growled William.

'He showed me the pocket knife,' said the girl, simply. 'And on another occasion he brought down two lions with one shot.'

William Mulliner's heart was heavy, but he struggled on.

'Very possibly he may have done these things,' he said, 'but surely marriage means more than this. Personally, if I were a girl, I would go rather for a certain steadiness and stability of character. To illustrate what I mean, did you happen to see me win the Egg-and-Spoon race at the ship's sports? Now there, it seems to me, in what I might call microcosm, was an exhibition of all the qualities a married man most requires – intense coolness, iron resolution, and a quiet, unassuming courage. The man who under test conditions has carried an egg one and a half times round a deck in a small spoon, is a man who can be trusted.'

She seemed to waver, but only for a moment.

'I must think,' she said. 'I must think.'

'Certainly,' said William. 'You will let me see something of you at the hotel, after we have landed?'

'Of course. And if – I mean to say, whatever happens, I shall always look on you as a dear, dear friend.'

'M'yes,' said William Mulliner.

For three days my Uncle William's stay in San Francisco was as pleasant as could reasonably be expected, considering that Desmond Franklyn was also stopping at his and Miss Banks's hotel. He contrived to get the girl to himself to quite a satisfactory extent; and they spent many happy hours together in the Golden Gate Park and at the Cliff House, watching the seals basking on the rocks. But on the evening of the third day the blow fell.

'Mr Mulliner,' said Myrtle Banks, 'I want to tell you something.'

'Anything,' breathed William tenderly, 'except that you are going to marry that perisher Franklyn.'

'But that is exactly what I was going to tell you, and I must not let you call him a perisher, for he is a very brave, intrepid man.'

'When did you decide on this rash act?' asked William dully.

'Scarcely an hour ago. We were talking in the garden, and somehow or other we got on to the subject of rhinoceroses. He then told me how he had once been chased up a tree by a rhinoceros in Africa and escaped by throwing pepper in the brute's eyes. He most fortunately chanced to be eating his lunch when the animal arrived, and he had a hard-boiled egg and the pepper pot in his hands. When I heard this story, like Desdemona, I loved him for the dangers he had passed, and he loved me that I did pity them. The wedding is to be in June.'

William Mulliner ground his teeth in a sudden access of jealous rage.

'Personally,' he said, 'I consider that the story you have just related reveals this man Franklyn in a very dubious – I might almost say sinister – light. On his own showing, the leading trait in his character appears to be cruelty to animals. The fellow seems totally incapable of meeting a shark or a rhinoceros or any other of our dumb friends without instantly going out of his way to inflict bodily injury on it. The last thing I would wish is to be indelicate, but I cannot refrain from pointing out that, if your union is blessed, your children will probably be the sort of children who kick cats and tie tin cans to dogs' tails. If you take my advice, you will write the man a little note, saying that you are sorry but you have changed your mind.'

The girl rose in a marked manner.

'I do not require your advice, Mr Mulliner,' she said, coldly. 'And I have not changed my mind.'

Instantly William Mulliner was all contrition. There is a certain stage in the progress of a man's love when he feels like curling up in a ball and making little bleating noises if the object of his affections so much as looks squiggle-eyed at him; and this stage my Uncle William had reached. He followed her as she paced proudly away through the hotel lobby, and stammered incoherent apologies. But Myrtle Banks was adamant.

'Leave me, Mr Mulliner,' she said, pointing at the revolving door that led into the street. 'You have maligned a better man than yourself, and I wish to have nothing more to do with you. Go!'

William went, as directed. And so great was the confusion of his mind that he got stuck in the revolving door and had gone round in it no fewer than eleven times before the hall porter came to extricate him.

'I would have removed you from the machinery earlier, sir,' said the hall porter deferentially, having deposited him safely in the street, 'but my bet with my mate in there called for ten laps. I waited till you had completed eleven so that there should be no argument.'

William looked at him dazedly.

'Hall porter,' he said.

'Sir?'

'Tell me, hall porter,' said William, 'suppose the only girl you have ever loved had gone and got engaged to another, what would you do?'

The hall porter considered.

'Let me get this right,' he said. 'The proposition is, if I have followed you correctly, what would I do supposing the Jane on whom I had always looked as a steady mamma had handed me the old skimmer and told me to take all the air I needed because she had gotten another sweetie?'

'Precisely.'

'Your question is easily answered,' said the hall porter. 'I would go around the corner and get me a nice stiff drink at Mike's Place.'

'A drink?'

'Yes, sir. A nice stiff one.'

'At – where did you say?'

'Mike's Place, sir. Just round the corner. You can't miss it.'

William thanked him and walked away. The man's words had started a new, and in many ways interesting, train of thought. A drink? And a nice stiff one? There might be something in it.

William Mulliner had never tasted alcohol in his life. He had promised his late mother that he would not do so until he was either twenty-one or forty-one – he could never remember which. He was at present twenty-nine; but wishing to be on the safe side in case he had got his figures wrong, he had remained a teetotaller. But now, as he walked listlessly along the street towards the corner, it seemed to him that his mother in the special circumstances could not reasonably object if he took a slight snort. He raised his eyes to heaven, as though to ask her if a couple of quick ones might not be permitted; and he fancied that a faint, far-off voice whispered, 'Go to it!'

And at this moment he found himself standing outside a brightly lighted saloon.

For an instant he hesitated. Then, as a twinge of anguish in the region of his broken heart reminded him of the necessity for immediate remedies, he pushed open the swing doors and went in.

The principal feature of the cheerful, brightly lit room in which he found himself was a long counter, at which were standing a number of the citizenry, each with an elbow on the woodwork and a foot upon the neat brass rail which ran below. Behind the counter appeared the upper section of one of the most benevolent and kindly looking men that William had ever seen. He had a large smooth face, and he wore a white coat, and he eyed William, as he advanced, with a sort of reverent joy.

'Is this Mike's Place?' asked William.

'Yes, sir,' replied the white-coated man.

'Are you Mike?'

'No, sir. But I am his representative, and have full authority to act on his behalf. What can I have the pleasure of doing for you?'

The man's whole attitude made him seem so like a large-hearted elder brother that William felt no diffidence about confiding in him. He placed an elbow on the counter and a foot on the rail, and spoke with a sob in his voice.

'Suppose the only girl you had ever loved had gone and got engaged to another, what in your view would best meet the case?'

The gentlemanly bartender pondered for some moments.

'Well,' he replied at length, 'I advance it, you understand, as a purely personal opinion, and I shall not be in the least offended if you decide not to act upon it; but my suggestion – for what it is worth – is that you try a Dynamite Dew-Drop.'

One of the crowd that had gathered sympathetically round shook his head. He was a charming man with a black eye, who had shaved on the preceding Thursday.

'Much better give him a Dreamland Special.'

A second man, in a sweater and a cloth cap, had yet another theory.

'You can't beat an Undertaker's Joy.'

They were all so perfectly delightful and appeared to have his interests so unselfishly at heart that William could not bring himself to choose between them. He solved the problem in diplomatic fashion by playing no favourites and ordering all three of the beverages recommended.

The effect was instantaneous and gratifying. As he drained the first glass, it seemed to him that a torchlight procession, of whose existence he had hitherto not been aware, had begun to march down his throat and explore the recesses of his stomach. The second glass, though slightly too heavily charged with molten lava, was extremely palatable. It helped the torchlight procession along by adding to it a brass band of singular power and sweetness of tone. And with the third somebody began to touch off fireworks inside his head.

William felt better – not only spiritually but physically. He seemed to himself to be a bigger, finer man, and the loss of Myrtle Banks had somehow in a flash lost nearly all its importance. After all, as he said to the man with the black eye, Myrtle Banks wasn't everybody.

'Now what do you recommend?' he asked the man with the sweater, having turned the last glass upside down.

The other mused, one forefinger thoughtfully pressed against the side of his face.

'Well, I'll tell you,' he said. 'When my brother Elmer lost his girl, he drank straight rye. Yes, sir. That's what he drank – straight rye. "I've lost my girl," he said, "and I'm going to drink straight rye." That's what he said. Yes, sir, straight rye.'

'And was your brother Elmer,' asked William, anxiously, 'a man whose example in your opinion should be followed? Was he a man you could trust?'

'He owned the biggest duck-farm in the southern half of Illinois.'

'That settles it,' said William. 'What was good enough for a duck who owned half Illinois is good enough for me. Oblige me,' he said to the gentlemanly bartender, 'by asking these gentlemen what they will have, and start pouring.'

The bartender obeyed, and William, having tried a pint or two of the strange liquid just to see if he liked it, found that he did, and ordered some. He then began to move about among his new friends, patting one on the shoulder, slapping another affably on the back, and asking a third what his Christian name was.

'I want you all,' he said, climbing on to the counter so that his voice should carry better, 'to come and stay with me in England. Never in my life have I met men whose faces I liked so much. More like brothers than anything is the way I regard you. So just you pack up a few things and come along and put up at my little place for as long as you can manage. You particularly, my dear old chap,' he added, beaming at the man in the sweater.

'Thanks,' said the man with the sweater.

'What did you say?' said William.

'I said, "Thanks."'

William slowly removed his coat and rolled up his shirtsleeves.

'I call you gentlemen to witness,' he said, quietly, 'that I have been grossly insulted by this gentleman who has just grossly insulted me. I am not a quarrelsome man, but if anybody wants a row they can have it. And when it comes to being cursed and sworn at by an ugly bounder in a sweater and a cloth cap, it is time to take steps.'

And with these spirited words William Mulliner sprang from the counter, grasped the other by the throat, and bit him sharply on the right ear. There was a confused interval, during which somebody attached himself to the collar of William's waistcoat and the seat of William's trousers, and then a sense of swift movement and rush of cool air.

William discovered that he was seated on the pavement outside the saloon. A hand emerged from the swing door and threw his hat out. And he was alone with the night and his meditations.

These were, as you may suppose, of a singularly bitter nature. Sorrow and disillusionment racked William Mulliner like a physical pain. That his friends inside there, in spite of the fact that he had been all sweetness and light and had not done a thing to them, should have thrown him out into the hard street was the saddest thing he had ever heard of; and for some minutes he sat there, weeping silently.

Presently he heaved himself to his feet and, placing one foot with infinite delicacy in front of the other, and then drawing the other one up and placing it with infinite delicacy in front of that, he began to walk back to his hotel.

At the corner he paused. There were some railings on his right. He clung to them and rested a while.

The railings to which William Mulliner had attached himself belonged to a brownstone house of the kind that seems destined from the first moment of its building to receive guests, both resident and transient, at a moderate weekly rental. It was, in fact, as he would have discovered had he been clear-sighted enough to read the card over the door, Mrs Beulah O'Brien's Theatrical Boarding-House ('A Home from Home – No Cheques Cashed – This Means You').

But William was not in the best of shape for reading cards. A sort of mist had obscured the world, and he was finding it difficult to keep his eyes open. And presently, his chin wedged into the railings, he fell into a dreamless sleep.

He was awakened by light flashing in his eyes; and, opening them, saw that a window opposite where he was standing had become brightly illuminated. His slumbers had cleared his vision; and he was able to observe that the room into which he was looking was a dining room. The long table was set for the evening meal; and to William, as he gazed, the sight of that cosy apartment, with the gas-light falling on the knives and forks and spoons, seemed the most pathetic and poignant that he had ever beheld.

A mood of the most extreme sentimentality now had him in its grip. The thought that he would never own a little home like that racked him from stem to stern with an almost unbearable torment. What, argued William, clinging to the railings and crying weakly, could compare, when you came right down to it, with a little home? A man with a little home is all right, whereas a man without a little home is just a bit of flotsam on the ocean of life. If Myrtle Banks had only consented to marry him, he would have had a little home. But she had refused to marry him, so he would never have a little home. What Myrtle Banks wanted, felt William, was a good swift clout on the side of the head.

The thought pleased him. He was feeling physically perfect again now, and seemed to have shaken off completely the slight indisposition from which he had been suffering. His legs had lost their tendency to act independently of the rest of his body. His head felt clearer, and he had a sense of overwhelming strength. If ever, in short, there was a moment when he could administer that clout on the side of the head to Myrtle Banks as it should be administered, that moment was now.

He was on the point of moving off to find her and teach her what it meant to stop a man like himself from having a little home, when someone entered the room into which he was looking, and he paused to make further inspection.

The new arrival was a coloured maidservant. She staggered to the head of the table beneath the weight of a large tureen containing, so William suspected, hash. A moment later a stout woman with bright golden hair came in and sat down opposite the tureen.

The instinct to watch other people eat is one of the most deeply implanted in the human bosom, and William lingered, intent. There was, he told himself, no need to hurry. He knew which was Myrtle's room in the hotel. It was just across the corridor from his own. He could pop in any time, during the night, and give her that clout. Meanwhile, he wanted to watch these people eat hash.

And then the door opened again, and there filed into the room a little procession. And William, clutching the railings, watched it with bulging eyes.

The procession was headed by an elderly man in a check suit with a carnation in his buttonhole. He was about three feet six in height, though the military jauntiness with which he carried himself made him seem fully three feet seven. He was followed by a younger man who wore spectacles and whose height was perhaps three feet four. And behind these two came, in single file, six others, scaling down by degrees until, bringing up the rear of the procession, there entered a rather stout man in tweeds and bedroom slippers who could not have measured more than two feet eight.

They took their places at the table. Hash was distributed to all. And the man in tweeds, having inspected his plate with obvious relish, removed his slippers and, picking up his knife and fork with his toes, fell to with a keen appetite.

William Mulliner uttered a soft moan, and tottered away.

It was a black moment for my Uncle William. Only an instant before he had been congratulating himself on having shaken off the effects of his first indulgence in alcohol after an abstinence of twenty-nine years; but now he perceived that he was still intoxicated.

Intoxicated? The word did not express it by a mile. He was oiled, boiled, fried, plastered, whiffled, sozzled, and blotto. Only by the exercise of the most consummate caution and address could he hope to get back to his hotel and reach his bedroom without causing an open scandal.

Of course, if his walk that night had taken him a few yards farther down the street than the door of Mike's Place, he would have seen that there was a very simple explanation of the spectacle which he had just witnessed. A walk so extended would have brought him to the San Francisco Palace of Varieties, outside which large posters proclaimed the exclusive engagement for two weeks of

MURPHY'S MIDGETS.

BIGGER AND BETTER THAN EVER.

But of the existence of these posters he was not aware; and it is not too much to say that the iron entered into William Mulliner's soul.

That his legs should have become temporarily unscrewed at the joints was a phenomenon which he had been able to bear with fortitude. That his head should be feeling as if a good many bees had decided to use it as a hive was unpleasant, but not unbearably so. But that his brain should have gone off its castors and be causing him to see visions was the end of all things.

William had always prided himself on the keenness of his mental powers. All through the long voyage on the ship, when Desmond Franklyn had related anecdotes illustrative of his prowess as a man of Action, William Mulliner had always consoled himself by feeling that in the matter of brain he could give Franklyn three bisques and a beating any time he chose to start. And now, it seemed, he had lost even this advantage over his rival. For Franklyn, dull-witted clod though he might be, was not such an absolute minus quantity that he would imagine he had seen a man of two feet eight cutting up hash with his toes. That hideous depth of mental decay had been reserved for William Mulliner.

Moodily he made his way back to his hotel. In a corner of the Palm Room he saw Myrtle Banks deep in conversation with Franklyn, but all desire to give her a clout on the side of the head had now left him. With his chin sunk on his breast, he entered the elevator and was carried up to his room.

Here as rapidly as his quivering fingers would permit, he undressed; and, climbing into the bed as it came round for the second time, lay for a space with wide-open eyes. He had been too shaken to switch his light off, and the rays of the lamp shone on the handsome ceiling which undulated above him. He gave himself up to thought once more.

No doubt, he felt, thinking it over now, his mother had had some very urgent reason for withholding him from alcoholic drink. She must have known of some family secret, sedulously guarded from his infant ears – some dark tale of a fatal Mulliner taint. 'William must never learn of this!' she had probably said when they told her the old legend of how every Mulliner for centuries back had died a maniac, victim at last to the fatal fluid. And tonight, despite her gentle care, he had found out for himself.

He saw now that this derangement of his eyesight was only the first step in the gradual dissolution which was the Mulliner Curse. Soon his sense of hearing would go, then his sense of touch.

He sat up in bed. It seemed to him that, as he gazed at the ceiling, a considerable section of it had parted from the parent body and fallen with a crash to the floor.

William Mulliner stared dumbly. He knew, of course, that it was an illusion. But what a perfect illusion! If he had not had the special knowledge which he possessed, he would have stated without fear of contradiction that there was a gap six feet wide above him and a mass of dust and plaster on the carpet below.

And even as his eyes deceived him, so did his ears. He seemed to be conscious of a babel of screams and shouts. The corridor, he could have sworn, was full of flying feet.

The world appeared to be all bangs and crashes and thuds. A cold fear gripped at William's heart. His sense of hearing was playing tricks with him already.

His whole being recoiled from making the final experiment, but he forced himself out of bed. He reached a finger towards the nearest heap of plaster and drew it back with a groan. Yes, it was as he feared, his sense of touch had gone wrong too. That heap of plaster, though purely a figment of his disordered brain, had felt solid.

So there it was. One little moderately festive evening at Mike's Place, and the Curse of the Mulliners had got him. Within an hour of absorbing the first drink of his life, it had deprived him of his sight, his hearing, and his sense of touch. Quick service, felt William Mulliner.

As he climbed back into bed, it appeared to him that two of the walls fell out. He shut his eyes, and presently sleep, which has been well called Tired Nature's Sweet Restorer, brought oblivion. His last waking thought was that he imagined he had heard another wall go.

William Mulliner was a sound sleeper, and it was many hours before consciousness returned to him. When he awoke, he looked about him in astonishment. The haunting horror of the night had passed; and now, though conscious of a rather severe headache, he knew that he was seeing things as they were.

And yet it seemed odd to think that what he beheld was not the remains of some nightmare. Not only was the world slightly yellow and a bit blurred about the edges, but it had changed in its very essentials overnight. Where eight hours before there had been a wall, only an open space appeared, with bright sunlight streaming through it.

The ceiling was on the floor, and almost the only thing remaining of what had been an expensive bedroom in a first-class hotel was the bed. Very strange, he thought, and very irregular.

A voice broke in upon his meditations.

'Why, Mr Mulliner!'

William turned, and being, like all the Mulliners, the soul of modesty, dived abruptly beneath the bedclothes. For the voice was the voice of Myrtle Banks. And she was in his room!

'Mr Mulliner!'

William poked his head out cautiously. And then he perceived that the proprieties had not been outraged as he had imagined. Miss Banks was not in his room, but in the corridor. The intervening wall had disappeared. Shaken, but relieved, he sat up in bed, the sheet drawn round his shoulders.

'You don't mean to say you're still in bed?' gasped the girl.

'Why, is it awfully late?' said William.

'Did you actually stay up here all through it?'

'Through what?'

'The earthquake.'

'What earthquake?'

'The earthquake last night.'

'Oh, that earthquake?' said William, carelessly. 'I did notice some sort of an earthquake. I remember seeing the ceiling come down and saying to myself, "I shouldn't wonder if that wasn't an earthquake." And then the walls fell out, and I said, "Yes, I believe it *is* an earthquake." And then I turned over and went to sleep.'

Myrtle Banks was staring at him with eyes that reminded him partly of twin stars and partly of a snail's.

'You must be the bravest man in the world!'

William gave a curt laugh.

'Oh, well,' he said, 'I may not spend my whole life persecuting unfortunate sharks with pocket knives, but I find I generally manage to keep my head fairly well in a crisis. We Mulliners are like that. We do not say much, but we have the right stuff in us.'

He clutched his head. A sharp spasm had reminded him how much of the right stuff he had in him at that moment.

'My hero!' breathed the girl, almost inaudibly.

'And how is your fiancé this bright, sunny morning?' asked William, nonchalantly. It was torture to refer to the man, but he must show her that a Mulliner knew how to take his medicine.

She gave a little shudder.

'I have no fiancé,' she said.

'But I thought you told me you and Franklyn . . .'

'I am no longer engaged to Mr Franklyn. Last night, when the earthquake started, I cried to him to help me; and he with a hasty "Some other time!" over his shoulder, disappeared into the open like something shot out of a gun. I never saw a man run so fast. This morning I broke off the engagement.' She uttered a scornful laugh.

'Sharks and pocket knives! I don't believe he ever killed a shark in his life.'

'And even if he did,' said William, 'what of it? I mean to say, how infrequently in married life must the necessity for killing sharks with pocket knives arise! What a husband needs is not some purely adventitious gift like that – a parlour trick, you might almost call it – but a steady character, a warm and generous disposition, and a loving heart.'

'How true!' she murmured, dreamily.

'Myrtle,' said William, 'I would be a husband like that. The steady character, the warm and generous disposition, and the loving heart to which I have alluded are at your disposal. Will you accept them?'

'I will,' said Myrtle Banks.

And that (concluded Mr Mulliner) is the story of my Uncle William's romance. And you will readily understand, having heard it, how his eldest son, my cousin, J. S. F. E. Mulliner, got his name.

'J. S. F. E.?' I said.

'John San Francisco Earthquake Mulliner,' explained my friend.

'There never was a San Francisco earthquake,' said the Californian. 'Only a fire.'

May

Jeeves Exerts the Old Cerebellum

'Morning, Jeeves,' I said.

'Good morning, sir,' said Jeeves.

He put the good old cup of tea softly on the table by my bed, and I took a refreshing sip. Just right, as usual. Not too hot, not too sweet, not too weak, not too strong, not too much milk, and not a drop spilled in the saucer. A most amazing cove, Jeeves. So dashed competent in every respect. I've said it before, and I'll say it again. I mean to say, take just one small instance. Every other valet I've ever had used to barge into my room in the morning while I was still asleep, causing much misery: but Jeeves seems to know when I'm awake by a sort of telepathy. He always floats in with the cup exactly two minutes after I come to life. Makes a deuce of a lot of difference to a fellow's day.

'How's the weather, Jeeves?'

'Exceptionally clement, sir.'

'Anything in the papers?'

'Some slight friction threatening in the Balkans, sir. Otherwise, nothing.'

'I say, Jeeves, a man I met at the club last night told me to put my shirt on Privateer for the two o'clock race this afternoon. How about it?'

'I should not advocate it, sir. The stable is not sanguine.'

That was enough for me. Jeeves knows. How, I couldn't say, but he knows. There was a time when I would laugh lightly, and go ahead, and lose my little all against his advice, but not now.

'Talking of shirts,' I said, 'have those mauve ones I ordered arrived yet?'

'Yes, sir. I sent them back.'

'Sent them back?'

'Yes, sir. They would not have become you.'

Well, I must say I'd thought fairly highly of those shirtings, but I bowed to superior knowledge. Weak? I don't know. Most fellows, no doubt, are all for having their valets confine their activities to creasing trousers and what not without trying to run the home; but it's different with Jeeves. Right from the first day he came to me, I have looked on him as a sort of guide, philosopher, and friend.

'Mr Little rang up on the telephone a few moments ago, sir. I informed him that you were not yet awake.'

'Did he leave a message?'

'No, sir. He mentioned that he had a matter of importance to discuss with you, but confided no details.'

'Oh, well, I expect I shall be seeing him at the club.'

'No doubt, sir.'

I wasn't what you might call in a fever of impatience. Bingo Little is a chap I was at school with, and we see a lot of each other still. He's the nephew of old Mortimer Little, who retired from business recently with a goodish pile. (You've probably heard of Little's Liniment – It Limbers Up the Legs.) Bingo biffs about London on a pretty comfortable allowance given him by his uncle, and leads on the whole a fairly unclouded life. It wasn't likely that anything which he described as a matter of importance would turn out to be really so frightfully important. I took it that he had discovered some new brand of cigarette which he wanted me to try, or something like that, and didn't spoil my breakfast by worrying.

After breakfast I lit a cigarette and went to the open window to inspect the day. It certainly was one of the best and brightest.

'Jeeves,' I said.

'Sir?' said Jeeves. He had been clearing away the breakfast things, but at the sound of the young master's voice cheesed it courteously.

'You were absolutely right about the weather. It is a juicy morning.'

'Decidedly, sir.'

'Spring and all that.'

'Yes, sir.'

'In the spring, Jeeves, a livelier iris gleams upon the burnished dove.'

'So I have been informed, sir.'

'Right ho! Then bring me my whangee, my yellowest shoes, and the old green Homburg. I'm going into the Park to do pastoral dances.'

I don't know if you know that sort of feeling you get on these days round about the end of April and the beginning of May, when the sky's a light blue, with cotton-wool clouds, and there's a bit of a breeze blowing from the west? Kind of uplifted feeling. Romantic, if you know what I mean. I'm not much of a ladies' man, but on this particular morning it seemed to me that what I really wanted was some charming girl to buzz up and ask me to save her from assassins or something. So that it was a bit of an anticlimax when I merely ran into young Bingo Little, looking perfectly foul in a crimson satin tie decorated with horseshoes.

'Hallo, Bertie,' said Bingo.

'My God, man!' I gargled. 'The cravat! The gent's neckwear! Why? For what reason?'

'Oh, the tie?' He blushed. 'I – er – I was given it.'

He seemed embarrassed, so I dropped the subject. We toddled along a bit, and sat down on a couple of chairs by the Serpentine.

'Jeeves tells me you want to talk to me about something,' I said.

'Eh?' said Bingo, with a start. 'Oh yes, yes. Yes.'

I waited for him to unleash the topic of the day, but he didn't seem to want to get along. Conversation languished. He stared straight ahead of him in a glassy sort of manner.

'I say, Bertie,' he said, after a pause of about an hour and a quarter.

'Hallo!'

'Do you like the name Mabel?'

'No.'

'No?'

'No.'

'You don't think there's a kind of music in the word, like the wind rustling gently through the tree-tops?'

'No.'

He seemed disappointed for a moment; then cheered up.

'Of course, you wouldn't. You always were a fatheaded worm without any soul, weren't you?'

'Just as you say. Who is she? Tell me all.'

For I realised now that poor old Bingo was going through it once again. Ever since I have known him – and we were at school together – he has been perpetually falling in love with someone, generally in the spring, which seems to act on him like magic. At school he had the finest collection of actresses' photographs of anyone of his time; and at Oxford his romantic nature was a byword.

'You'd better come along and meet her at lunch,' he said, looking at his watch.

'A ripe suggestion,' I said. 'Where are you meeting her? At the Ritz?'

'Near the Ritz.'

He was geographically accurate. About fifty yards east of the Ritz there is one of those blighted tea-and-bun shops you see dotted about all over London, and into this, if you'll believe me, young Bingo dived like a homing rabbit; and before I had time to say a word we were wedged in at a table, on the brink of a silent pool of coffee left there by an early luncher.

I'm bound to say I couldn't quite follow the development of the scenario. Bingo, while not absolutely rolling in the stuff, has always had a fair amount of the ready. Apart from what he got from his uncle, I knew that he had finished up the jumping season well on the right side of the ledger. Why, then, was he lunching the girl at this Godforsaken eatery? It couldn't be because he was hard up.

Just then the waitress arrived. Rather a pretty girl.

'Aren't we going to wait—?' I started to say to Bingo, thinking it somewhat thick that, in addition to asking a girl to lunch with him in a place like this, he should fling himself on the foodstuffs before she turned up, when I caught sight of his face, and stopped.

The man was goggling. His entire map was suffused with a rich blush. He looked like the Soul's Awakening done in pink.

'Hullo, Mabel!' he said, with a sort of gulp.

'Hallo!' said the girl.

'Mabel,' said Bingo, 'this is Bertie Wooster, a pal of mine.'

'Pleased to meet you,' she said. 'Nice morning.'

'Fine,' I said.

'You see I'm wearing the tie,' said Bingo.

'It suits you beautiful,' said the girl.

Personally, if anyone had told me that a tie like that suited me, I should have risen and struck them on the mazzard, regardless of their age and sex; but poor old Bingo simply got all flustered with gratification, and smirked in the most gruesome manner.

'Well, what's it going to be today?' asked the girl, introducing the business touch into the conversation.

Bingo studied the menu devoutly.

'I'll have a cup of cocoa, cold veal and ham pie, slice of fruit cake, and a macaroon. Same for you, Bertie?'

I gazed at the man, revolted. That he could have been a pal of mine all these years and think me capable of insulting the old tum with this sort of stuff cut me to the quick.

'Or how about a bit of hot steak-pudding, with a sparkling limado to wash it down?' said Bingo.

You know, the way love can change a fellow is really frightful to contemplate. This chappie before me, who spoke in that absolutely careless way of macaroons and limado, was the man I had seen in happier days telling the head waiter at Claridge's exactly how he wanted the chef to prepare the *sole frite au gourmet aux champignons*, and saying he would jolly well sling it back if it wasn't just right. Ghastly! Ghastly!

A roll and butter and a small coffee seemed the only things on the list that hadn't been specially prepared by the nastier-minded members of the Borgia family for people they had a particular grudge against, so I chose them, and Mabel hopped it.

'Well?' said Bingo rapturously.

I took it that he wanted my opinion of the female poisoner who had just left us.

'Very nice,' I said.

He seemed dissatisfied.

'You don't think she's the most wonderful girl you ever saw?' he said wistfully.

'Oh, absolutely!' I said, to appease the blighter. 'Where did you meet her?'

'At a subscription dance at Camberwell.'

'What on earth were you doing at a subscription dance at Camberwell?'

'Your man Jeeves asked me if I would buy a couple of tickets. It was in aid of some charity or other.'

'Jeeves? I didn't know he went in for that sort of thing.'

'Well, I suppose he has to relax a bit every now and then. Anyway, he was there, swinging a dashed efficient shoe. I hadn't meant to go at first, but I turned up for a lark. Oh, Bertie, think what I might have missed!'

'What might you have missed?' I asked, the old lemon being slightly clouded.

'Mabel, you chump. If I hadn't gone I shouldn't have met Mabel.'

'Oh, ah!'

At this point Bingo fell into a species of trance, and only came out of it to wrap himself round the pie and the macaroon.

'Bertie,' he said, 'I want your advice.'

'Carry on.'

'At least, not your advice, because that wouldn't be much good to anybody. I mean, you're a pretty consummate old ass, aren't you? Not that I want to hurt your feelings, of course.'

'No, no, I see that.'

'What I wish you would do is to put the whole thing to that fellow Jeeves of yours, and see what he suggests. You've often told me that he has helped other pals of yours out of messes. From what you tell me, he's by way of being the brains of the family.'

'He's never let me down yet.'

'Then put my case to him.'

'What case?'

'My problem.'

'What problem?'

'Why, you poor fish, my uncle, of course. What do you think my uncle's going to say to all this? If I sprang it on him cold, he'd tie himself in knots on the hearthrug.'

'One of these emotional johnnies, eh?'

'Somehow or other his mind has got to be prepared to receive the news. But how?'

'Ah!'

'That's a lot of help, that "ah"! You see, I'm pretty well

dependent on the old boy. If he cut off my allowance, I should be very much in the soup. So you put the whole binge to Jeeves and see if he can't scare up a happy ending somehow. Tell him my future is in his hands, and that, if the wedding bells ring out, he can rely on me, even unto half my kingdom. Well, call it ten quid. Jeeves would exert himself with ten quid on the horizon, what?'

'Undoubtedly,' I said.

I wasn't in the least surprised at Bingo wanting to lug Jeeves into his private affairs like this. It was the first thing I would have thought of doing myself if I had been in a hole of any description. As I have frequently had occasion to observe, he is a bird of the ripest intellect, full of bright ideas. If anybody could fix things for poor old Bingo, he could.

I stated the case to him that night after dinner.

'Jeeves.'

'Sir?'

'Are you busy just now?'

'No, sir.'

'I mean, not doing anything in particular?'

'No, sir. It is my practice at this hour to read some improving book; but, if you desire my services, this can easily be postponed, or, indeed, abandoned altogether.'

'Well, I want your advice. It's about Mr Little.'

'Young Mr Little, sir, or the elder Mr Little, his uncle, who lives in Pounceby Gardens?'

Jeeves seemed to know everything. Most amazing thing. I'd been pally with Bingo practically all my life, and yet I didn't remember having heard that his uncle lived anywhere in particular.

'How did you know he lived in Pounceby Gardens?' I said.

'I am on terms of some intimacy with the elder Mr Little's cook, sir. In fact, there is an understanding.'

I'm bound to say that this gave me a bit of a start. Somehow I'd never thought of Jeeves going in for that sort of thing.

'Do you mean you're engaged?'

'It may be said to amount to that, sir.'

'Well, well!'

'She is a remarkably excellent cook, sir,' said Jeeves, as though he felt called on to give some explanation. 'What was it you wished to ask me about Mr Little?'

I sprang the details on him.

'And that's how the matter stands, Jeeves,' I said. 'I think we ought to rally round a trifle and help poor old Bingo put the thing through. Tell me about old Mr Little. What sort of a chap is he?'

'A somewhat curious character, sir. Since retiring from business he has become a great recluse, and now devotes himself almost entirely to the pleasures of the table.'

'Greedy hog, you mean?'

'I would not, perhaps, take the liberty of describing him in precisely those terms, sir. He is what is usually called a gourmet. Very particular about what he eats, and for that reason sets a high value on Miss Watson's services.'

'The cook?'

'Yes, sir.'

'Well, it looks to me as though our best plan would be to shoot young Bingo in on him after dinner one night. Melting mood, I mean to say, and all that.'

'The difficulty is, sir, that at the moment Mr Little is on a diet, owing to an attack of gout.'

'Things begin to look wobbly.'

'No, sir, I fancy that the elder Mr Little's misfortune may be turned to the younger Mr Little's advantage. I was speaking only the other day to Mr Little's valet, and he was telling me that it has become his principal duty to read to Mr Little in the evenings. If I were in your place, sir, I should send young Mr Little to read to his uncle.'

'Nephew's devotion, you mean? Old man touched by kindly action, what?'

'Partly that, sir. But I would rely more on young Mr Little's choice of literature.'

'That's no good. Jolly old Bingo has a kind face, but when it comes to literature he stops at the *Sporting Times*.'

'That difficulty may be overcome. I would be happy to select books for Mr Little to read. Perhaps I might explain my idea a little further?'

'I can't say I quite grasp it yet.'

'The method which I advocate is what, I believe, the advertisers call Direct Suggestion, sir, consisting as it does of driving an idea home by constant repetition. You may have had experience of the system?'

'You mean they keep on telling you that some soap or other is the best, and after a bit you come under the influence and charge round the corner and buy a cake?'

'Exactly, sir. The same method was the basis of all the most valuable propaganda during the recent war. I see no reason why it should not be adopted to bring about the desired result with regard to the subject's views on class distinctions. If young Mr Little were to read day after day to his uncle a series of narratives in which marriage with young persons of an inferior social status was held up as both feasible and admirable, I fancy it would prepare the elder Mr Little's mind for the reception of the information that his nephew wishes to marry a waitress in a tea-shop.'

'*Are* there any books of that sort nowadays? The only ones I ever see mentioned in the papers are about married couples who find life grey, and can't stick each other at any price.'

'Yes, sir, there are a great many, neglected by the reviewers but widely read. You have never encountered *All for Love*, by Rosie M. Banks?'

'No.'

'Nor *A Red, Red Summer Rose*, by the same author?'

'No.'

'I have an aunt, sir, who owns an almost complete set of Rosie M. Banks'. I could easily borrow as many volumes as young Mr Little might require. They make very light, attractive reading.'

'Well, it's worth trying.'

'I should certainly recommend the scheme, sir.'

'All right, then. Toddle round to your aunt's tomorrow and grab a couple of the fruitiest. We can but have a dash at it.'

'Precisely, sir.'

To find out what happens next, see Chapter 2 of *The Inimitable Jeeves*.

June

Mr Potter Takes a Rest Cure

Mr John Hamilton Potter, founder and proprietor of the well-known New York publishing house of J. H. Potter, Inc., laid down the typescript which had been engaging his leisurely attention, and from the depths of his basket-chair gazed dreamily across the green lawns and gleaming flower beds to where Skeldings Hall basked in the pleasant June sunshine. He was feeling quietly happy. The waters of the moat glittered like liquid silver; a gentle breeze brought to his nostrils the scent of newly cut grass; the doves in the immemorial elms cooed with precisely the right gentlemanly intonation; and he had not seen Clifford Gandle since luncheon. God, it seemed to Mr Potter, was in His Heaven and all was right with the world.

And how near, he reflected, he had come to missing all this delightful old-world peace. When, shortly after his arrival in England, he had met Lady Wickham at a Pen and Ink Club dinner and she had invited him to pay a visit to Skeldings, his first impulse had been to decline. His hostess was a woman of rather markedly overwhelming personality; and, inasmuch as he had only recently recovered from a nervous breakdown and had been ordered by his doctor complete rest and tranquillity, it had seemed to him that at close range and over an extended period of time she might be a little too much for the old system. Furthermore, she wrote novels: and that instinct of self-preservation which lurks in every publisher had suggested to him that behind her invitation lay a sinister desire to read these to him one by one with a view to getting him to produce them in America. Only the fact that he was a lover of the old and picturesque, coupled with the fact that Skeldings Hall dated back to the time of the Tudors, had caused him to accept.

Not once, however – not even when Clifford Gandle was expressing to him with a politician's trained verbosity his views on the Gold Standard and other weighty matters – had he regretted his decision. When he looked back on his life of the past eighteen months – a life spent in an inferno of shrilling telephones and authors, many of them female, popping in to abuse him for not advertising their books better – he could almost fancy that he had been translated to Paradise.

A Paradise, moreover, which was not without its Peri. For at this moment there approached Mr Potter across the lawn, walking springily as if she were constructed of whalebone and indiarubber, a girl. She was a boyish-looking girl, slim and graceful, and the red hair on her bare head glowed pleasingly in the sun.

'Hullo, Mr Potter!' she said.

The publisher beamed upon her. This was Roberta Wickham, his hostess's daughter, who had returned to her ancestral home two days ago from a visit to friends in the North. A friendly young thing, she had appealed to Mr Potter from the first.

'Well, well, well!' said Mr Potter.

'Don't get up. What are you reading?' Bobbie Wickham picked up the manuscript. '*Ethics of Suicide*,' she read. 'Cheery!'

Mr Potter laughed indulgently.

'No doubt it seems an odd thing to be reading on such a day and in such surroundings. But a publisher is never free. This was sent over for my decision from my New York office. They won't leave me alone, you see, even when I am on vacation.'

Bobbie Wickham's hazel eyes clouded pensively.

'There's a lot to be said for suicide,' she murmured. 'If I had to see much of Clifford Gandle, I'd commit suicide myself.'

Mr Potter started. He had always liked this child, but he had never dreamed that she was such a completely kindred soul.

'Don't you like Mr Gandle?'

'No.'

'Nor do I.'

'Nor does anyone,' said Bobbie, 'except Mother.' Her eyes clouded again. 'Mother thinks he's wonderful.'

'She does?'

'Yes.'

'Well, well!' said Mr Potter.

Bobbie brooded.

'He's a member of Parliament, you know.'

'Yes.'

'And they say he may be in the Cabinet any day.'

'So he gave me to understand.'

'And all that sort of thing is very bad for a man, don't you think? I mean, it seems to make him so starchy.'

'The very word.'

'And pompous.'

'The exact adjective I would have selected,' agreed Mr Potter. 'In our frequent conversations, before you arrived, he addressed me as if I were a half-witted deputation of his constituents.'

'Did you see much of him before I came?'

'A great deal, though I did my best to avoid him.'

'He's a difficult man to avoid.'

'Yes.' Mr Potter chuckled sheepishly. 'Shall I tell you something that happened a day or two ago? You must not let it go any farther, of course. I was coming out of the smoking room one morning, and I saw him approaching me along the passage. So – so I jumped back and – ha, ha! – hid in a small cupboard.'

'Jolly sensible.'

'Yes. But unfortunately he opened the cupboard door and discovered me. It was exceedingly embarrassing.'

'What did you say?'

'There was nothing much I could say. I'm afraid he must have thought me out of my senses.'

'Well, I— All right, Mother. Coming.'

The rich contralto of a female novelist calling to its young had broken the stillness of the summer afternoon. Mr Potter looked up with a start. Lady Wickham was standing on the lawn. It seemed to Mr Potter that, as his little friend moved towards her, something of the springiness had gone out of her walk. It was as if she moved reluctantly.

'Where have you been, Roberta?' asked Lady Wickham, as her daughter came within earshot of the normal tone of voice. 'I have been looking everywhere for you.'

'Anything special, Mother?'

'Mr Gandle wants to go to Hertford. He has to get some books. I think you had better drive him in your car.'

'Oh, Mother!'

Mr Potter, watching from his chair, observed a peculiar expression flit into Lady Wickham's face. Had he been her English publisher, instead of merely her prospective American publisher, he would have been familiar with that look. It meant that Lady Wickham was preparing to exercise her celebrated willpower.

'Roberta,' she said, with dangerous quiet, 'I particularly wish you to drive Mr Gandle to Hertford.'

'But I had promised to go over and play tennis at the Crufts'.'

'Mr Gandle is a much better companion for you than a young waster like Algy Crufts. You must run over and tell him that you cannot play today.'

A few minutes later a natty two-seater drew up at the front door of the Crufts' residence down the road; and Bobbie Wickham, seated at the wheel, gave tongue.

'Algy!'

The flannel-clad form of Mr Algernon Crufts appeared at a window.

'Hullo! Down in a jiffy.'

There was an interval. Then Mr Crufts joined her on the drive.

'Hullo! I say, you haven't brought your racquet, you poor chump,' he said.

'Tennis is off,' announced Bobbie briefly. 'I've got to drive Clifford Gandle in to Hertford.' She paused. 'I say, Algy, shall I tell you something?'

'What?'

'Between ourselves.'

'Absolutely.'

'Mother wants me to marry Clifford Gandle.'

Algy Crufts uttered a strangled exclamation. Such was his emotion that he nearly swallowed the first eight inches of his cigarette-holder.

'Marry Clifford Gandle!'

'Yes. She's all for it. She says he would have a steadying influence on me.'

'Ghastly! Take my advice and give the project the most absolute go-by. I was up at Oxford with the man. A blighter, if ever there was one. He was President of the Union and all sorts of frightful things.'

'It's all very awkward. I don't know what to do.'

'Kick him in the eye and tell him to go to blazes. That's the procedure.'

'But it's so hard not to do anything Mother wants you to do. You know Mother.'

'I do,' said Mr Crufts, who did.

'Oh, well,' said Bobbie, 'you never know. There's always the chance that she may take a sudden dislike to him for some reason or other. She does take sudden dislikes to people.'

'She does,' said Mr Crufts. Lady Wickham had disliked him at first sight.

'Well, let's hope she will suddenly dislike Clifford Gandle. But I don't mind telling you, Algy, that at the moment things are looking pretty black.'

'Keep smiling,' urged Mr Crufts.

'What's the good of smiling, you fathead?' said Bobbie morosely.

Night had fallen on Skeldings Hall. Lady Wickham was in her study, thinking those great thoughts which would subsequently be copyrighted in all languages, including the Scandinavian. Bobbie was strolling somewhere in the grounds, having eluded Mr Gandle after dinner. And Mr Gandle, baffled but not defeated, had donned a light overcoat and gone out to try to find Bobbie.

As for Mr Potter, he was luxuriating in restful solitude in a punt under a willow by the bank of the moat.

From the first moment he had set eyes on it, Hamilton Potter had loved the moat at Skeldings Hall. Here, by the willow, it broadened out almost into the dimensions of a lake; and there was in the glitter of stars on its surface and the sleepy rustling of birds in the trees along its bank something infinitely soothing. The healing darkness wrapped the publisher about like a blanket; the cool night-wind fanned caressingly a forehead a little heated by Lady Wickham's fine old port; and gradually, lulled by the beauty of the scene, Mr Potter allowed himself to float into one of those reveries which come to publishers at moments such as this.

He mused on jackets and remainders and modes of distribution; on royalties and advertisements and spring lists and booksellers' discounts. And his random thoughts, like fleeting thistledown, had just drifted to the question of the growing price of pulp-paper, when from somewhere nearby there came the sound of a voice, jerking him back to the world again.

'Oh, let the solid ground not fail beneath my feet before that I have found what some have found so sweet,' said the voice.

A moderate request, one would have supposed; and yet it irritated Mr Potter like the bite of a mosquito. For the voice was the voice of Clifford Gandle.

'Robertah,' proceeded the voice, and Mr Potter breathed again. He had taken it for granted that the man had perceived and was addressing himself. He gathered now that his presence had not been discovered.

'Robertah,' said Mr Gandle, 'surely you cannot have been blind to the na-chah of my feelings? Surely you must have guessed that it was love that—'

Hamilton Potter congealed into a solid mass of frozen horror. He was listening in on a proposal of marriage.

The emotions of any delicate-minded man who finds himself in such a position cannot fail to be uncomfortable; and the greater his delicacy of mind the more acute must the discomfort be. Mr Potter, being, as are all publishers, more like a shrinking violet than anything else in the world, nearly swooned. His scalp tingled; his jaw fell; and his toes began to open and shut like poppet-valves.

'Heart of my heart—' said Mr Gandle.

Mr Potter gave a convulsive shudder. And the puntpole, which had been resting on the edge of the boat, clattered down with a noise like a machine gun.

There was a throbbing silence. Then Mr Gandle spoke sharply.

'Is anybody they-ah?'

There are situations in which a publisher can do only

one thing. Raising himself noiselessly, Mr Potter wriggled to the side of the punt and lowered himself into the water.

'Who is they-ah?'

Mr Potter with a strong effort shut his mouth, which was trying to emit a howl of anguish. He had never supposed that water could be so cold. Silently he waded out towards the opposite bank. The only thing that offered any balm in this black moment was the recollection that his hostess had informed him that the moat was not more than four feet deep.

But what Lady Wickham had omitted to inform him was that in one or two places there were ten-foot holes. It came, therefore, as a surprise to Mr Potter, when, after he had travelled some six yards, there happened to him that precise disaster which Mr Gandle, in his recent remarks, had expressed himself as so desirous of avoiding. As the publisher took his next step forward, the solid ground failed beneath his feet.

'Oosh!' ejaculated Mr Potter.

Clifford Gandle was a man of swift intuition. Hearing the cry and becoming aware at the same time of loud splashing noises, he guessed in one masterly flash of inductive reasoning that someone had fallen in. He charged down the bank and perceived the punt. He got into the punt. Bobbie Wickham got into the punt. Mr Gandle seized the pole and propelled the punt out into the waste of waters.

'Are you they-ah?' inquired Mr Gandle.

'Glub!' exclaimed Mr Potter.

'I see him,' said Bobbie. 'More to the left.'

Clifford Gandle drove the rescuing craft more to the

left, and was just digging the pole into the water when Mr Potter, coming up for the third time, found it within his reach. The partiality of drowning men for straws is proverbial; but, as a class, they are broad-minded and will clutch at punt-poles with equal readiness. Mr Potter seized the pole and pulled strongly; and Clifford Gandle, who happened to be leaning his whole weight on it at the moment, was not proof against what practically amounted to a formal invitation. A moment later he had joined Mr Potter in the depths.

Bobbie Wickham rescued the punt-pole, which was floating away on the tide, and peered down through the darkness. Stirring things were happening below. Clifford Gandle had grasped Mr Potter. Mr Potter had grasped Clifford Gandle. And Bobbie, watching from above, was irresistibly reminded of a picture she had seen in her childhood of alligators fighting in the River Hooghly. She raised the pole, and, with the best intentions, prodded at the tangled mass.

The treatment proved effective. The pole, taking Clifford Gandle shrewdly in the stomach, caused him to release his grip on Mr Potter; and Mr Potter, suddenly discovering that he was in shallow water again, did not hesitate. By the time Clifford Gandle had scrambled into the punt he was on dry land, squelching rapidly towards the house.

A silence followed his departure. Then Mr Gandle, expelling the last pint of water from his mouth, gave judgement.

'The man must be mad!'

He found some more water which he had overlooked, and replaced it.

'Stark, staring mad!' he repeated. 'He must have deliberately flung himself in.'

Bobbie Wickham was gazing out into the night; and, had the visibility been better, her companion might have observed in her expression the raptness of inspiration.

'There is no other explanation. The punt was they-ah, by the bank, and he was hee-yah, right out in the middle of the moat. I've suspected for days that he was unbalanced. Once I found him hiding in a cupboard. Crouching there with a wild gleam in his eyes. And that brooding look of his. That strange brooding look. I've noticed it every time I've been talking to him.'

Bobbie broke the silence, speaking in a low, grave voice.

'Didn't you know about poor Mr Potter?'

'Eh?'

'That he has suicidal mania?'

Clifford Gandle drew in his breath sharply.

'You can't blame him,' said Bobbie. 'How would you feel if you came home one day and found your wife and your two brothers and a cousin sitting round the dinner table stone dead?'

'What!'

'Poisoned. Something in the curry.' She shivered. 'This morning I found him in the garden gloating over a book called *Ethics of Suicide*.'

Clifford Gandle ran his fingers through his dripping hair.

'Something ought to be done!'

'What can you do? The thing isn't supposed to be known. If you mention it to him, he will simply go away; and then Mother will be furious, because she wants him to publish her books in America.'

'I shall keep the closest watch on the man.'

'Yes, that's the thing to do,' agreed Bobbie.

She pushed the punt to the shore. Mr Gandle, who had begun to feel chilly, leaped out and sped to the house to change his clothes. Bobbie, following at a more leisurely pace, found her mother standing in the passage outside her study. Lady Wickham's manner was perturbed.

'Roberta!'

'Yes, Mother?'

'What in the world has been happening? A few moments ago Mr Potter ran past my door, dripping wet. And now Clifford Gandle has just gone by, also soaked to the skin. What have they been doing?'

'Fighting in the moat, Mother.'

'Fighting in the moat? What do you mean?'

'Mr Potter jumped in to try and get away from Mr Gandle, and then Mr Gandle went in after him and seized him round the neck, and they grappled together for quite a long time, struggling furiously. I think they must have had a quarrel.'

'What on earth would they quarrel about?'

'Well, you know what a violent man Clifford Gandle is.'

This was an aspect of Mr Gandle's character which Lady Wickham had not perceived. She opened her penetrating eyes.

'Clifford Gandle violent?'

'I think he's the sort of man who takes sudden dislikes to people.'

'Nonsense!'

'Well, it all seems very queer to me,' said Bobbie.

She passed on her way upstairs; and, reaching the first

landing, turned down the corridor till she came to the principal guest room. She knocked delicately. There were movements inside, and presently the door opened, revealing Hamilton Potter in a flowered dressing gown.

'Thank Heaven you're safe!' said Bobbie.

The fervour of her tone touched Mr Potter. His heart warmed to the child.

'If I hadn't been there when Mr Gandle was trying to drown you—'

Mr Potter started violently.

'Trying to drown me?' he gasped.

Bobbie's eyebrows rose.

'Hasn't anybody told you about Mr Gandle – warned you? Didn't you know he was one of the mad Gandles?'

'The – the—'

'Mad Gandles. You know what some of these very old English families are like. All the Gandles have been mad for generations back.'

'You don't mean – you can't mean—' Mr Potter gulped. 'You can't mean that Mr Gandle is homicidal?'

'Not normally. But he takes sudden dislikes to people.'

'I think he likes me,' said Mr Potter, with a certain nervous satisfaction. 'He has made a point of seeking me out and giving me his views on – er – various matters.'

'Did you ever yawn while he was doing it?'

Mr Potter blenched.

'Would – would he mind that very much?'

'Mind it! You lock your door at night, don't you, Mr Potter?'

'But this is terrible.'

'He sleeps in this corridor.'

'But why is the man at large?'

'He hasn't done anything yet. You can't shut a man up till he has done something.'

'Does Lady Wickham know of this?'

'For goodness' sake don't say a word to Mother. It would only make her nervous. Everything will be quite all right, if you're only careful. You had better try not to let him get you alone.'

'Yes,' said Mr Potter.

The last of the mad Gandles, meanwhile, having peeled off the dress-clothes moistened during the recent water-carnival, had draped his bony form in a suit of orange-coloured pyjamas, and was now devoting the full force of a legislator's mind to the situation which had arisen.

He was a long, thin young man with a curved nose which even in his lighter moments gave him the appearance of disapproving things in general; and there had been nothing in the events of the last hour to cause any diminution of this look of disapproval. For we cannot in fairness but admit that, if ever a mad Gandle had good reason to be mad, Clifford Gandle had at this juncture. He had been interrupted at the crucial point of proposal of marriage. He had been plunged into water and prodded with a punt-pole. He had sown the seeds of a cold in the head. And he rather fancied that he had swallowed a newt. These things do not conduce to sunniness in a man.

Nor did an inspection of the future do anything to remove his gloom. He had come to Skeldings for rest and recuperation after the labours of an exhausting Session, and now it seemed that, instead of passing his time pleasantly in the society of Roberta Wickham, he would be compelled to devote himself to acting as a guardian to a misguided publisher.

It was not as if he liked publishers, either. His relations with Prodder and Wiggs, who had sold forty-three copies of his book of political essays – 'Watchman, What of the Night?' – had not been agreeable.

Nevertheless, this last of the Gandles was a conscientious man. He had no intention of shirking the call of duty. The question of whether it was worth while preventing a publisher committing suicide did not present itself to him.

That was why Bobbie's note, when he read it, produced such immediate results.

Exactly when the missive had been delivered, Clifford Gandle could not say. Much thought had rendered him distrait, and the rustle of the paper as it was thrust under his door did not reach his consciousness. It was only when, after a considerable time, he rose with the intention of going to bed that he perceived lying on the floor an envelope.

He stooped and picked it up. He examined it with a thoughtful stare. He opened it.

The letter was brief. It ran as follows: –

'*What about his razors?*'

A thrill of dismay shot through him.

Razors!

He had forgotten them.

Clifford Gandle did not delay. Already it might be that

he was too late. He hurried down the passage and tapped at Mr Potter's door.

'Who's there?'

Clifford Gandle was relieved. He was in time.

'Can I come in?'

'Who is that?'

'Gandle.'

'What do you want?'

'Can you – er – lend me a razah?'

'A what?'

'A razah.'

There followed a complete silence from within. Mr Gandle tapped again.

'Are you they-ah?'

The silence was broken by an odd rumbling sound. Something heavy knocked against the woodwork. But that the explanation seemed so improbable, Mr Gandle would have said that this peculiar publisher had pushed a chest of drawers against the door.

'Mr Pottah!'

More silence.

'Are you they-ah, Mr Pottah?'

Additional stillness. Mr Gandle, wearying of a profitless vigil, gave the thing up and returned to his room.

The task that lay before him, he now realised, was to wait awhile and then make his way along the balcony which joined the windows of the two rooms; enter while the other slept, and abstract his weapon or weapons.

He looked at his watch. The hour was close on midnight. He decided to give Mr Potter till two o'clock.

*

Clifford Gandle sat down to wait.

Mr Potter's first action, after the retreating footsteps had told him that his visitor had gone, was to extract a couple of nerve pills from the box by his bed and swallow them. This was a rite which, by the orders of his medical adviser, he had performed thrice a day since leaving America – once half an hour before breakfast, once an hour before luncheon, and again on retiring to rest.

In spite of the fact that he now consumed these pills, it seemed to Mr Potter that he could scarcely be described as retiring to rest. After the recent ghastly proof of Clifford Gandle's insane malevolence, he could not bring himself to hope that even the most fitful slumber would come to him this night. The horror of the thought of that awful man padding softly to his door and asking for razors chilled Hamilton Potter to the bone.

Nevertheless, he did his best. He switched off the light and, closing his eyes, began to repeat in a soft undertone a formula which he had often found efficacious.

'Day by day,' murmured Mr Potter, 'in every way, I am getting better and better. Day by day, in every way, I am getting better and better.'

It would have astonished Clifford Gandle, yawning in his room down the corridor, if he could have heard such optimistic sentiments proceeding from those lips.

'Day by day, in every way, I am getting better and better.'

Mr Potter's mind performed an unfortunate side-slip. He lay there tingling. Suppose he *was* getting better and better, what of it? What was the use of getting better and better if at any moment a mad Gandle might spring out with a razor and end it all?

He forced his thoughts away from these uncomfortable channels. He clenched his teeth and whispered through them with a touch of defiance.

'Day by day, in every way, I am getting better and better. Day by day, in every way—'

A pleasant drowsiness stole over Mr Potter.

'Day by day, in every way,' he murmured, 'I am getting better and better. Day by day, in every way, I am betting getter and getter. Bay by day, in every way, I am betting getter and wetter. Way by day—'

Mr Potter slept.

Over the stables the clock chimed the hour of two, and Clifford Gandle stepped out on to the balcony.

It has been well said by many thinkers that in human affairs you can never be certain that some little trifling obstacle will not undo the best-laid of schemes. It was the sunken road at Hougoumont that undid the French cavalry at Waterloo, and it was something very similar that caused Clifford Gandle's plan of action to go wrong now – a jug of water, to wit, which the maid who had brought Mr Potter's hot-water can before dinner had placed immediately beneath the window.

Clifford Gandle, insinuating himself with the extreme of caution through the window and finding his foot resting on something hard, assumed that he was touching the floor, and permitted his full weight to rest upon that foot. Almost immediately afterwards the world collapsed with a crash and a deluge of water; and light, flooding the room, showed Mr Potter sitting up in bed, blinking.

Mr Potter stared at Clifford Gandle. Clifford Gandle stared at Mr Potter.

'Er – hullo!' said Clifford Gandle.

Mr Potter uttered a low, curious sound like a cat with a fish-bone in its throat.

'I – er – just looked in,' said Clifford Gandle.

Mr Potter made a noise like a second and slightly larger cat with another fish-bone in its throat.

'I've come for the razah,' said Clifford Gandle. 'Ah, there it is,' he said, and, moving towards the dressing table, secured it.

Mr Potter leaped from his bed. He looked about him for a weapon. The only one in sight appeared to be the typescript of *Ethics of Suicide*, and that, while it would have made an admirable instrument for swatting flies, was far too flimsy for the present crisis. All in all, it began to look to Mr Potter like a sticky evening.

'Good night,' said Clifford Gandle.

Mr Potter was amazed to see that his visitor was withdrawing towards the window. It seemed incredible. For a moment he wondered whether Bobbie Wickham had not made some mistake about this man. Nothing could be more temperate than his behaviour at the moment.

And then, as he reached the window, Clifford Gandle smiled, and all Mr Potter's fears leaped into being again.

The opinion of Clifford Gandle regarding this smile was that it was one of those kindly, reassuring smiles – the sort of smile to put the most nervous melancholiac at his ease. To Mr Potter it seemed precisely the kind of maniac grin which he would have expected from such a source.

'Good night,' said Clifford Gandle.

He smiled again, and was gone. And Mr Potter, having stood rooted to the spot for some minutes, crossed the floor and closed the window. He then bolted the window. He perceived a pair of shutters, and shut them. He moved the wash-hand stand till it rested against the shutters. He placed two chairs and a small bookcase against the wash-hand stand. Then he went to bed, leaving the light burning.

'Day by day, in every way,' said Mr Potter, 'I am getting better and better.'

But his voice lacked the ring of true conviction.

Sunshine filtering in through the shutters, and the song of birds busy in the ivy outside his window, woke Mr Potter at an early hour next morning; but it was some time before he could bring himself to spring from his bed to greet another day. His disturbed night had left him heavy and lethargic. When finally he had summoned up the energy to rise and remove the zareba in front of the window and open the shutters, he became aware that a glorious morning was upon the world. The samples of sunlight that had crept into the room had indicated only feebly the golden wealth without.

But there was no corresponding sunshine in Mr Potter's heart. Spiritually as well as physically he was at a low ebb. The more he examined the position of affairs, the less he liked it. He went down to breakfast in pensive mood.

Breakfast at Skeldings was an informal meal, and visitors were expected to take it when they pleased, irrespective of the movements of their hostess, who was a late riser. In the dining room, when Mr Potter entered it, only the daughter of the house was present.

Bobbie was reading the morning paper. She nodded cheerfully to him over its top.

'Good morning, Mr Potter. I hope you slept well.'

Mr Potter winced.

'Miss Wickham,' he said, 'last night an appalling thing occurred.'

A startled look came into Bobbie's eyes.

'You don't mean – Mr Gandle?'

'Yes.'

'Oh, Mr Potter, what?'

'Just as I was going to bed, the man knocked at my door and asked if he could borrow my razah – I mean my razor.'

'You didn't lend it to him?'

'No, I did not,' replied Mr Potter, with a touch of asperity. 'I barricaded the door.'

'How wise of you!'

'And at two in the morning he came in through the window!'

'How horrible!'

'He took my razor. Why he did not attack me, I cannot say. But, having obtained it, he grinned at me in a ghastly way and went out.'

There was a silence.

'Have an egg or something,' said Bobbie, in a hushed voice.

'Thank you, I will take a little ham,' whispered Mr Potter.

There was another silence.

'I'm afraid,' said Bobbie at length, 'you will have to go.'

'That is what I think.'

'It is quite evident that Mr Gandle has taken one of his uncontrollable dislikes to you.'

'Yes.'

'What I think you ought to do is to leave quite quietly, without saying goodbye or anything, so that he won't know where you've gone and won't be able to follow you. Then you could write Mother a letter, saying that you had to go because of Mr Gandle's persecution.'

'Exactly.'

'You needn't say anything about his being mad. She knows that. Just say that he ducked you in the moat and then came into your room at two in the morning and made faces at you. She will understand.'

'Yes. I—'

'Hush!'

Clifford Gandle came into the room.

'Good morning,' said Bobbie.

'Good morning,' said Mr Gandle.

He helped himself to poached egg; and, glancing across the table at the publisher, was concerned to note how wan and sombre was his aspect. If ever a man looked as if he were on the verge of putting an end to everything, that man was John Hamilton Potter.

Clifford Gandle was not feeling particularly festive himself at the moment, for he was a man who depended greatly for his well-being on a placid eight hours of sleep; but he exerted himself to be bright and optimistic.

'What a lovely morning!' he trilled.

'Yes,' said Mr Potter.

'Surely such weather is enough to make any man happy and satisfied with life.'

'Yes,' said Mr Potter doubtfully.

'Who, with all Na-chah smiling, could seriously contemplate removing himself from so bright a world?'

'George Philibert, of 32, Acacia Road, Cricklewood, did,' said Bobbie, who had resumed her study of the paper.

'Eh?' said Mr Gandle.

'George Philibert, of 32, Acacia Road, Cricklewood, was had up before the beak yesterday, charged with attempted suicide. He stated that—'

Mr Gandle cast a reproachful look at her. He had always supposed Roberta Wickham to be a girl of fair intelligence, as women go; and it seemed to him that he had over-estimated her good sense. He did his best to cover up her blunder.

'Possibly,' he said, 'with some really definite and serious reason—'

'I can never understand,' said Mr Potter, coming out of what had all the outward appearance of a trance, 'why the idea arose that suicide is wrong.'

He spoke with a curious intensity. The author of *Ethics of Suicide* had wielded a plausible pen, and the subject was one on which he now held strong views. And, even if he had not already held them, his mood this morning was of a kind to breed them in his bosom.

'The author of a very interesting book which I intend to publish shortly,' he said, 'points out that none but the votaries of the monotheistic religions look upon suicide as a crime.'

'Yes,' said Mr Gandle, 'but—'

'If, he goes on to say, the criminal law forbids suicide, that is not an argument valid in the Church. And, besides, the prohibition is ridiculous, for what penalty can frighten a man who is not afraid of death itself?'

'George Philibert got fourteen days,' said Bobbie.

'Yes, but—' said Mr Gandle.

'The ancients were very far from regarding the matter in the modern light. Indeed, in Massilia and on the island of Cos, the man who could give valid reasons for relinquishing his life was handed the cup of hemlock by the magistrate, and that, too, in public.'

'Yes, but—'

'And why,' said Mr Potter, 'suicide should be regarded as cowardly is beyond me. Surely no man who had not an iron nerve—'

He broke off. The last two words had tapped a chord in his memory. Abruptly it occurred to him that here he was, halfway through breakfast, and he had not taken those iron nerve-pills which his doctor had so strictly ordered him to swallow thirty minutes before the morning meal.

'Yes,' said Mr Gandle. He lowered his cup, and looked across the table. 'But—'

His voice died away. He sat staring before him in horror-struck silence. Mr Potter, with a strange, wild look in his eyes, was in the very act of raising to his lips a sinister-looking white pellet. And, even as Mr Gandle gazed, the wretched man's lips closed over the horrid thing and a movement of his Adam's apple showed that the deed was done.

'Surely,' said Mr Potter, 'no man who—'

It seemed that Fate was inflexibly bent on preventing him from finishing that particular sentence this morning. For he had got thus far when Clifford Gandle, seizing the mustard pot, rose with a maniac screech and bounded, wild-eyed, round the table at him.

Lady Wickham came downstairs and made her way like a stately galleon under sail towards the dining room. Unlike others of the household, she was feeling particularly cheerful this morning. She liked fine weather, and the day was unusually fine. Also, she had resolved that after breakfast she would take Mr Potter aside and use the full force of her commanding personality to extract from him something in the nature of an informal contract.

She would not, she decided, demand too much at first. If he would consent to undertake the American publication of 'Agatha's Vow', 'A Strong Man's Love', and – possibly – 'A Man For A' That', she would be willing to postpone discussion of 'Meadow-sweet', 'Fetters of Fate', and the rest of her works. But if he thought he could eat her bread and salt and sidestep 'Agatha's Vow', he had grievously under-estimated the power of her cold grey eye when it came to subduing such members of the animal kingdom as publishers.

There was a happy smile, therefore, on Lady Wickham's face as she entered the room. She was not actually singing, but she stopped only just short of it.

She was surprised to find that, except for her daughter Roberta, the dining room was empty.

'Good morning, Mother,' said Bobbie.

'Good morning. Has Mr Potter finished his breakfast?'

Bobbie considered the question.

'I don't know if he had actually finished,' she said. 'But he didn't seem to want any more.'

'Where is he?'

'I don't know, Mother.'

'When did he go?'

'He's only just left.'

'I didn't meet him.'

'He went out of the window.'

The sunshine faded from Lady Wickham's face.

'Out of the window? Why?'

'I think it was because Clifford Gandle was between him and the door.'

'What do you mean? Where is Clifford Gandle?'

'I don't know, Mother. He went out of the window, too. They were both running down the drive when I last saw them.' Bobbie's face grew pensive. 'Mother, I've been thinking,' she said. 'Are you really sure that Clifford Gandle would be such a steadying influence for me? He seems to me rather eccentric.'

'I cannot understand a word of what you are saying.'

'Well, he is eccentric. At two o'clock this morning, Mr Potter told me, he climbed in through Mr Potter's window, made faces at him, and climbed out again. And just now—'

'Made faces at Mr Potter?'

'Yes, Mother. And just now Mr Potter was peacefully eating his breakfast, when Clifford Gandle suddenly uttered a loud cry and sprang at him. Mr Potter jumped out of the window and Clifford Gandle jumped out after him and chased him down the drive. I thought Mr Potter ran awfully well for an elderly man, but that sort of thing can't be good for him in the middle of breakfast.'

Lady Wickham subsided into a chair.

'Is everybody mad?'

'I think Clifford Gandle must be. You know, these men who do wonderful things at the University often do crack up suddenly. I was reading a case only yesterday about a man in America. He took every possible prize at Harvard or wherever it was, and then, just as everybody was predicting the most splendid future for him, he bit his aunt. He—'

'Go and find Mr Potter,' cried Lady Wickham. 'I must speak to him.'

'I'll try. But I don't believe it will be easy. I think he's gone for good.'

Lady Wickham uttered a bereaved cry, such as a tigress might who sees its prey snatched from it.

'Gone!'

'He told me he was thinking of going. He said he couldn't stand Clifford Gandle's persecution any longer. And that was before breakfast, so I don't suppose he has changed his mind. I think he means to go on running.'

A sigh like the whistling of the wind through the cracks in a broken heart escaped Lady Wickham.

'Mother,' said Bobbie, 'I've something to tell you. Last night Clifford Gandle asked me to marry him. I hadn't time to answer one way or the other, because just after he had proposed he jumped into the moat and tried to drown Mr Potter; but if you really think he would be a steadying influence for me—'

Lady Wickham uttered a snort of agony.

'I forbid you to dream of marrying this man!'

'Very well, Mother,' said Bobbie dutifully. She rose and moved to the sideboard. 'Would you like an egg, Mother?'

'No!'

'Some ham?'

'No!'

'Very well.' Bobbie paused at the door. 'Don't you think it would be a good idea,' she said, 'if I were to go and find Clifford Gandle and tell him to pack up and go away? I'm sure you won't like having him about after this.'

Lady Wickham's eyes flashed fire.

'If that man dares to come back, I'll – I'll— Yes. Tell him to go. Tell him to go away and never let me set eyes on him again.'

'Very well, Mother,' said Bobbie.

July

Pig-Hoo-o-o-o-ey

Thanks to the publicity given to the matter by *The Bridgnorth, Shifnal and Albrighton Argus* (with which is incorporated *The Wheat-Growers' Intelligencer and Stock Breeders' Gazette*), the whole world today knows that the silver medal in the Fat Pigs class at the eighty-seventh annual Shropshire Agricultural Show was won by the Earl of Emsworth's black Berkshire sow, Empress of Blandings.

Very few people, however, are aware how near that splendid animal came to missing the coveted honour.

Now it can be told.

This brief chapter of Secret History may be said to have begun on the night of the eighteenth of July, when George Cyril Wellbeloved (twenty-nine), pig-man in the employ of Lord Emsworth, was arrested by Police Constable Evans of Market Blandings for being drunk and disorderly in the taproom of the Goat and Feathers. On July the nineteenth, after first offering to apologise, then explaining that it had been his birthday, and finally attempting to prove an alibi, George Cyril was very properly jugged for fourteen days without the option of a fine.

On July the twentieth, Empress of Blandings, always hitherto a hearty and even a boisterous feeder, for the first time on record declined all nourishment. And on the morning of July the twenty-first, the veterinary surgeon called in to diagnose and deal with this strange asceticism, was compelled to confess to Lord Emsworth that the thing was beyond his professional skill.

Let us just see, before proceeding, that we have got these dates correct:

July 18 – Birthday Orgy of Cyril Wellbeloved.
July 19 – Incarceration of Ditto.
July 20 – Pig Lays off the Vitamins.
July 21 – Veterinary Surgeon Baffled.
Right.

The effect of the veterinary surgeon's announcement on Lord Emsworth was overwhelming. As a rule, the wear and tear of our complex life left this vague and amiable peer unscathed. So long as he had sunshine, regular meals, and complete freedom from the society of his younger son Frederick, he was placidly happy. But there were chinks in his armour, and one of these had been pierced this morning. Dazed by the news he had received, he stood at the window of the great library of Blandings Castle, looking out with unseeing eyes.

As he stood there, the door opened. Lord Emsworth turned; and having blinked once or twice, as was his habit when confronted suddenly with anything, recognised in the handsome and imperious-looking woman who had entered his sister, Lady Constance Keeble. Her demeanour, like his own, betrayed the deepest agitation.

'Clarence,' she cried, 'an awful thing has happened!'

Lord Emsworth nodded dully.

'I know. He's just told me.'

'What! Has he been here?'

'Only this moment left.'

'Why did you let him go? You must have known I would want to see him.'

'What good would that have done?'

'I could at least have assured him of my sympathy,' said Lady Constance stiffly.

'Yes, I suppose you could,' said Lord Emsworth, having considered the point. 'Not that he deserves any sympathy. The man's an ass.'

'Nothing of the kind. A most intelligent young man, as young men go.'

'Young? Would you call him young? Fifty, I should have said, if a day.'

'Are you out of your senses? Heacham fifty?'

'Not Heacham. Smithers.'

As frequently happened to her when in conversation with her brother, Lady Constance experienced a swimming sensation in the head.

'Will you kindly tell me, Clarence, in a few simple words, what you imagine we are talking about?'

'I'm talking about Smithers. Empress of Blandings is refusing her food, and Smithers says he can't do anything about it. And he calls himself a vet!'

'Then you haven't heard? Clarence, a dreadful thing has happened. Angela has broken off her engagement to Heacham.'

'And the Agricultural Show on Wednesday week!'

'What on earth has that got to do with it?' demanded Lady Constance, feeling a recurrence of the swimming sensation.

'What has it got to do with it?' said Lord Emsworth

warmly. 'My champion sow, with less than ten days to prepare herself for a most searching examination in competition with all the finest pigs in the county, starts refusing her food—'

'Will you stop maundering on about your insufferable pig and give your attention to something that really matters? I tell you that Angela – your niece Angela – has broken off her engagement to Lord Heacham and expresses her intention of marrying that hopeless ne'er-do-well, James Belford.'

'The son of old Belford, the parson?'

'Yes.'

'She can't. He's in America.'

'He is not in America. He is in London.'

'No,' said Lord Emsworth, shaking his head sagely. 'You're wrong. I remember meeting his father two years ago out on the road by Meeker's twenty-acre field, and he distinctly told me the boy was sailing for America next day. He must be there by this time.'

'Can't you understand? He's come back.'

'Oh? Come back? I see. Come *back*?'

'You know there was once a silly sentimental sort of affair between him and Angela; but a year after he left she became engaged to Heacham and I thought the whole thing was over and done with. And now it seems that she met this young man Belford when she was in London last week, and it has started all over again. She tells me she has written to Heacham and broken the engagement.'

There was a silence. Brother and sister remained for a space plunged in thought. Lord Emsworth was the first to speak.

'We've tried acorns,' he said. 'We've tried skim milk. And we've tried potato peel. But, no, she won't touch them.'

Conscious of two eyes raising blisters on his sensitive skin, he came to himself with a start.

'Absurd! Ridiculous! Preposterous!' he said, hurriedly. 'Breaking the engagement? Pooh! Tush! What nonsense! I'll have a word with that young man. If he thinks he can go about the place playing fast and loose with my niece and jilting her without so much as a—'

'Clarence!'

Lord Emsworth blinked. Something appeared to be wrong, but he could not imagine what. It seemed to him that in his last speech he had struck just the right note – strong, forceful, dignified.

'Eh?'

'It is Angela who has broken the engagement.'

'Oh, Angela?'

'She is infatuated with this man Belford. And the point is, what are we to do about it?'

Lord Emsworth reflected.

'Take a strong line,' he said firmly. 'Stand no nonsense. Don't send 'em a wedding present.'

There is no doubt that, given time, Lady Constance would have found and uttered some adequately corrosive comment on this imbecile suggestion; but even as she was swelling preparatory to giving tongue, the door opened and a girl came in.

She was a pretty girl, with fair hair and blue eyes which in their softer moments probably reminded all sorts of people of twin lagoons slumbering beneath a southern sky. To Lord Emsworth, as they met his, they looked like something out of an oxyacetylene blowpipe; and, as far as he was capable of being disturbed by anything that was not his younger son Frederick, he was disturbed. Angela, it seemed to him, was upset about something; and he was sorry. He liked Angela.

To ease a tense situation, he said:

'Angela, my dear, do you know anything about pigs?'

The girl laughed. One of those sharp, bitter laughs which are so unpleasant just after breakfast.

'Yes, I do. You're one.'

'Me?'

'Yes, you. Aunt Constance says that, if I marry Jimmy, you won't let me have my money.'

'Money? Money?' Lord Emsworth was mildly puzzled. 'What money? You never lent me any money.'

Lady Constance's feelings found vent in a sound like an overheated radiator.

'I believe this absent-mindedness of yours is nothing but a ridiculous pose, Clarence. You know perfectly well that when poor Jane died she left you Angela's trustee.'

'And I can't touch my money without your consent till I'm twenty-five.'

'Well, how old are you?'

'Twenty-one.'

'Then what are you worrying about?' asked Lord Emsworth, surprised. 'No need to worry about it for another four years. God bless my soul, the money is quite safe. It is in excellent securities.'

Angela stamped her foot. An unladylike action, no

doubt, but how much better than kicking an uncle with it, as her lower nature prompted.

'I have told Angela,' explained Lady Constance, 'that, while we naturally cannot force her to marry Lord Heacham, we can at least keep her money from being squandered by this wastrel on whom she proposes to throw herself away.'

'He isn't a wastrel. He's got quite enough money to marry me on, but he wants some capital to buy a partnership in a—'

'He is a wastrel. Wasn't he sent abroad because—'

'That was two years ago. And since then—'

'My dear Angela, you may argue until—'

'I'm not arguing. I'm simply saying that I'm going to marry Jimmy, if we both have to starve in the gutter.'

'What gutter?' asked his lordship, wrenching his errant mind away from thoughts of acorns.

'Any gutter.'

'Now, please listen to me, Angela.'

It seemed to Lord Emsworth that there was a frightful amount of conversation going on. He had the sensation of having become a mere bit of flotsam upon a tossing sea of female voices. Both his sister and his niece appeared to have much to say, and they were saying it simultaneously and fortissimo. He looked wistfully at the door.

It was smoothly done. A twist of the handle, and he was where beyond those voices there was peace. Galloping gaily down the stairs, he charged out into the sunshine.

*

His gaiety was not long-lived. Free at last to concentrate itself on the really serious issues of life, his mind grew sombre and grim. Once more there descended upon him the cloud which had been oppressing his soul before all this Heacham-Angela-Belford business began. Each step that took him nearer to the sty where the ailing Empress resided seemed a heavier step than the last. He reached the sty; and, draping himself over the rails, peered moodily at the vast expanse of pig within.

For, even though she had been doing a bit of dieting of late, Empress of Blandings was far from being an ill-nourished animal. She resembled a captive balloon with ears and a tail, and was as nearly circular as a pig can be without bursting. Nevertheless, Lord Emsworth, as he regarded her, mourned and would not be comforted. A few more square meals under her belt, and no pig in all Shropshire could have held its head up in the Empress's presence. And now, just for lack of those few meals, the supreme animal would probably be relegated to the mean obscurity of an 'Honourably Mentioned'. It was bitter, bitter.

He became aware that somebody was speaking to him; and, turning, perceived a solemn young man in riding breeches.

'I say,' said the young man.

Lord Emsworth, though he would have preferred solitude, was relieved to find that the intruder was at least one of his own sex. Women are apt to stray off into side issues, but men are practical and can be relied on to stick to the fundamentals. Besides, young Heacham probably kept pigs himself and might have a useful hint or two up his sleeve.

'I say, I've just ridden over to see if there was anything I could do about this fearful business.'

'Uncommonly kind and thoughtful of you, my dear fellow,' said Lord Emsworth, touched. 'I fear things look very black.'

'It's an absolute mystery to me.'

'To me, too.'

'I mean to say, she was all right last week.'

'She was all right as late as the day before yesterday.'

'Seemed quite cheery and chirpy and all that.'

'Entirely so.'

'And this happens – out of a blue sky, as you might say.'

'Exactly. It is insoluble. We have done everything possible to tempt her appetite.'

'Her appetite? Is Angela ill?'

'Angela? No, I fancy not. She seemed perfectly well a few minutes ago.'

'You've seen her this morning, then? Did she say anything about this fearful business?'

'No. She was speaking about some money.'

'It's all so dashed unexpected.'

'Like a bolt from the blue,' agreed Lord Emsworth. 'Such a thing has never happened before. I fear the worst. According to the Wolff-Lehmann feeding standards, a pig, if in health, should consume daily nourishment amounting to fifty-seven thousand eight hundred calories, these to consist of proteins four pounds five ounces, carbohydrates twenty-five pounds—'

'What has that got to do with Angela?'

'Angela?'

'I came to find out why Angela has broken off our engagement.'

Lord Emsworth marshalled his thoughts. He had a misty idea that he had heard something mentioned about that. It came back to him.

'Ah, yes, of course. She has broken off the engagement, hasn't she? I believe it is because she is in love with someone else. Yes, now that I recollect, that was distinctly stated. The whole thing comes back to me quite clearly. Angela has decided to marry someone else. I knew there was some satisfactory explanation. Tell me, my dear fellow, what are your views on linseed meal.'

'What do you mean, linseed meal?'

'Why, linseed meal,' said Lord Emsworth, not being able to find a better definition. 'As a food for pigs.'

'Oh, curse all pigs!'

'What!' There was a sort of astounded horror in Lord Emsworth's voice. He had never been particularly fond of young Heacham, for he was not a man who took much to his juniors, but he had not supposed him capable of anarchistic sentiments like this. 'What did you say?'

'I said, "Curse all pigs!" You keep talking about pigs. I'm not interested in pigs. I don't want to discuss pigs. Blast and damn every pig in existence!'

Lord Emsworth watched him, as he strode away, with an emotion that was partly indignation and partly relief – indignation that a landowner and a fellow son of Shropshire could have brought himself to utter such words, and relief that one capable of such utterance was not going to marry into his family. He had always in his woollen-headed way been very fond of his niece Angela, and it was nice to think that the child had such solid good sense and so much cool discernment. Many girls of her age would have been carried away by the glamour of young Heacham's position and wealth; but she, divining with an intuition beyond her years that he was unsound on the subject of pigs, had drawn back while there was still time and refused to marry him.

A pleasant glow suffused Lord Emsworth's bosom, to be frozen out a few moments later as he perceived his sister Constance bearing down upon him. Lady Constance was a beautiful woman, but there were times when the charm of her face was marred by a rather curious expression; and from nursery days onward his lordship had learned that this expression meant trouble. She was wearing it now.

'Clarence,' she said, 'I have had enough of this nonsense of Angela and young Belford. The thing cannot be allowed to go drifting on. You must catch the two o'clock train to London.'

'What! Why?'

'You must see this man Belford and tell him that, if Angela insists on marrying him, she will not have a penny for four years. I shall be greatly surprised if that piece of information does not put an end to the whole business.'

Lord Emsworth scratched meditatively at the Empress's tank-like back. A mutinous expression was on his mild face.

'Don't see why she shouldn't marry that fellow,' he mumbled.

'Marry James Belford?'

'I don't see why not. Seems fond of him and all that.'

'You never have had a grain of sense in your head, Clarence. Angela is going to marry Heacham.'

'Can't stand that man. All wrong about pigs.'

'Clarence, I don't wish to have any more discussion and argument. You will go to London on the two o'clock train. You will see Mr Belford. And you will tell him about Angela's money. Is that quite clear?'

'Oh, all right,' said his lordship moodily. 'All right, all right, all right.'

The emotions of the Earl of Emsworth, as he sat next day facing his luncheon guest, James Batholomew Belford, across a table in the main dining room of the Senior Conservative Club, were not of the liveliest and most agreeable. It was bad enough to be in London at all on such a day of golden sunshine. To be charged, while there, with the task of blighting the romance of two young people for whom he entertained a warm regard was unpleasant to a degree.

For, now that he had given the matter thought, Lord Emsworth recalled that he had always liked this boy Belford. A pleasant lad, with, he remembered now, a healthy fondness for that rural existence which so appealed to himself. By no means the sort of fellow who, in the very presence and hearing of Empress of Blandings, would have spoken disparagingly and with oaths of pigs as a class. It occurred to Lord Emsworth, as it has occurred to so many people, that the distribution of money in this world is all wrong. Why should a man like pig-despising

Heacham have a rent roll that ran into the tens of thousands, while this very deserving youngster had nothing?

These thoughts not only saddened Lord Emsworth – they embarrassed him. He hated unpleasantness, and it was suddenly borne in upon him that, after he had broken the news that Angela's bit of capital was locked up and not likely to get loose, conversation with his young friend during the remainder of lunch would tend to be somewhat difficult.

He made up his mind to postpone the revelation. During the meal, he decided, he would chat pleasantly of this and that; and then, later, while bidding his guest goodbye, he would spring the thing on him suddenly and dive back into the recesses of the club.

Considerably cheered at having solved a delicate problem with such adroitness, he started to prattle.

'The gardens at Blandings,' he said, 'are looking particularly attractive this summer. My head gardener, Angus McAllister, is a man with whom I do not always find myself seeing eye to eye, notably in the matter of hollyhocks, on which I consider his views subversive to a degree; but there is no denying that he understands roses. The rose-garden—'

'How well I remember that rose-garden,' said James Belford, sighing slightly and helping himself to brussels sprouts. 'It was there that Angela and I used to meet on summer mornings.'

Lord Emsworth blinked. This was not an encouraging start, but the Emsworths were a fighting clan. He had another try.

'I have seldom seen such a blaze of colour as was to be

witnessed there during the month of June. Both McAllister and I adopted a very strong policy with the slugs and plant lice, with the result that the place was a mass of flourishing Damasks and Ayrshires and—'

'Properly to appreciate roses,' said James Belford, 'you want to see them as a setting for a girl like Angela. With her fair hair gleaming against the green leaves she makes a rose-garden seem a veritable Paradise.'

'No doubt,' said Lord Emsworth. 'No doubt. I am glad you like my rose-garden. At Blandings, of course, we have the natural advantage of loamy soil, rich in plant food and humus; but, as I often say to McAllister, and on this point we have never had the slightest disagreement, loamy soil by itself is not enough. You must have manure. If every autumn a liberal mulch of stable manure is spread upon the beds and the coarser parts removed in the spring before the annual forking—'

'Angela tells me,' said James Belford, 'that you have forbidden our marriage.'

Lord Emsworth choked dismally over his chicken. Directness of this kind, he told himself with a pang of self-pity, was the sort of thing young Englishmen picked up in America. Diplomatic circumlocution flourished only in a more leisurely civilisation, and in those energetic and forceful surroundings you learned to Talk Quick and Do It Now, and all sorts of uncomfortable things.

'Er – well, yes, now you mention it, I believe some informal decision of that nature was arrived at. You see, my dear fellow, my sister Constance feels rather strongly—'

'I understand. I suppose she thinks I'm a sort of prodigal.'

'No, no, my dear fellow. She never said that. Wastrel was the term she employed.'

'Well, perhaps I did start out in business on those lines. But you can take it from me that when you find yourself employed on a farm in Nebraska belonging to an applejack-nourished patriarch with strong views on work and a good vocabulary, you soon develop a certain liveliness.'

'Are you employed on a farm?'

'I was employed on a farm.'

'Pigs?' said Lord Emsworth in a low, eager voice.

'Among other things.'

Lord Emsworth gulped. His fingers clutched at the tablecloth.

'Then perhaps, my dear fellow, you can give me some advice. For the last two days my prize sow, Empress of Blandings, has declined all nourishment. And the Agricultural Show is on Wednesday week. I am distracted with anxiety.' James Belford frowned thoughtfully.

'What does your pig-man say about it?'

'My pig-man was sent to prison two days ago. Two days!' For the first time the significance of the coincidence struck him. 'You don't think that can have anything to do with the animal's loss of appetite?'

'Certainly. I imagine she is missing him and pining away because he isn't there.'

Lord Emsworth was surprised. He had only a distant acquaintance with George Cyril Wellbeloved, but from what he had seen of him he had not credited him with this fatal allure.

'She probably misses his afternoon call.'

Again his lordship found himself perplexed. He had had no notion that pigs were such sticklers for the formalities of social life.

'His call?'

'He must have had some special call that he used when he wanted her to come to dinner. One of the first things you learn on a farm is hog-calling. Pigs are temperamental. Omit to call them, and they'll starve rather than put on the nosebag. Call them right, and they will follow you to the ends of the earth with their mouths watering.'

'God bless my soul! Fancy that.'

'A fact, I assure you. These calls vary in different parts of America. In Wisconsin, for example, the words "Poig, Poig, Poig" bring home – in both the literal and the figurative sense – the bacon. In Illinois, I believe they call "Burp, Burp, Burp", while in Iowa the phrase "Kus, Kus, Kus" is preferred. Proceeding to Minnesota, we find "Peega, Peega, Peega" or, alternatively, "Oink, Oink, Oink", whereas in Milwaukee, so largely inhabited by those of German descent, you will hear the good old Teuton "Komm Schweine, Komm Schweine". Oh, yes, there are all sorts of pig-calls, from the Massachusetts "Phew, Phew, Phew" to the "Loo-ey, Loo-ey, Loo-ey" of Ohio, not counting various local devices such as beating on tin cans with axes or rattling pebbles in a suitcase. I knew a man out in Nebraska who used to call his pigs by tapping on the edge of the trough with his wooden leg.'

'Did he, indeed?'

'But a most unfortunate thing happened. One evening, hearing a woodpecker at the top of a tree, they started shinning up it; and when the man came out he found them all lying there in a circle with their necks broken.'

'This is no time for joking,' said Lord Emsworth, pained.

'I'm not joking. Solid fact. Ask anybody out there.'

Lord Emsworth placed a hand to his throbbing forehead.

'But if there is this wide variety, we have no means of knowing which call Wellbeloved . . .'

'Ah,' said James Belford, 'but wait. I haven't told you all. There is a master word.'

'A what?'

'Most people don't know it, but I had it straight from the lips of Fred Patzel, the hog-calling champion of the Western States. What a man! I've known him to bring pork chops leaping from their plates. He informed me that, no matter whether an animal has been trained to answer to the Illinois "Burp" or the Minnesota "Oink", it will always give immediate service in response to this magic combination of syllables. It is to the pig world what the Masonic grip is to the human. "Oink" in Illinois or "Burp" in Minnesota, and the animal merely raises its eyebrows and stares coldly. But go to either state and call "Pig-hoo-oo-ey!" . . .'

The expression on Lord Emsworth's face was that of a drowning man who sees a lifeline.

'Is that the master word of which you spoke?'

'That's it.'

'Pig—?'

'– hoo-oo-ey.'

'Pig-hoo-o-ey?'

'You haven't got it quite right. The first syllable should be short and staccato, the second long and rising into a falsetto, high but true.'

'Pig-hoo-o-o-ey.'

'Pig-hoo-o-o-ey.'

'Pig-hoo-o-o-ey!' yodelled Lord Emsworth, flinging his head back and giving tongue in a high, penetrating tenor which caused ninety-three Senior Conservatives, lunching in the vicinity, to congeal into living statues of alarm and disapproval.

'More body to the "hoo",' advised James Belford.

'Pig-hoo-o-o-o-ey!'

The Senior Conservative Club is one of the few places in London where lunchers are not accustomed to getting music with their meals. White-whiskered financiers gazed bleakly at bald-headed politicians, as if asking silently what was to be done about this. Bald-headed politicians stared back at white-whiskered financiers, replying in the language of the eye that they did not know. The general sentiment prevailing was a vague determination to write to the Committee about it.

'Pig-hoo-o-o-o-ey!' carolled Lord Emsworth. And, as he did so, his eye fell on the clock over the mantelpiece. Its hands pointed to twenty minutes to two.

He started convulsively. The best train in the day for Market Blandings was the one which left Paddington Station at two sharp. After that there was nothing till the five-five.

He was not a man who often thought; but, when he

did, to think was with him to act. A moment later he was scudding over the carpet, making for the door that led to the broad staircase.

Throughout the room which he had left, the decision to write in strong terms to the Committee was now universal; but from the mind, such as it was, of Lord Emsworth the past, with the single exception of the word 'Pig-hoo-o-o-o-ey!' had been completely blotted.

Whispering the magic syllables, he sped to the cloakroom and retrieved his hat. Murmuring them over and over again, he sprang into a cab. He was still repeating them as the train moved out of the station; and he would doubtless have gone on repeating them all the way to Market Blandings, had he not, as was his invariable practice when travelling by rail, fallen asleep after the first ten minutes of the journey.

The stopping of the train at Swindon Junction woke him with a start. He sat up, wondering, after his usual fashion on these occasions, who and where he was. Memory returned to him, but a memory that was, alas, incomplete. He remembered his name. He remembered that he was on his way home from a visit to London. But what it was that you said to a pig when inviting it to drop in for a bite of dinner he had completely forgotten.

It was the opinion of Lady Constance Keeble, expressed verbally during dinner in the brief intervals when they were alone, and by means of silent telepathy when Beach, the butler, was adding his dignified presence to the proceedings, that her brother Clarence, in his expedition to London to put matters plainly to James Belford, had made an outstanding idiot of himself.

There had been no need whatever to invite the man Belford to lunch; but, having invited him to lunch, to leave him sitting, without having clearly stated that Angela would have no money for four years, was the act of a congenital imbecile. Lady Constance had been aware ever since their childhood days that her brother had about as much sense as a—

Here Beach entered, superintending the bringing-in of the savoury, and she had been obliged to suspend her remarks.

This sort of conversation is never agreeable to a sensitive man, and his lordship had removed himself from the danger zone as soon as he could manage it. He was now seated in the library, sipping port and straining his brain which Nature had never intended for hard exercise in an effort to bring back that word of magic of which his unfortunate habit of sleeping in trains had robbed him.

'Pig—'

He could remember as far as that; but of what avail was a single syllable? Besides, weak as his memory was, he could recall that the whole gist or nub of the thing lay in the syllable that followed. The 'pig' was a mere preliminary.

Lord Emsworth finished his port and got up. He felt restless, stifled. The summer night seemed to call to him like some silver-voiced swineherd calling to his pig. Possibly, he thought, a breath of fresh air might stimulate his brain-cells. He wandered downstairs; and, having dug a shocking old slouch hat out of the cupboard where he hid it to keep his sister Constance from impounding and burning it, he strode heavily out into the garden.

He was pottering aimlessly to and fro in the parts adjacent to the rear of the castle when there appeared in his path a slender female form. He recognised it without pleasure. Any unbiased judge would have said that his niece Angela, standing there in the soft, pale light, looked like some dainty spirit of the moon. Lord Emsworth was not an unbiased judge. To him Angela merely looked like Trouble. The march of civilisation has given the modern girl a vocabulary and an ability to use it which her grandmother never had. Lord Emsworth would not have minded meeting Angela's grandmother a bit.

'Is that you, my dear?' he said nervously.

'Yes.'

'I didn't see you at dinner.'

'I didn't want any dinner. The food would have choked me. I can't eat.'

'It's precisely the same with my pig,' said his lordship. 'Young Belford tells me—'

Into Angela's queenly disdain there flashed a sudden animation.

'Have you seen Jimmy? What did he say?'

'That's just what I can't remember. It began with the word "Pig"—'

'But after he had finished talking about you, I mean. Didn't he say anything about coming down here?'

'Not that I remember.'

'I expect you weren't listening. You've got a very annoying habit, Uncle Clarence,' said Angela maternally, 'of switching your mind off and just going blah when people are talking to you. It gets you very much disliked on all sides. Didn't Jimmy say anything about me?'

'I fancy so. Yes, I am nearly sure he did.'

'Well, what.'

'I cannot remember.'

There was a sharp clicking noise in the darkness. It was caused by Angela's upper front teeth meeting her lower front teeth; and was followed by a sort of wordless exclamation. It seemed only too plain that the love and respect which a niece should have for an uncle were in the present instance at a very low ebb.

'I wish you wouldn't do that,' said Lord Emsworth plaintively.

'Do what?'

'Make clicking noises at me.'

'I will make clicking noises at you. You know perfectly well, Uncle Clarence, that you are behaving like a bohunkus.'

'A what?'

'A bohunkus,' explained his niece, coldly, 'is a very inferior sort of worm. Not the kind of worm that you see on lawns, which you can respect, but a really degraded species.'

'I wish you would go in, my dear,' said Lord Emsworth. 'The night air may give you a chill.'

'I won't go in. I came out here to look at the moon and think of Jimmy. What are you doing out here, if it comes to that?'

'I came here to think. I am greatly exercised about my pig, Empress of Blandings. For two days she has refused her food, and young Belford says she will not eat until she hears the proper call or cry. He very kindly taught it to me, but unfortunately I have forgotten it.'

'I wonder you had the nerve to ask Jimmy to teach you pig calls, considering the way you're treating him.'

'But—'

'Like a leper, or something. And all I can say is that, if you remember this call of his, and it makes the Empress eat, you ought to be ashamed of yourself if you still refuse to let me marry him.'

'My dear,' said Lord Emsworth earnestly, 'if through young Belford's instrumentality Empress of Blandings is induced to take nourishment once more, there is nothing I will refuse him – nothing.'

'Honour bright?'

'I give you my solemn word.'

'You won't let Aunt Constance bully you out of it?'

Lord Emsworth drew himself up.

'Certainly not,' he said proudly. 'I am always ready to listen to your Aunt Constance's view, but there are certain matters where I claim the right to act according to my own judgment.' He paused and stood musing. 'It began with the word "Pig—".'

From somewhere near at hand music made itself heard. The servants' hall, its day's labours ended, was refreshing itself with the housekeeper's gramophone. To Lord Emsworth the strains were merely an additional annoyance. He was not fond of music. It reminded him of his younger son Frederick, a flat but persevering songster both in and out of the bath.

'Yes, I can distinctly recall as much as that. Pig – Pig—'

'WHO—'

Lord Emsworth leaped in the air. It was as if an electric shock had been applied to his person.

'WHO stole my heart away?' howled the gramophone. 'WHO—?'

The peace of the summer night was shattered by a triumphant shout.

'Pig-HOO-o-o-o-ey!'

A window opened. A large, bald head appeared. A dignified voice spoke.

'Who is there? Who is making that noise?'

'Beach!' cried Lord Emsworth. 'Come out here at once.'

'Very good, your lordship.'

And presently the beautiful night was made still more lovely by the added attraction of the butler's presence.

'Beach, listen to this.'

'Very good, your lordship.'

'Pig-hoo-o-o-o-ey!'

'Very good, your lordship.'

'Now you do it.'

'I, your lordship?'

'Yes. It's a way you call pigs.'

'I do not call pigs, your lordship,' said the butler coldly.

'What do you want Beach to do it for?' asked Angela.

'Two heads are better than one. If we both learn it, it will not matter should I forget it again.'

'By Jove, yes! Come on, Beach. Push it over the thorax,' urged the girl eagerly. 'You don't know it, but this is a matter of life and death. At-a-boy, Beach! Inflate the lungs and go to it.'

It had been the butler's intention, prefacing his remarks with the statement that he had been in service at the Castle for eighteen years, to explain frigidly to Lord Emsworth that it was not his place to stand in the moonlight practising pig calls. If, he would have gone on to add, his lordship saw the matter from a different angle, then it was his, Beach's, painful duty to tender his resignation, to become effective one month from that day.

But the intervention of Angela made this impossible to a man of chivalry and heart. A paternal fondness for the girl, dating from the days when he had stooped to enacting – and very convincingly, too, for his was a figure that lent itself to the impersonation – the *role* of a hippopotamus for her childish amusement, checked the words he would have uttered. She was looking at him with bright eyes, and even the rendering of pig noises seemed a small sacrifice to make for her sake.

'Very good, your lordship,' he said in a low voice, his face pale and set in the moonlight. 'I shall endeavour to give satisfaction. I would merely advance the suggestion, your lordship, that we move a few steps farther away from the vicinity of the servants' hall. If I were to be overheard by any of the lower domestics, it would weaken my position as a disciplinary force.'

'What chumps we are!' cried Angela, inspired. 'The place to do it is outside the Empress's sty. Then, if it works, we'll see it working.'

Lord Emsworth found this a little abstruse, but after a moment he got it.

'Angela,' he said, 'You are a very intelligent girl. Where you get your brains from, I don't know. Not from my side of the family.'

The bijou residence of the Empress of Blandings

looked very snug and attractive in the moonlight. But beneath even the beautiful things of life there is always an underlying sadness. This was supplied in the present instance by a long, low trough, only too plainly full to the brim of succulent mash and acorns. The fast, obviously, was still in progress.

The sty stood some considerable distance from the Castle walls, so that there had been ample opportunity for Lord Emsworth to rehearse his little company during the journey. By the time they had ranged themselves against the rails, his two assistants were letter-perfect.

'Now,' said his lordship.

There floated out upon the summer night a strange composite sound that sent the birds roosting in the trees above shooting off their perches like rockets. Angela's clear soprano rang out like the voice of the village blacksmith's daughter. Lord Emsworth contributed a reedy tenor. And the bass notes of Beach probably did more to startle the birds than any other one item in the programme.

They paused and listened. Inside the Empress's boudoir there sounded the movement of a heavy body. There was an inquiring grunt. The next moment the sacking that covered the doorway was pushed aside, and the noble animal emerged.

'Now!' said Lord Emsworth again.

Once more that musical cry shattered the silence of the night. But it brought no responsive movement from Empress of Blandings. She stood there motionless, her nose elevated, her ears hanging down, her eyes everywhere but on the trough where, by rights, she should now have been digging in and getting hers. A chill disappointment crept over Lord Emsworth, to be succeeded by a gust of petulant anger.

'I might have known it,' he said bitterly. 'That young scoundrel was deceiving me. He was playing a joke on me.'

'He wasn't,' cried Angela indignantly. 'Was he, Beach?'

'Not knowing the circumstances, miss, I cannot venture an opinion.'

'Well, why has it no effect, then?' demanded Lord Emsworth.

'You can't expect it to work right away. We've got her stirred up, haven't we? She's thinking it over, isn't she? Once more will do the trick. Ready, Beach?'

'Quite ready, miss.'

'Then when I say three. And this time, Uncle Clarence, do please for goodness' sake not yowl like you did before. It was enough to put any pig off. Let it come out quite easily and gracefully. Now, then, one, two – three!'

The echoes died away. And as they did so a voice spoke.

'Community singing!'

'Jimmy!' cried Angela, whisking round.

'Hullo, Angela. Hullo, Lord Emsworth. Hullo, Beach.'

'Good evening, sir. Happy to see you once more.'

'Thanks. I'm spending a few days at the Vicarage with my father. I got down here by the five-five.'

Lord Emsworth cut peevishly in upon these civilities.

'Young man,' he said, 'what do you mean by telling me that my pig would respond to that cry? It does nothing of the kind.'

'You can't have done it right.'

'I did it precisely as you instructed me. I have had, moreover, the assistance of Beach here and my niece Angela—'

'Let's hear a sample.'

Lord Emsworth cleared his throat.

'Pig-hoo-o-o-o-ey!'

James Belford shook his head.

'Nothing like it,' he said. 'You want to begin the "Hoo" in a low minor of two quarter notes in four-four time. From this build gradually to a higher note, until at last the voice is soaring in full crescendo, reaching F sharp on the natural scale and dwelling for two retarded half-notes, then breaking into a shower of accidental grace notes.'

'God bless my soul!' said Lord Emsworth, appalled. 'I shall never be able to do it.'

'Jimmy will do it for you,' said Angela. 'Now that he's engaged to me, he'll be one of the family and always popping about here. He can do it every day till the show is over.'

James Belford nodded.

'I think that would be the wisest plan. It is doubtful if an amateur could ever produce real results. You need a voice that has been trained on the open prairie and that has gathered richness and strength from competing with tornadoes. You need a manly, sunburned, wind-scorched voice with a suggestion in it of the crackling of corn husks and the whisper of evening breezes in the fodder. Like this!'

Resting his hands on the rail before him, James Belford swelled before their eyes like a young balloon. The muscles on his cheekbones stood out, his forehead became corrugated, his ears seemed to shimmer. Then, at the very height of the tension, he let it go like, as the poet beautifully puts it, the sound of a great Amen.

'Pig-HOOOOO-OOO-OOO-O-O-ey!'

They looked at him, awed. Slowly, fading off across hill and dale, the vast bellow died away. And suddenly, as it died, another, softer sound succeeded it. A sort of gulpy, gurgly, ploddy, squishy, wofflesome sound, like a thousand eager men drinking soup in a foreign restaurant. And, as he heard it, Lord Emsworth uttered a cry of rapture.

The Empress was feeding.

August

Lord Emsworth and the Girl Friend

The day was so warm, so fair, so magically a thing of sunshine and blue skies and birdsong that anyone acquainted with Clarence, ninth Earl of Emsworth, and aware of his liking for fine weather, would have pictured him going about the place on this summer morning with a beaming smile and an uplifted heart. Instead of which, humped over the breakfast table, he was directing at a blameless kippered herring a look of such intense bitterness that the fish seemed to sizzle beneath it. For it was August Bank Holiday, and Blandings Castle on August Bank Holiday became, in his lordship's opinion, a miniature Inferno.

This was the day when his park and grounds broke out into a noisome rash of swings, roundabouts, marquees, toy balloons and paper bags; when a tidal wave of the peasantry and its squealing young engulfed those haunts of immemorial peace. On August Bank Holiday he was not allowed to potter pleasantly about his gardens in an old coat: forces beyond his control shoved him into a stiff collar and a top hat and told him to go out and be genial. And in the cool of the quiet evenfall they put him on a platform and made him make a speech. To a man with a day like that in front of him fine weather was a mockery.

His sister, Lady Constance Keeble, looked brightly at him over the coffee pot.

'What a lovely morning!' she said.

Lord Emsworth's gloom deepened. He chafed at being called upon – by this woman of all others – to behave as if everything was for the jolliest in the jolliest of all possible worlds. But for his sister Constance and her hawk-like vigilance, he might, he thought, have been able at least to dodge the top hat.

'Have you got your speech ready?'

'Yes.'

'Well, mind you learn it by heart this time and don't stammer and dodder as you did last year.'

Lord Emsworth pushed plate and kipper away. He had lost his desire for food.

'And don't forget you have to go to the village this morning to judge the cottage gardens.'

'All right, all right, all right,' said his lordship testily. 'I've not forgotten.'

'I think I will come to the village with you. There are a number of those Fresh Air London children staying there now, and I must warn them to behave properly when they come to the Fête this afternoon. You know what London children are. McAllister says he found one of them in the gardens the other day, picking his flowers.'

At any other time the news of this outrage would, no doubt, have affected Lord Emsworth profoundly. But now, so intense was his self-pity, he did not even shudder. He drank coffee with the air of a man who regretted that it was not hemlock.

'By the way, McAllister was speaking to me again last

night about that gravel path through the yew alley. He seems very keen on it.'

'Glug!' said Lord Emsworth – which, as any philologist will tell you, is the sound which peers of the realm make when stricken to the soul while drinking coffee.

Concerning Glasgow, that great commercial and manufacturing city in the county of Lanarkshire in Scotland, much has been written. So lyrically does the Encyclopædia Britannica deal with the place that it covers twenty-seven pages before it can tear itself away and go on to Glass, Glastonbury, Glatz and Glauber. The only aspect of it, however, which immediately concerns the present historian is the fact that the citizens it breeds are apt to be grim, dour, persevering, tenacious men; men with red whiskers who know what they want and mean to get it. Such a one was Angus McAllister, head gardener at Blandings Castle.

For years Angus McAllister had set before himself as his earthly goal the construction of a gravel path through the Castle's famous yew alley. For years he had been bringing the project to the notice of his employer, though in anyone less whiskered the latter's unconcealed loathing would have caused embarrassment. And now, it seemed, he was at it again.

'Gravel path!' Lord Emsworth stiffened through the whole length of his stringy body. Nature, he had always maintained, intended a yew alley to be carpeted with a mossy growth. And, whatever Nature felt about it, he personally was dashed if he was going to have men with Clydeside accents and faces like dissipated potatoes coming along and mutilating that lovely expanse of green velvet. 'Gravel path, indeed! Why not asphalt? Why not a few hoardings with advertisements of liver pills and a filling station? That's what the man would really like.'

Lord Emsworth felt bitter, and when he felt bitter he could be terribly sarcastic.

'Well, I think it is a very good idea,' said his sister. 'One could walk there in wet weather then. Damp moss is ruinous to shoes.'

Lord Emsworth rose. He could bear no more of this. He left the table, the room and the house and, reaching the yew alley some minutes later, was revolted to find it infested by Angus McAllister in person. The head gardener was standing gazing at the moss like a high priest of some ancient religion about to stick the gaff into the human sacrifice.

'Morning, McAllister,' said Lord Emsworth coldly.

'Good morrrrning, your lorrudsheep.'

There was a pause. Angus McAllister, extending a foot that looked like a violin-case, pressed it on the moss. The meaning of the gesture was plain. It expressed contempt, dislike, a generally anti-moss spirit: and Lord Emsworth, wincing, surveyed the man unpleasantly through his pince-nez. Though not often given to theological speculation, he was wondering why Providence, if obliged to make head gardeners, had found it necessary to make them so Scotch. In the case of Angus McAllister, why, going a step farther, have made him a human being at all? All the ingredients of a first-class mule simply thrown away. He felt that he might have liked Angus McAllister if he had been a mule.

'I was speaking to her leddyship yesterday.'

'Oh?'

'About the gravel path I was speaking to her leddyship.'
'Oh?'
'Her leddyship likes the notion fine.'
'Indeed! Well . . .'

Lord Emsworth's face had turned a lively pink, and he was about to release the blistering words which were forming themselves in his mind when suddenly he caught the head gardener's eye and paused. Angus McAllister was looking at him in a peculiar manner, and he knew what that look meant. Just one crack, his eye was saying – in Scotch, of course – just one crack out of you and I tender my resignation. And with a sickening shock it came home to Lord Emsworth how completely he was in this man's clutches.

He shuffled miserably. Yes, he was helpless. Except for that kink about gravel paths, Angus McAllister was a head gardener in a thousand, and he needed him. He could not do without him. That, unfortunately, had been proved by experiment. Once before, at the time when they were grooming for the Agricultural Show that pumpkin which had subsequently romped home so gallant a winner, he had dared to flout Angus McAllister. And Angus had resigned, and he had been forced to plead – yes, plead – with him to come back. An employer cannot hope to do this sort of thing and still rule with an iron hand. Filled with the coward rage that dares to burn but does not dare to blaze, Lord Emsworth coughed a cough that was undisguisedly a bronchial white flag.

'I'll – er – I'll think it over, McAllister.'
'Mphm.'
'I have to go to the village now. I will see you later.'

'Mphm.'

'Meanwhile, I will – er – think it over.'

'Mphm.'

The task of judging the floral displays in the cottage gardens of the little village of Blandings Parva was one to which Lord Emsworth had looked forward with pleasurable anticipation. It was the sort of job he liked. But now, even though he had managed to give his sister Constance the slip and was free from her threatened society, he approached the task with a downcast spirit. It is always unpleasant for a proud man to realise that he is no longer captain of his soul; that he is to all intents and purposes ground beneath the number twelve heel of a Glaswegian head gardener; and, brooding on this, he judged the cottage gardens with a distrait eye. It was only when he came to the last on his list that anything like animation crept into his demeanour.

This, he perceived, peering over its rickety fence, was not at all a bad little garden. It demanded closer inspection. He unlatched the gate and pottered in. And a dog, dozing behind a water-butt, opened one eye and looked at him. It was one of those hairy, nondescript dogs, and its gaze was cold, wary and suspicious, like that of a stockbroker who thinks someone is going to play the confidence trick on him.

Lord Emsworth did not observe the animal. He had pottered to a bed of wallflowers and now, stooping, he took a sniff at them.

As sniffs go, it was an innocent sniff, but the dog for some reason appeared to read into it criminality of a high order. All the indignant householder in him woke in a flash. The next moment the world had become full of hideous noises, and Lord Emsworth's preoccupation was swept away in a passionate desire to save his ankles from harm.

As these chronicles of Blandings Castle have already shown, he was not at his best with strange dogs. Beyond saying 'Go away, sir!' and leaping to and fro with an agility surprising in one of his years, he had accomplished little in the direction of a reasoned plan of defence when the cottage door opened and a girl came out.

'Hoy!' cried the girl.

And on the instant, at the mere sound of her voice, the mongrel, suspending hostilities, bounded at the newcomer and writhed on his back at her feet with all four legs in the air. The spectacle reminded Lord Emsworth irresistibly of his own behaviour when in the presence of Angus McAllister.

He blinked at his preserver. She was a small girl, of uncertain age – possibly twelve or thirteen, though a combination of London fogs and early cares had given her face a sort of wizened motherliness which in some odd way caused his lordship from the first to look on her as belonging to his own generation. She was the type of girl you see in back streets carrying a baby nearly as large as herself and still retaining sufficient energy to lead one little brother by the hand and shout recrimination at another in the distance. Her cheeks shone from recent soaping, and she was dressed in a velveteen frock which was obviously the pick of her wardrobe. Her hair, in defiance of the prevailing mode, she wore drawn tightly back into a short pigtail.

'Er – thank you,' said Lord Emsworth.

'Thank you, sir,' said the girl.

For what she was thanking him, his lordship was not able to gather. Later, as their acquaintance ripened, he was to discover that this strange gratitude was a habit with his new friend. She thanked everybody for everything. At the moment, the mannerism surprised him. He continued to blink at her through his pince-nez.

Lack of practice had rendered Lord Emsworth a little rusty in the art of making conversation to members of the other sex. He sought in his mind for topics.

'Fine day.'

'Yes, sir. Thank you, sir.'

'Are you' – Lord Emsworth furtively consulted his list – 'are you the daughter of – ah – Ebenezer Sprockett?' he asked, thinking, as he had often thought before, what ghastly names some of his tenantry possessed.

'No, sir. I'm from London, sir.'

'Ah? London, eh? Pretty warm it must be there.' He paused. Then, remembering a formula of his youth: 'Er – been out much this Season?'

'No, sir.'

'Everybody out of town now, I suppose? What part of London?'

'Drury Line, sir.'

'What's your name? Eh, what?'

'Gladys, sir. Thank you, sir. This is Ern.'

A small boy had wandered out of the cottage, a rather hard-boiled specimen with freckles, bearing surprisingly in his hand a large and beautiful bunch of flowers. Lord Emsworth bowed courteously and with the addition of this third party to the *tête-à-tête* felt more at his ease.

'How do you do,' he said. 'What pretty flowers.'

With her brother's advent, Gladys, also, had lost diffidence and gained conversational aplomb.

'A treat, ain't they?' she agreed eagerly. 'I got 'em for 'im up at the big 'ahse. Coo! The old josser the plice belongs to didn't arf chase me. 'E found me picking 'em and 'e sharted somefin at me and come runnin' after me, but I copped 'im on the shin wiv a stone and 'e stopped to rub it and I come away.'

Lord Emsworth might have corrected her impression that Blandings Castle and its gardens belonged to Angus McAllister, but his mind was so filled with admiration and gratitude that he refrained from doing so. He looked at the girl almost reverently. Not content with controlling savage dogs with a mere word, this super-woman actually threw stones at Angus McAllister — a thing which he had never been able to nerve himself to do in an association which had lasted nine years — and, what was more, copped him on the shin with them. What nonsense, Lord Emsworth felt, the papers talked about the Modern Girl. If this was a specimen, the Modern Girl was the highest point the sex had yet reached.

'Ern,' said Gladys, changing the subject, 'is wearin' 'air-oil todiy.'

Lord Emsworth had already observed this and had, indeed, been moving to windward as she spoke.

'For the Feet,' explained Gladys.

'For the feet?' It seemed unusual.

'For the Feet in the pork this afternoon.'

'Oh, you are going to the Fête?'

'Yes, sir, thank you, sir.'

For the first time, Lord Emsworth found himself regarding that grisly social event with something approaching favour.

'We must look out for one another there,' he said cordially. 'You will remember me again? I shall be wearing' – he gulped – 'a top hat.'

'Ern's going to wear a stror penamaw that's been give 'im.'

Lord Emsworth regarded the lucky young devil with frank envy. He rather fancied he knew that panama. It had been his constant companion for some six years and then had been torn from him by his sister Constance and handed over to the vicar's wife for her rummage-sale.

He sighed.

'Well, goodbye.'

'Goodbye, sir. Thank you, sir.'

Lord Emsworth walked pensively out of the garden and, turning into the little street, encountered Lady Constance.

'Oh, there you are, Clarence.'

'Yes,' said Lord Emsworth, for such was the case.

'Have you finished judging the gardens?'

'Yes.'

'I am just going into this end cottage here. The vicar tells me there is a little girl from London staying there. I want to warn her to behave this afternoon. I have spoken to the others.'

Lord Emsworth drew himself up. His pince-nez were slightly askew, but despite this his gaze was commanding and impressive.

'Well, mind what you say,' he said authoritatively. 'None of your district-visiting stuff, Constance.'

'What do you mean?'

'You know what I mean. I have the greatest respect for the young lady to whom you refer. She behaved on a certain recent occasion – on two recent occasions – with notable gallantry and resource, and I won't have her bally-ragged. Understand that!'

The technical title of the orgy which broke out annually on the first Monday in August in the park of Blandings Castle was the Blandings Parva School Treat, and it seemed to Lord Emsworth, wanly watching the proceedings from under the shadow of his top hat, that if this was the sort of thing schools looked on as pleasure he and they were mentally poles apart. A function like the Blandings Parva School Treat blurred his conception of Man as Nature's Final Word.

The decent sheep and cattle to whom this park normally belonged had been hustled away into regions unknown, leaving the smooth expanse of turf to children whose vivacity scared Lord Emsworth and adults who appeared to him to have cast aside all dignity and every other noble quality which goes to make a one hundred per cent British citizen. Look at Mrs Rossiter over there, for instance, the wife of Jno. Rossiter, Provisions, Groceries and Home-Made Jams. On any other day of the year, when you met her, Mrs Rossiter was a nice, quiet, docile woman who gave at the knees respectfully as you passed. Today, flushed in the face and with her bonnet on one side, she seemed to have gone completely native. She was wandering to and fro drinking lemonade out of a bottle and employing her mouth, when not so occupied, to make a devastating noise with what he believed was termed a squeaker.

The injustice of the thing stung Lord Emsworth. This park was his own private park. What right had people to come and blow squeakers in it? How would Mrs Rossiter like it if one afternoon he suddenly invaded her neat little garden in the High Street and rushed about over her lawn, blowing a squeaker?

And it was always on these occasions so infernally hot. July might have ended in a flurry of snow, but directly the first Monday in August arrived and he had to put on a stiff collar out came the sun, blazing with tropic fury.

Of course, admitted Lord Emsworth, for he was a fair-minded man, this cut both ways. The hotter the day, the more quickly his collar lost its starch and ceased to spike him like a javelin. This afternoon, for instance, it had resolved itself almost immediately into something which felt like a wet compress. Severe as were his sufferings, he was compelled to recognise that he was that much ahead of the game.

A masterful figure loomed at his side.

'Clarence!'

Lord Emsworth's mental and spiritual state was now such that not even the advent of his sister Constance could add noticeably to his discomfort.

'Clarence, you look a perfect sight.'

'I know I do. Who wouldn't in a rig-out like this? Why in the name of goodness you always insist . . .'

'Please don't be childish, Clarence. I cannot understand the fuss you make about dressing for once in your life like a reasonable English gentleman and not like a tramp.'

'It's this top hat. It's exciting the children.'

'What on earth do you mean, exciting the children?'

'Well, all I can tell you is that just now, as I was passing the place where they're playing football – Football! In weather like this! – a small boy called out something derogatory and threw a portion of a coconut at it.'

'If you will identify the child,' said Lady Constance warmly, 'I will have him severely punished.'

'How the dickens,' replied his lordship with equal warmth, 'can I identify the child? They all look alike to me. And if I did identify him, I would shake him by the hand. A boy who throws coconuts at top hats is fundamentally sound in his views. And stiff collars . . .'

'Stiff! That's what I came to speak to you about. Are you aware that your collar looks like a rag? Go in and change it at once.'

'But, my dear Constance . . .'

'At once, Clarence. I simply cannot understand a man having so little pride in his appearance. But all your life you have been like that. I remember when we were children . . .'

Lord Emsworth's past was not of such a purity that he was prepared to stand and listen to it being lectured on by a sister with a good memory.

'Oh, all right, all right, all right,' he said. 'I'll change it, I'll change it.'

'Well, hurry. They are just starting tea.'

Lord Emsworth quivered.

'Have I got to go into that tea-tent?'

'Of course you have. Don't be so ridiculous. I do wish you would realise your position. As master of Blandings Castle . . .'

A bitter, mirthless laugh from the poor peon thus ludicrously described drowned the rest of the sentence.

It always seemed to Lord Emsworth, in analysing these entertainments, that the August Bank Holiday Saturnalia at Blandings Castle reached a peak of repulsiveness when tea was served in the big marquee. Tea over, the agony abated, to become acute once more at the moment when he stepped to the edge of the platform and cleared his throat and tried to recollect what the deuce he had planned to say to the goggling audience beneath him. After that, it subsided again and passed until the following August.

Conditions during the tea hour, the marquee having stood all day under a blazing sun, were generally such that Shadrach, Meshach and Abednego, had they been there, could have learned something new about burning fiery furnaces. Lord Emsworth, delayed by the revision of his toilet, made his entry when the meal was half over and was pleased to find that his second collar almost instantaneously began to relax its iron grip. That, however, was the only gleam of happiness which was to be vouchsafed him. Once in the tent, it took his experienced eye but a moment to discern that the present feast was eclipsing in frightfulness all its predecessors.

Young Blandings Parva, in its normal form, tended rather to the stolidly bovine than the riotous. In all villages, of course, there must of necessity be an occasional tough egg – in the case of Blandings Parva the names of Willie Drake and Thomas (Rat-Face) Blenkiron spring to the mind – but it was seldom that the local infants offered anything beyond the power of a curate to control. What was giving the present gathering its striking resemblance to a reunion of *sans-culottes* at the height of the French Revolution was the admixture of the Fresh Air London visitors.

About the London child, reared among the tin cans and cabbage stalks of Drury Lane and Clare Market, there is a breezy insouciance which his country cousin lacks. Years of back-chat with annoyed parents and relatives have cured him of any tendency he may have had towards shyness, with the result that when he requires anything he grabs for it, and when he is amused by any slight peculiarity in the personal appearance of members of the governing classes he finds no difficulty in translating his thoughts into speech. Already, up and down the long tables, the curate's unfortunate squint was coming in for hearty comment, and the front teeth of one of the schoolteachers ran it a close second for popularity. Lord Emsworth was not, as a rule, a man of swift inspirations, but it occurred to him at this juncture that it would be a prudent move to take off his top hat before his little guests observed it and appreciated its humorous possibilities.

The action was not, however, necessary. Even as he raised his hand a rock cake, singing through the air like a shell, took it off for him.

Lord Emsworth had had sufficient. Even Constance, unreasonable woman though she was, could hardly expect him to stay and beam genially under conditions like this. All civilised laws had obviously gone by the board and Anarchy reigned in the marquee. The curate was doing his best to form a provisional government consisting of himself and the two schoolteachers, but there was only one man who could have coped adequately with the situation and that was King Herod, who – regrettably – was not among those present. Feeling like some aristocrat of the old *régime* sneaking away from the tumbril, Lord Emsworth edged to the exit and withdrew.

Outside the marquee the world was quieter, but only comparatively so. What Lord Emsworth craved was solitude, and in all the broad park there seemed to be but one spot where it was to be had. This was a red-tiled shed, standing beside a small pond, used at happier times as a lounge or retiring room for cattle. Hurrying thither, his lordship had just begun to revel in the cool, cow-scented dimness of its interior when from one of the dark corners, causing him to start and bite his tongue, there came the sound of a subdued sniff.

He turned. This was persecution. With the whole park to mess about in, why should an infernal child invade this one sanctuary of his? He spoke with angry sharpness. He came of a line of warrior ancestors and his fighting blood was up.

'Who's that?'

'Me, sir. Thank you, sir.'

Only one person of Lord Emsworth's acquaintance was capable of expressing gratitude for having been barked at in such a tone. His wrath died away and remorse took its place. He felt like a man who in error has kicked a favourite dog.

'God bless my soul!' he exclaimed. 'What in the world are you doing in a cowshed?'

'Please, sir, I was put.'

'Put? How do you mean, put? Why?'

'For pinching things, sir.'

'Eh? What? Pinching things? Most extraordinary. What did you – er – pinch?'

'Two buns, two jem-sengwiches, two apples and a slicer cake.'

The girl had come out of her corner and was standing correctly at attention. Force of habit had caused her to intone the list of the purloined articles in the sing-song voice in which she was wont to recite the multiplication-table at school, but Lord Emsworth could see that she was deeply moved. Tear-stains glistened on her face, and no Emsworth had ever been able to watch unstirred a woman's tears. The ninth Earl was visibly affected.

'Blow your nose,' he said, hospitably extending his handkerchief.

'Yes, sir. Thank you, sir.'

'What did you say you had pinched? Two buns . . .'

'. . . Two jem-sengwiches, two apples and a slicer cake.'

'Did you eat them?'

'No, sir. They wasn't for me. They was for Ern.'

'Ern? Oh, ah, yes. Yes, to be sure. For Ern, eh?'

'Yes, sir.'

'But why the dooce couldn't Ern have – er – pinched them for himself? Strong, able-bodied young feller, I mean.'

Lord Emsworth, a member of the old school, did not like this disposition on the part of the modern young man to shirk the dirty work and let the woman pay.

'Ern wasn't allowed to come to the treat, sir.'

'What! Not allowed? Who said he mustn't?'

'The lidy, sir.'

'What lidy?'

'The one that come in just after you'd gorn this morning.'

A fierce snort escaped Lord Emsworth. Constance! What the devil did Constance mean by taking it upon herself to revise his list of guests without so much as a . . . Constance, eh? He snorted again. One of these days Constance would go too far.

'Monstrous!' he cried.

'Yes, sir.'

'High-handed tyranny, by Gad. Did she give any reason?'

'The lidy didn't like Ern biting 'er in the leg, sir.'

'Ern bit her in the leg?'

'Yes, sir. Pliying 'e was a dorg. And the lidy was cross and Ern wasn't allowed to come to the treat, and I told 'im I'd bring 'im back somefing nice.'

Lord Emsworth breathed heavily. He had not supposed that in these degenerate days a family like this existed. The sister copped Angus McAllister on the shin with stones, the brother bit Constance in the leg . . . It was like listening to some grand old saga of the exploits of heroes and demigods.

'I thought if I didn't 'ave nothing myself it would make it all right.'

'Nothing?' Lord Emsworth started. 'Do you mean to tell me you have not had tea?'

'No, sir. Thank you, sir. I thought if I didn't 'ave none, then it would be all right Ern 'aving what I would 'ave 'ad if I 'ad 'ave 'ad.'

His lordship's head, never strong, swam a little. Then it resumed its equilibrium. He caught her drift.

'God bless my soul!' said Lord Emsworth. 'I never heard anything so monstrous and appalling in my life. Come with me immediately.'

'The lidy said I was to stop 'ere, sir.'

Lord Emsworth gave vent to his loudest snort of the afternoon.

'Confound the lidy!'

'Yes, sir. Thank you, sir.'

Five minutes later Beach, the butler, enjoying a siesta in the housekeeper's room, was roused from his slumbers by the unexpected ringing of a bell. Answering its summons, he found his employer in the library, and with him a surprising young person in a velveteen frock, at the sight of whom his eyebrows quivered and, but for his iron self-restraint, would have risen.

'Beach!'

'Your lordship?'

'This young lady would like some tea.'

'Very good, your lordship.'

'Buns, you know. And apples, and jem – I mean jam-sandwiches, and cake, and that sort of thing.'

'Very good, your lordship.'

'And she has a brother, Beach.'

'Indeed, your lordship?'

'She will want to take some stuff away for him.' Lord Emsworth turned to his guest. 'Ernest would like a little chicken, perhaps?'

'Coo!'

'I beg your pardon?'

'Yes, sir. Thank you, sir.'

'And a slice or two of ham?'

'Yes, sir. Thank you, sir.'

'And – he has no gouty tendency?'

'No, sir. Thank you, sir.'

'Capital! Then a bottle of that new lot of port, Beach. It's some stuff they've sent me down to try,' explained his lordship. 'Nothing special, you understand,' he added apologetically, 'but quite drinkable. I should like your brother's opinion of it. See that all that is put together in a parcel, Beach, and leave it on the table in the hall. We will pick it up as we go out.'

A welcome coolness had crept into the evening air by the time Lord Emsworth and his guest came out of the great door of the castle. Gladys, holding her host's hand and clutching the parcel, sighed contentedly. She had done herself well at the tea table. Life seemed to have nothing more to offer.

Lord Emsworth did not share this view. His spacious mood had not yet exhausted itself.

'Now, is there anything else you can think of that Ernest would like?' he asked. 'If so, do not hesitate to mention it. Beach, can you think of anything?'

The butler, hovering respectfully, was unable to do so.

'No, your lordship. I ventured to add – on my own responsibility, your lordship – some hard-boiled eggs and a pot of jam to the parcel.'

'Excellent! You are sure there is nothing else?'

A wistful look came into Gladys's eyes.

'Could he 'ave some flarze?'

'Certainly,' said Lord Emsworth. 'Certainly, certainly, certainly. By all means. Just what I was about to suggest my – er – what *is* flarze?'

Beach, the linguist, interpreted.

'I think the young lady means flowers, your lordship.'

'Yes, sir. Thank you, sir. Flarze.'

'Oh?' said Lord Emsworth. 'Oh? Flarze?' he said slowly. 'Oh, ah, yes. Yes. I see. H'm!'

He removed his pince-nez, wiped them thoughtfully, replaced them, and gazed with wrinkling forehead at the gardens that stretched gaily out before him. Flarze! It would be idle to deny that those gardens contained flarze in full measure. They were bright with Achillea, Bignonia Radicans, Campanula, Digitalis, Euphorbia, Funkia, Gypsophila, Helianthus, Iris, Liatris, Monarda, Phlox Drummondi, Salvia, Thalictrum, Vinca and Yucca. But the devil of it was that Angus McAllister would have a fit if they were picked. Across the threshold of this Eden the ginger whiskers of Angus McAllister lay like a flaming sword.

As a general rule, the procedure for getting flowers out of Angus McAllister was as follows. You waited till he was in one of his rare moods of complaisance, then you led the conversation gently round to the subject of interior decoration, and then, choosing your moment, you asked if he could possibly spare a few to be put in vases. The last thing you thought of doing was to charge in and start helping yourself.

'I – er . . .' said Lord Emsworth.

He stopped. In a sudden blinding flash of clear vision he had seen himself for what he was – the spineless, unspeakably unworthy descendant of ancestors who, though they may have had their faults, had certainly known how to handle employees. It was 'How now, varlet!' and 'Marry come up, thou malapert knave!' in the days of previous Earls of Emsworth. Of course, they had possessed certain advantages which he lacked. It undoubtedly helped a man in his dealings with the domestic staff to have, as they had had, the rights of the high, the middle and the low justice – which meant, broadly, that if you got annoyed with your head gardener you could immediately divide him into four head gardeners with a battleaxe and no questions asked – but even so, he realised that they were better men than he was and that, if he allowed craven fear of Angus McAllister to stand in the way of this delightful girl and her charming brother getting all the flowers they required, he was not worthy to be the last of their line.

Lord Emsworth wrestled with his tremors.

'Certainly, certainly, certainly,' he said, though not without a qualm. 'Take as many as you want.'

And so it came about that Angus McAllister, crouched in his potting shed like some dangerous beast in its den, beheld a sight which first froze his blood and then sent it boiling through his veins. Flitting to and fro through his sacred gardens, picking his sacred flowers, was a small girl in a velveteen frock. And – which brought apoplexy a step closer – it was the same small girl who two days before had copped him on the shin with a stone. The stillness of the summer evening was shattered by a roar that sounded like boilers exploding, and Angus McAllister came out of the potting shed at forty-five miles per hour.

Gladys did not linger. She was a London child, trained from infancy to bear herself gallantly in the presence of alarms and excursions, but this excursion had been so sudden that it momentarily broke her nerve. With a horrified yelp she scuttled to where Lord Emsworth stood and, hiding behind him, clutched the tails of his morning coat.

'Oo-er!' said Gladys.

Lord Emsworth was not feeling so frightfully good himself. We have pictured him a few moments back drawing inspiration from the nobility of his ancestors and saying, in effect, 'That for McAllister!' but truth now compels us to admit that this hardy attitude was largely due to the fact that he believed the head gardener to be a safe quarter of a mile away among the swings and roundabouts of the Fête. The spectacle of the man charging vengefully down on him with gleaming eyes and bristling whiskers made him feel like a nervous English infantryman at the Battle of Bannockburn. His knees shook and the soul within him quivered.

And then something happened, and the whole aspect of the situation changed.

It was, in itself, quite a trivial thing, but it had an astoundingly stimulating effect on Lord Emsworth's morale. What happened was that Gladys, seeking further protection, slipped at this moment a small, hot hand into his.

It was a mute vote of confidence, and Lord Emsworth intended to be worthy of it.

'He's coming,' whispered his lordship's Inferiority Complex agitatedly.

'What of it?' replied Lord Emsworth stoutly.

'Tick him off,' breathed his lordship's ancestors in his other ear.

'Leave it to me,' replied Lord Emsworth.

He drew himself up and adjusted his pince-nez. He felt

filled with a cool masterfulness. If the man tendered his resignation, let him tender his damned resignation.

'Well, McAllister?' said Lord Emsworth coldly.

He removed his top hat and brushed it against his sleeve.

'What is the matter, McAllister?'

He replaced his top hat.

'You appear agitated, McAllister.'

He jerked his head militantly. The hat fell off. He let it lie. Freed from its loathsome weight he felt more masterful than ever. It had just needed that to bring him to the top of his form.

'This young lady,' said Lord Emsworth, 'has my full permission to pick all the flowers she wants, McAllister. If you do not see eye to eye with me in this matter, McAllister, say so and we will discuss what you are going to do about it, McAllister. These gardens, McAllister, belong to me, and if you do not – er – appreciate that fact you will, no doubt, be able to find another employer – ah – more in tune with your views. I value your services highly, McAllister, but I will not be dictated to in my own garden, McAllister. Er – dash it,' added his lordship, spoiling the whole effect.

A long moment followed in which Nature stood still, breathless. The Achillea stood still. So did the Bignonia Radicans. So did the Campanula, the Digitalis, the Euphorbia, the Funkia, the Gypsophila, the Helianthus, the Iris, the Liatris, the Monarda, the Phlox Drummondi, the Salvia, the Thalictrum, the Vinca and the Yucca. From far off in the direction of the park there sounded the happy howls of children who were probably breaking things, but even these seemed hushed. The evening breeze had died away.

Angus McAllister stood glowering. His attitude was that of one sorely perplexed. So might the early bird have looked if the worm earmarked for its breakfast had suddenly turned and snapped at it. It had never occurred to him that his employer would voluntarily suggest that he sought another position, and now that he had suggested it Angus McAllister disliked the idea very much. Blandings Castle was in his bones. Elsewhere, he would feel an exile. He fingered his whiskers, but they gave him no comfort.

He made his decision. Better to cease to be a Napoleon than be a Napoleon in exile.

'Mphm,' said Angus McAllister.

'Oh, and by the way, McAllister,' said Lord Emsworth, 'that matter of the gravel path through the yew alley. I've been thinking it over, and I won't have it. Not on any account. Mutilate my beautiful moss with a beastly gravel path? Make an eyesore of the loveliest spot in one of the finest and oldest gardens in the United Kingdom? Certainly not. Most decidedly not. Try to remember, McAllister, as you work in the gardens of Blandings Castle, that you are not back in Glasgow, laying out recreation grounds. That is all, McAllister. Er – dash it – that is all.'

'Mphm,' said Angus McAllister.

He turned. He walked away. The potting shed swallowed him up. Nature resumed its breathing. The breeze began to blow again. And all over the gardens birds who had stopped on their high note carried on according to plan.

Lord Emsworth took out his handkerchief and dabbed with it at his forehead. He was shaken, but a novel sense of being a man among men thrilled him. It might seem bravado, but he almost wished – yes, dash it, he almost wished – that his sister Constance would come along and start something while he felt like this.

He had his wish.

'Clarence!'

Yes, there she was, hurrying towards him up the garden path. She, like McAllister, seemed agitated. Something was on her mind.

'Clarence!'

'Don't keep saying "Clarence!" as if you were a dashed parrot,' said Lord Emsworth haughtily. 'What the dickens is the matter, Constance?'

'Matter? Do you know what the time is? Do you know that everybody is waiting down there for you to make your speech?'

Lord Emsworth met her eye sternly.

'I do not,' he said. 'And I don't care. I'm not going to make any dashed speech. If you want a speech, let the vicar make it. Or make it yourself. Speech! I never heard such dashed nonsense in my life.' He turned to Gladys. 'Now, my dear,' he said, 'if you will just give me time to get out of these infernal clothes and this ghastly collar and put on something human, we'll go down to the village and have a chat with Ern.'

September

The Début of Battling Billson

It becomes increasingly difficult, I have found, as time goes by, to recall the exact circumstances in which one first became acquainted with this man or that; for as a general thing I lay no claim to the possession of one of those hair-trigger memories which come from subscribing to the correspondence courses advertised in the magazines. And yet I can state without doubt or hesitation that the individual afterwards known as Battling Billson entered my life at half-past four on the afternoon of Saturday, September the tenth, two days after my twenty-seventh birthday. For there was that about my first sight of him which has caused the events to remain photographically lined on the tablets of my mind when a yesterday has faded from its page. Not only was our meeting dramatic and even startling, but it had in it something of the quality of the last straw, the final sling or arrow of outrageous Fortune. It seemed to put the lid on the sadness of life.

Everything had been going steadily wrong with me for more than a week. I had been away, paying a duty visit to uncongenial relatives in the country, and it had rained and rained and rained. There had been family prayers before breakfast and bezique after dinner. On the journey back to London my carriage had been full of babies, the train had stopped everywhere, and I had had nothing to eat but a bag of buns. And when finally I let myself into my lodgings in Ebury Street and sought the soothing haven of my sitting room, the first thing I saw on opening the door was this enormous red-headed man lying on the sofa.

He made no move as I came in, for he was asleep; and I can best convey the instantaneous impression I got of his formidable physique by saying that I had no desire to wake him. The sofa was a small one, and he overflowed it in every direction. He had a broken nose, and his jaw was the jaw of a Wild West motion-picture star registering Determination. One hand was under his head; the other, hanging down to the floor, looked like a strayed ham congealed into stone. What he was doing in my sitting room I did not know; but, passionately as I wished to know, I preferred not to seek first-hand information. There was something about him that seemed to suggest that he might be one of those men who are rather cross when they first wake up. I crept out and stole softly downstairs to make inquiries of Bowles, my landlord.

'Sir?' said Bowles, in his fruity ex-butler way, popping up from the depths accompanied by a rich smell of finnan haddie.

'There's someone in my room,' I whispered.

'That would be Mr Ukridge, sir.'

'It wouldn't be anything of the kind,' I replied, with asperity. I seldom had the courage to contradict Bowles, but this statement was so wildly inaccurate that I could not let it pass. 'It's a huge red-headed man.'

'Mr Ukridge's friend, sir. He joined Mr Ukridge here yesterday.'

'How do you mean, joined Mr Ukridge here yesterday?'

'Mr Ukridge came to occupy your rooms in your absence, sir, on the night after your departure. I assumed that he had your approval. He said, if I remember correctly, that "it would be all right".'

For some reason or other which I had never been able to explain, Bowles's attitude towards Ukridge from their first meeting had been that of an indulgent father towards a favourite son. He gave the impression now of congratulating me on having such a friend to rally round and sneak into my rooms when I went away.

'Would there be anything further, sir?' inquired Bowles, with a wistful half-glance over his shoulder. He seemed reluctant to tear himself away for long from the finnan haddie.

'No,' I said. 'Er – no. When do you expect Mr Ukridge back?'

'Mr Ukridge informed me that he would return for dinner, sir. Unless he has altered his plans, he is now at a *matinée* performance at the Gaiety Theatre.'

The audience was just beginning to leave when I reached the Gaiety. I waited in the Strand, and presently was rewarded by the sight of a yellow mackintosh working its way through the crowd.

'Hallo, laddie!' said Stanley Featherstonehaugh Ukridge, genially. 'When did you get back? I say, I want you to remember this tune, so that you can remind me of it tomorrow, when I'll be sure to have forgotten it. This is how it goes.' He poised himself flat-footedly in the surging tide of pedestrians and, shutting his eyes and raising his chin, began to yodel in a loud and dismal tenor. 'Tumty-tumty-tumty-tum, tum

tum tum,' he concluded. 'And now, old horse, you may lead me across the street to the Coal Hole for a short snifter. What sort of a time have you had?'

'Never mind what sort of a time I've had. Who's the fellow you've dumped down in my rooms?'

'Red-haired man?'

'Good Lord! Surely even you wouldn't inflict more than one on me?'

Ukridge looked at me a little pained.

'I don't like this tone,' he said, leading me down the steps of the Coal Hole. 'Upon my Sam, your manner wounds me, old horse. I little thought that you would object to your best friend laying his head on your pillow.'

'I don't mind your head. At least I do, but I suppose I've got to put up with it. But when it comes to your taking in lodgers —'

'Order two tawny ports, laddie,' said Ukridge, 'and I'll explain all about that. I had an idea all along that you would want to know. It's like this,' he proceeded, when the tawny ports had arrived. 'That bloke's going to make my everlasting fortune.'

'Well, can't he do it somewhere else except in my sitting room?'

'You know me, old horse,' said Ukridge, sipping luxuriously. 'Keen, alert, far-sighted. Brain never still. Always getting ideas – *bing* – like a flash. The other day I was in a pub down Chelsea way having a bit of bread and cheese, and a fellow came in smothered with jewels. Smothered, I give you my word. Rings on his fingers and a tie-pin you could have lit your cigar at. I made inquiries and found that he was Tod Bingham's manager.'

'Who's Tod Bingham?'

'My dear old son, you must have heard of Tod Bingham. The new middle-weight champion. Beat Alf Palmer for the belt a couple of weeks ago. And this bloke, as opulent-looking a bloke as ever I saw, was his manager. I suppose he gets about fifty per cent of everything Tod makes, and you know the sort of purses they give for big fights nowadays. And then there's music-hall tours and the movies and all that. Well, I see no reason why, putting the thing at the lowest figures, I shouldn't scoop in thousands. I got the idea two seconds after they told me who this fellow was. And what made the thing seem almost as if it was meant to be was the coincidence that I should have heard only that morning that the *Hyacinth* was in.'

The man seemed to me to be rambling. In my reduced and afflicted state his cryptic method of narrative irritated me.

'I don't know what you're talking about,' I said. 'What's the *Hyacinth*? In where?'

'Pull yourself together, old horse,' said Ukridge, with the air of one endeavouring to be patient with a half-witted child. 'You remember the *Hyacinth*, the tramp steamer I took that trip on a couple of years ago. Many's the time I've told you all about the *Hyacinth*. She docked in the Port of London the night before I met this opulent bloke, and I had been meaning to go down next day and have a chat with the lads. The fellow you found in your rooms is one of the trimmers. As decent a bird as ever you met. Not much conversation, but a heart of gold. And it came across me like a thunderbolt the moment they told me who the jewelled cove was that, if I could only induce this man Billson to take up scrapping seriously, with me as his manager, my fortune was made. Billson is the man who invented fighting.'

'He looks it.'

'Splendid chap – you'll like him.'

'I bet I shall. I made up my mind to like him the moment I saw him.'

'Never picks a quarrel, you understand – in fact, used to need the deuce of a lot of provocation before he would give of his best; but once he started – golly! I've seen that man clean out a bar at Marseilles in a way that fascinated you. A bar filled to overflowing with A.B.'s and firemen, mind you, and all capable of felling oxen with a blow. Six of them there were, and they kept swatting Billson with all the vim and heartiness at their disposal, but he just let them bounce off, and went on with the business in hand. The man's a champion, laddie, nothing less. You couldn't hurt him with a hatchet, and every time he hits anyone all the undertakers in the place jump up and make bids for the body. And the amazing bit of luck is that he was looking for a job ashore. It appears he's fallen in love with one of the barmaids at the Crown in Kennington. Not,' said Ukridge, so that all misapprehension should be avoided, 'the one with the squint. The other one. Flossie. The girl with yellow hair.'

'I don't know the barmaids at the Crown in Kennington,' I said.

'Nice girls,' said Ukridge, paternally. 'So it was all right, you see. Our interests were identical. Good old Billson isn't what you'd call a very intelligent chap, but I managed to make him understand after an hour or so, and we drew up the contract. I'm to get fifty per cent of everything in consideration of managing him, fixing up fights, and looking after him generally.'

'And looking after him includes tucking him up on my sofa and singing him to sleep?'

Again that pained look came into Ukridge's face. He gazed at me as if I had disappointed him.

'You keep harping on that, laddie, and it isn't the right spirit. Anyone would think that we had polluted your damned room.'

'Well, you must admit that having this coming champion of yours in the home is going to make things a bit crowded.'

'Don't worry about that, my dear old man,' said Ukridge, reassuringly. 'We move to the White Hart at Barnes tomorrow, to start training. I've got Billson an engagement in one of the preliminaries down at Wonderland two weeks from tonight.'

'No; really?' I said, impressed by this enterprise. 'How did you manage it?'

'I just took him along and showed him to the management. They jumped at him. You see, the old boy's appearance rather speaks for itself. Thank goodness, all this happened just when I had a few quid tucked away. By the greatest good luck I ran into George Tupper at the very moment when he had had word that they were going to make him an under-secretary or something – I can't remember the details, but it's something they give these Foreign Office blokes when they show a bit of class – and Tuppy parted with a tenner without a murmur. Seemed sort of dazed. I believe now I could have had twenty if I'd had the presence of mind to ask for it. Still,' said Ukridge, with a manly resignation which did him credit, 'it can't be helped now, and ten will see me through. The only thing that's worrying me at the moment is what to call Billson.'

'Yes, I should be careful what I called a man like that.'

'I mean, what name is he to fight under?'

'Why not his own?'

'His parents, confound them,' said Ukridge, moodily, 'christened him Wilberforce. I ask you, can you see the crowd at Wonderland having Wilberforce Billson introduced to them?'

'Willie Billson,' I suggested. 'Rather snappy.'

Ukridge considered the proposal seriously, with knit brows, as becomes a manager.

'Too frivolous,' he decided at length. 'Might be all right for a bantam, but – no, I don't like it. I was thinking of something like Hurricane Hicks or Rock-Crusher Riggs.'

'Don't do it,' I urged, 'or you'll kill his career right from the start. You never find a real champion with one of these fancy names. Bob Fitzsimmons, Jack Johnson, James J. Corbett, James J. Jeffries —'

'James J. Billson?'

'Rotten.'

'You don't think,' said Ukridge, almost with timidity, 'that Wildcat Wix might do?'

'No fighter with an adjective in front of his name ever boxed in anything except a three-round preliminary.'

'How about Battling Billson?'

I patted him on the shoulder.

'Go no farther,' I said. 'The thing is settled. Battling Billson is the name.'

'Laddie,' said Ukridge in a hushed voice, reaching across the table and grasping my hand, 'this is genius. Sheer genius. Order another couple of tawny ports, old man.'

I did so, and we drank deep to the Battler's success.

My formal introduction to my godchild took place on our return to Ebury Street, and – great as had been my respect for the man before – it left me with a heightened appreciation of the potentialities for triumph awaiting him in his selected profession. He was awake by this time and moving ponderously about the sitting room, and he looked even more impressive standing than he had appeared when lying down. At our first meeting, moreover, his eyes had been closed in sleep; they were now open, green in colour, and of a peculiarly metallic glint which caused them, as we shook hands, to seem to be exploring my person for good spots to hit. What was probably intended to be the smile that wins appeared to me a grim and sardonic twist of the lip. Take him for all in all, I had never met a man so calculated to convert the most truculent swashbuckler to pacifism at a glance; and when I recalled Ukridge's story of the little unpleasantness at Marseilles and realised that a mere handful of half a dozen able-bodied seamen had had the temerity to engage this fellow in personal conflict, it gave me a thrill of patriotic pride. There must be good stuff in the British Merchant Marine, I felt. Hearts of oak.

Dinner, which followed the introduction, revealed the Battler rather as a capable trencherman than as a sparkling conversationalist. His long reach enabled him to grab salt, potatoes, pepper, and other necessaries without the necessity of asking for them; and on other topics he seemed to possess no views which he deemed worthy of exploitation. A strong, silent man.

That there was a softer side to his character was, however, made clear to me when, after smoking one of my cigars and talking for a while of this and that, Ukridge went out on one of those mysterious errands of his which were always summoning him at all hours and left my guest and myself alone together. After a bare half-hour's silence, broken only by the soothing gurgle of his pipe, the coming champion cocked an intimidating eye at me and spoke.

'You ever been in love, mister?'

I was thrilled and flattered. Something in my appearance, I told myself, some nebulous something that showed me a man of sentiment and sympathy, had appealed to this man, and he was about to pour out his heart in intimate confession. I said yes, I had been in love many times. I went on to speak of love as a noble emotion of which no man need be ashamed. I spoke at length and with fervour.

''R!' said Battling Billson.

Then, as if aware that he had been chattering in an undignified manner to a comparative stranger, he withdrew into the silence again and did not emerge till it was time to go to bed, when he said 'Good night, mister,' and disappeared. It was disappointing. Significant, perhaps, the conversation had been, but I had been rather hoping for something which could have been built up into a human document, entitled 'The Soul of the Abysmal Brute', and sold to some editor for that real money which was always so badly needed in the home.

Ukridge and his *protégé* left next morning for Barnes, and, as that riverside resort was somewhat off my beat, I saw no more of the Battler until the fateful night at Wonderland. From time to time Ukridge would drop in at my rooms to purloin cigars and socks, and on these occasions he always spoke with the greatest confidence of his man's prospects. At first, it seemed, there had been a little difficulty owing to the other's rooted idea that plug tobacco was an indispensable adjunct to training: but towards the end of the first week the arguments of wisdom had prevailed and he had consented to abandon smoking until after his *début*. By this concession the issue seemed to Ukridge to have been sealed as a certainty, and he was in sunny mood as he borrowed the money from me to pay our fares to the Underground station at which the pilgrim alights who wishes to visit that Mecca of East End boxing, Wonderland.

The Battler had preceded us, and when we arrived was in the dressing room, stripped to a breath-taking semi-nudity. I had not supposed that it was possible for a man to be larger than was Mr Billson when arrayed for the street, but in trunks and boxing shoes he looked like his big brother. Muscles resembling the hawsers of an Atlantic liner coiled down his arms and rippled along his massive shoulders. He seemed to dwarf altogether the by no means flimsy athlete who passed out of the room as we came in.

'That's the bloke,' announced Mr Billson, jerking his red head after this person.

We understood him to imply that the other was his opponent, and the spirit of confidence which had animated us waxed considerably. Where six of the pick of the Merchant Marine had failed, this stripling could scarcely hope to succeed.

'I been talkin' to 'im,' said Battling Billson.

I took this unwonted garrulity to be due to a slight nervousness natural at such a moment.

''E's 'ad a lot of trouble, that bloke,' said the Battler.

The obvious reply was that he was now going to have a lot more, but before either of us could make it a hoarse voice announced that Squiffy and the Toff had completed their three-round bout and that the stage now waited for our nominee. We hurried to our seats. The necessity of taking a look at our man in his dressing room had deprived us of the pleasure of witnessing the passage of arms between Squiffy and the Toff, but I gathered that it must have been lively and full of entertainment, for the audience seemed in excellent humour. All those who were not too busy eating jellied eels were babbling happily or whistling between their fingers to friends in distant parts of the hall. As Mr Billson climbed into the ring in all the glory of his red hair and jumping muscles, the babble rose to a roar. It was plain that Wonderland had stamped our Battler with its approval on sight.

The audiences which support Wonderland are not disdainful of science. Neat footwork wins their commendation, and a skilful ducking of the head is greeted with knowing applause. But what they esteem most highly is the punch. And one sight of Battling Billson seemed to tell them that here was the Punch personified. They sent the fighters off to a howl of ecstasy, and settled back in their seats to enjoy the pure pleasure of seeing two of their fellow-men hitting each other very hard and often.

The howl died away.

I looked at Ukridge with concern. Was this the hero of Marseilles, the man who cleaned out bar-rooms and on whom undertakers fawned? Diffident was the only word to describe our Battler's behaviour in that opening round. He pawed lightly at his antagonist. He embraced him like a brother. He shuffled about the ring, innocuous.

'What's the matter with him?' I asked.

'He always starts slow,' said Ukridge, but his concern was manifest. He fumbled nervously at the buttons of his mackintosh. The referee was warning Battling Billson. He was speaking to him like a disappointed father. In the cheaper and baser parts of the house enraged citizens were whistling 'Comrades'. Everywhere a chill had fallen on the house. That first fine fresh enthusiasm had died away, and the sounding of the gong for the end of the round was greeted with censorious catcalls. As Mr Billson lurched back to his corner, frank unfriendliness was displayed on all sides.

With the opening of the second round considerably more spirit was introduced into the affair. The same strange torpidity still held our Battler in its grip, but his opponent was another man. During round one he had seemed a little nervous and apprehensive. He had behaved as if he considered it prudent not to stir Mr Billson. But now this distaste for direct action had left him. There was jauntiness in his demeanour as he moved to the centre of the ring; and, having reached it, he uncoiled a long left and smote Mr Billson forcefully on the nose. Twice he smote him, and twice Mr Billson blinked like one who has had bad news from home. The man who had had a lot of trouble leaned sideways and brought his right fist squarely against the Battler's ear.

All was forgotten and forgiven. A moment before, the audience had been solidly anti-Billson. Now they were as unanimously pro. For these blows, while they appeared to have affected him not at all physically, seemed to have awakened Mr Billson's better feelings as if somebody had turned on a tap. They had aroused in Mr Billson's soul that zest for combat which had been so sadly to seek in round one. For an instant after the receipt of that buffet on the ear the Battler stood motionless on his flat feet, apparently in deep thought. Then, with the air of one who has suddenly remembered an important appointment, he plunged forward. Like an animated windmill he cast himself upon the bloke of troubles. He knocked him here, he bounced him there. He committed mayhem upon his person. He did everything to him that a man can do who is hampered with boxing-gloves, until presently the troubled one was leaning heavily against the ropes, his head hanging dazedly, his whole attitude that of a man who would just as soon let the matter drop. It only remained for the Battler to drive home the final punch, and a hundred enthusiasts, rising to their feet, were pointing out to him desirable locations for it.

But once more that strange diffidence had descended upon our representative. While every other man in the building seemed to know the correct procedure and was sketching it out in nervous English, Mr Billson appeared the victim of doubt. He looked uncertainly at his opponent and inquiringly at the referee.

The referee, obviously a man of blunted sensibilities, was unresponsive. Do It Now was plainly his slogan. He was a business man, and he wanted his patrons to get good value for their money. He was urging Mr Billson to make a thorough job of it. And finally Mr Billson approached his man and drew back his right arm. Having done this, he looked over his shoulder once more at the referee.

It was a fatal blunder. The man who had had a lot of trouble may have been in poor shape, but, like most of his profession, he retained, despite his recent misadventures, a reserve store of energy. Even as Mr Billson turned his head, he reached down to the floor with his gloved right hand, then, with a final effort, brought it up in a majestic sweep against the angle of the other's jaw. And then, as the fickle audience, with swift change of sympathy, cheered him on, he buried his left in Mr Billson's stomach on the exact spot where the well-dressed man wears the third button of his waistcoat.

Of all human experiences this of being smitten in this precise locality is the least agreeable. Battling Billson drooped like a stricken flower, settled slowly down, and spread himself out. He lay peacefully on his back with outstretched arms like a man floating in smooth water. His day's work was done.

A wailing cry rose above the din of excited patrons of sport endeavouring to explain to their neighbours how it had all happened. It was the voice of Ukridge mourning over his dead.

At half-past eleven that night, as I was preparing for bed, a drooping figure entered my room. I mixed a silent, sympathetic Scotch-and-soda, and for a while no word was spoken.

'How is the poor fellow?' I asked at length.

'He's all right,' said Ukridge, listlessly. 'I left him eating fish and chips at a coffee-stall.'

'Bad luck his getting pipped on the post like that.'

'Bad luck!' boomed Ukridge, throwing off his lethargy with a vigour that spoke of mental anguish. 'What do you mean, bad luck? It was just dam' bone-headedness. Upon my Sam, it's a little hard. I invest vast sums in this man, I support him in luxury for two weeks, asking nothing of him in return except to sail in and knock somebody's head off, which he could have done in two minutes if he had liked, and he lets me down purely and simply because the other fellow told him that he had been up all night looking after his wife who had burned her hand at the jam factory. Infernal sentimentalism!'

'Does him credit,' I argued.

'Bah!'

'Kind hearts,' I urged, 'are more than coronets.'

'Who the devil wants a pugilist to have a kind heart? What's the use of this man Billson being able to knock out an elephant if he's afflicted with this damned maudlin mushiness? Who ever heard of a mushy pugilist? It's the wrong spirit. It doesn't make for success.'

'It's a handicap, of course,' I admitted.

'What guarantee have I,' demanded Ukridge, 'that if I go to enormous trouble and expense getting him another match, he won't turn aside and brush away a silent tear in the first round because he's heard that the blighter's wife has got an ingrowing toenail?'

'You could match him only against bachelors.'

'Yes, and the first bachelor he met would draw him into a corner and tell him his aunt was down with whooping cough, and the chump would heave a sigh and stick his chin out to be walloped. A fellow's got no business to have red hair if he isn't going to live up to it. And yet,' said Ukridge, wistfully, 'I've seen that man – it was in a dance hall at Naples – I've seen him take on at least eleven Italians simultaneously. But then, one of them stuck a knife about three inches into his leg. He seems to need something like that to give him ambition.'

'I don't see how you are going to arrange to have him knifed just before each fight.'

'No,' said Ukridge, mournfully.

'What are you going to do about his future? Have you any plans?'

'Nothing definite. My aunt was looking for a companion to attend to her correspondence and take care of the canary last time I saw her. I might try to get the job for him.'

And with a horrid, mirthless laugh Stanley Featherstonehaugh Ukridge borrowed five shillings and passed out into the night.

I did not see Ukridge for the next few days, but I had news of him from our mutual friend George Tupper, whom I met prancing in uplifted mood down Whitehall.

'I say,' said George Tupper without preamble, and with a sort of dazed fervour, 'they've given me an under-secretaryship.'

I pressed his hand. I would have slapped him on the back, but one does not slap the backs of eminent Foreign

Office officials in Whitehall in broad daylight, even if one has been at school with them.

'Congratulations,' I said. 'There is no one whom I would more gladly see under-secretarying. I heard rumours of this from Ukridge.'

'Oh, yes, I remember I told him it might be coming off. Good old Ukridge! I met him just now and told him the news, and he was delighted.'

'How much did he touch you for?'

'Eh? Oh, only five pounds. Till Saturday. He expects to have a lot of money by then.'

'Did you ever know the time when Ukridge didn't expect to have a lot of money?'

'I want you and Ukridge to come and have a bit of dinner with me to celebrate. How would Wednesday suit you?'

'Splendidly.'

'Seven-thirty at the Regent Grill, then. Will you tell Ukridge?'

'I don't know where he's got to. I haven't seen him for nearly a week. Did he tell you where he was?'

'Out at some place at Barnes. What was the name of it?'

'The White Hart?'

'That's it.'

'Tell me,' I said, 'how did he seem? Cheerful?'

'Very. Why?'

'The last time I saw him he was thinking of giving up the struggle. He had had reverses.'

I proceeded to the White Hart immediately after lunch. The fact that Ukridge was still at that hostelry and had regained his usual sunny outlook on life seemed to point to the fact that the clouds enveloping the future of Mr Billson had cleared away, and that the latter's hat was still in the ring. That this was so was made clear to me directly I arrived. Inquiring for my old friend, I was directed to an upper room, from which, as I approached, there came a peculiar thudding noise. It was caused, as I perceived on opening the door, by Mr Billson. Clad in flannel trousers and a sweater, he was earnestly pounding a large leather object suspended from a wooden platform. His manager, seated on a soapbox in a corner, regarded him the while with affectionate proprietorship.

'Hallo, old horse!' said Ukridge, rising as I entered. 'Glad to see you.'

The din of Mr Billson's bag-punching, from which my arrival had not caused him to desist, was such as to render conversation difficult. We moved to the quieter retreat of the bar downstairs, where I informed Ukridge of the under-secretary's invitation.

'I'll be there,' said Ukridge. 'There's one thing about good old Billson, you can trust him not to break training if you take your eye off him. And, of course, he realises that this is a big thing. It'll be the making of him.'

'Your aunt is considering engaging him, then?'

'My aunt? What on earth are you talking about? Collect yourself, laddie.'

'When you left me you were going to try to get him the job of looking after your aunt's canary.'

'Oh, I was feeling rather sore then. That's all over. I had an earnest talk with the poor zimp, and he means business from now on. And so he ought to, dash it, with a magnificent opportunity like this.'

'Like what?'

'We're on to a big thing now, laddie, the dickens of a big thing.'

'I hope you've made sure the other man's a bachelor. Who is he?'

'Tod Bingham.'

'Tod Bingham?' I groped in my memory. 'You don't mean the middle-weight champion?'

'That's the fellow.'

'You don't expect me to believe that you've got a match on with a champion already?'

'It isn't exactly a match. It's like this. Tod Bingham is going round the East End halls offering two hundred quid to anyone who'll stay four rounds with him. Advertisement stuff. Good old Billson is going to unleash himself at the Shoreditch Empire next Saturday.'

'Do you think he'll be able to stay four rounds?'

'Stay four rounds!' cried Ukridge. 'Why, he could stay four rounds with a fellow armed with a Gatling gun and a couple of pickaxes. That money's as good as in our pockets, laddie. And once we're through with this job, there isn't a boxing-place in England that won't jump at us. I don't mind telling you in confidence, old horse, that in a year from now I expect to be pulling in hundreds a week. Clean up a bit here first, you know, and then pop over to America and make an enormous fortune. Damme. I shan't know how to spend the money!'

'Why not buy some socks? I'm running a bit short of them.'

'Now, laddie, laddie,' said Ukridge, reprovingly, 'need we strike a jarring note? Is this the moment to fling your beastly socks in an old friend's face? A broader-minded spirit is what I would like to see.'

I was ten minutes late in arriving at the Regent Grill on the Wednesday of George Tupper's invitation, and the spectacle of George in person standing bareheaded at the Piccadilly entrance filled me with guilty remorse. George was the best fellow in the world, but the atmosphere of the Foreign Office had increased the tendency he had always had from boyhood to a sort of precise fussiness, and it upset him if his affairs did not run exactly on schedule. The thought that my unpunctuality should have marred this great evening sent me hurrying towards him full of apologies.

'Oh, there you are,' said George Tupper. 'I say, it's too bad —'

'I'm awfully sorry. My watch —'

'Ukridge!' cried George Tupper, and I perceived that it was not I who had caused his concern.

'Isn't he coming?' I asked, amazed. The idea of Ukridge evading a free meal was one of those that seem to make the solid foundations of the world rock.

'He's come. And he's brought a girl with him!'

'A *girl*!'

'In pink, with yellow hair,' wailed George Tupper. 'What am I to do?'

I pondered the point.

'It's a weird thing for even Ukridge to have done,' I said, 'but I suppose you'll have to give her dinner.'

'But the place is full of people I know, and this girl's so – so spectacular.'

I felt for him deeply, but I could see no way out of it.

'You don't think I could say I had been taken ill?'

'It would hurt Ukridge's feelings.'

'I should enjoy hurting Ukridge's feelings, curse him!' said George Tupper, fervently.

'And it would be an awful slam for the girl, whoever she is.'

George Tupper sighed. His was a chivalrous nature. He drew himself up as if bracing himself for a dreadful ordeal.

'Oh, well, I suppose there's nothing to do,' he said. 'Come along. I left them drinking cocktails in the lounge.'

George had not erred in describing Ukridge's addition to the festivities as spectacular. Flamboyant would have been a suitable word. As she preceded us down the long dining room, her arm linked in George Tupper's – she seemed to have taken a liking to George – I had ample opportunity for studying her, from her patent-leather shoes to the mass of golden hair beneath her picture-hat. She had a loud, clear voice, and she was telling George Tupper the rather intimate details of an internal complaint which had recently troubled an aunt of hers. If George had been the family physician, she could not have been franker; and I could see a dull glow spreading over his shapely ears.

Perhaps Ukridge saw it, too, for he seemed to experience a slight twinge of conscience.

'I have an idea, laddie,' he whispered, 'that old Tuppy is a trifle peeved at my bringing Flossie along. If you get a chance, you might murmur to him that it was military necessity.'

'Who is she?' I asked.

'I told you about her. Flossie, the barmaid at the Crown in Kennington. Billson's *fiancée*.'

I looked at him in amazement.

'Do you mean to tell me that you're courting death by flirting with Battling Billson's girl?'

'My dear old man, nothing like that,' said Ukridge, shocked. 'The whole thing is, I've got a particular favour to ask of her – rather a rummy request – and it was no good springing it on her in cold blood. There had to be a certain amount of champagne in advance, and my funds won't run to champagne. I'm taking her on to the Alhambra after dinner. I'll look you up tonight and tell you all about it.'

We then proceeded to dine. It was not one of the pleasantest meals of my experience. The future Mrs Billson prattled agreeably throughout, and Ukridge assisted her in keeping the conversation alive; but the shattered demeanour of George Tupper would have taken the sparkle out of any banquet. From time to time he pulled himself together and endeavoured to play the host, but for the most part he maintained a pale and brooding silence; and it was a relief when Ukridge and his companion rose to leave.

'Well! –' began George Tupper in a strangled voice, as they moved away down the aisle.

I lit a cigar and sat back dutifully to listen.

Ukridge arrived in my rooms at midnight, his eyes gleaming through their pince-nez with a strange light. His manner was exuberant.

'It's all right,' he said.

'I'm glad you think so.'
'Did you explain to Tuppy?'
'I didn't get a chance. He was talking too hard.'
'About me?'
'Yes. He said everything I've always felt about you, only far, far better than I could ever have put it.'

Ukridge's face clouded for a moment, but cheerfulness returned.

'Oh, well, it can't be helped. He'll simmer down in a day or two. It had to be done, laddie. Life and death matter. And it's all right. Read this.'

I took the letter he handed me. It was written in a scrawly hand.

'What's this?'
'Read it, laddie. I think it will meet the case.'
I read.
'"*Wilberforce*." Who on earth's Wilberforce?'
'I told you that was Billson's name.'
'Oh, yes.'
I returned to the letter.

Wilberforce,
I take my pen in hand to tell you that I can never be yours. You will no doubt be surprised to hear that I love another and a better man, so that it can never be. He loves me, and he is a better man than you.

Hoping this finds you in the pink as it leaves me at present.

Yours faithfully,
Florence Burns

'I told her to keep it snappy,' said Ukridge.

'Well, she's certainly done it,' I replied, handing back the letter. 'I'm sorry. From the little I saw of her, I thought her a nice girl – for Billson. Do you happen to know the other man's address? Because it would be a kindly act to send him a postcard advising him to leave England for a year or two.'

'The Shoreditch Empire will find him this week.'

'What!'

'The other man is Tod Bingham.'

'Tod Bingham!' The drama of the situation moved me. 'Do you mean to say that Tod Bingham is in love with Battling Billson's girl?'

'No. He's never seen her!'

'What do you mean?'

Ukridge sat down creakingly on the sofa. He slapped my knee with sudden and uncomfortable violence.

'Laddie,' said Ukridge, 'I will tell you all. Yesterday afternoon I found old Billson reading a copy of the *Daily Sportsman*. He isn't much of a reader as a rule, so I was rather interested to know what had gripped him. And do you know what it was, old horse?'

'I do not.'

'It was an article about Tod Bingham. One of those damned sentimental blurbs they print about pugilists nowadays, saying what a good chap he was in private life and how he always sent a telegram to his old mother after each fight and gave her half the purse. Damme, there ought to be a censorship of the Press. These blighters don't mind *what* they print. I don't suppose Tod Bingham has *got* an old mother, and if he has I'll bet he doesn't give her a bob.

There were tears in that chump Billson's eyes as he showed me the article. Salt tears, laddie! "Must be a nice feller!" he said. Well, I ask you! I mean to say, it's a bit thick when the man you've been pouring out money for and watching over like a baby sister starts getting sorry for a champion three days before he's due to fight him. A champion, mark you! It was bad enough his getting mushy about that fellow at Wonderland, but when it came to being soft-hearted over Tod Bingham something had to be done. Well, you know me. Brain like a buzz-saw. I saw the only way of counteracting this pernicious stuff was to get him so mad with Tod Bingham that he would forget all about his old mother, so I suddenly thought: Why not get Flossie to pretend that Bingham had cut him out with her? Well, it's not the sort of thing you can ask a girl to do without preparing the ground a bit, so I brought her along to Tuppy's dinner. It was a master stroke, laddie. There's nothing softens the delicately nurtured like a good dinner, and there's no denying that old Tuppy did us well. She agreed the moment I put the thing to her, and sat down and wrote that letter without a blink. I think she thinks it's all a jolly practical joke. She's a light-hearted girl.'

'Must be.'

'It'll give poor old Billson a bit of a jar for the time being, I suppose, but it'll make him spread himself on Saturday night, and he'll be perfectly happy on Sunday morning when she tells him she didn't mean it and he realises that he's got a hundred quid of Tod Bingham's in his trousers pocket.'

'I thought you said it was two hundred quid that Bingham was offering.'

'I get a hundred,' said Ukridge, dreamily.

'The only flaw is, the letter doesn't give the other man's name. How is Billson to know it's Tod Bingham?'

'Why, damme, laddie, do use your intelligence. Billson isn't going to sit down and yawn when he gets that letter. He'll buzz straight down to Kennington and ask Flossie.'

'And then she'll give the whole thing away.'

'No, she won't. I slipped her a couple of quid to promise she wouldn't. And that reminds me, old man, it has left me a bit short, so if you could possibly manage —'

'Good night,' I said.

'But, laddie —'

'And God bless you,' I added, firmly.

The Shoreditch Empire is a roomy house, but it was crowded to the doors when I reached it on the Saturday night. In normal circumstances I suppose there would always have been a large audience on a Saturday, and this evening the lure of Tod Bingham's personal appearance had drawn more than capacity. In return for my shilling I was accorded the privilege of standing against the wall at the back, a position from which I could not see a great deal of the performance.

From the occasional flashes which I got of the stage between the heads of my neighbours, however, and from the generally restless and impatient attitude of the audience I gathered that I was not missing much. The programme of the Shoreditch Empire that week was essentially a one-man affair. The patrons had the air of suffering the preliminary acts as unavoidable obstacles that stand between them and the headliner. It was Tod Bingham whom they had come to see, and they were not cordial to the unfortunate serio-comics, tramp cyclists, jugglers, acrobats, and ballad singers who intruded themselves during the earlier part of the evening. The cheer that arose as the curtain fell on a dramatic sketch came from the heart, for the next number on the programme was that of the star.

A stout man in evening dress with a red handkerchief worn ambassadorially athwart his shirt front stepped out from the wings.

'Ladies and gentlemen!'

''Ush!' cried the audience.

'Ladies and gentlemen!'

A Voice: 'Good ole Tod!' ('Cheese it!')

'Ladies and gentlemen,' said the ambassador for the third time. He scanned the house apprehensively. 'Deeply regret have unfortunate disappointment to announce. Tod Bingham unfortunately unable to appear before you tonight.'

A howl like the howl of wolves balked of their prey or of an amphitheatre full of Roman citizens on receipt of the news that the supply of lions had run out greeted these words. We stared at each other with a wild surmise. Could this thing be, or was it not too thick for human belief?

'Wot's the matter with 'im?' demanded the gallery, hoarsely.

'Yus, wot's the matter with 'im?' echoed we of the better element on the lower floor.

The ambassador sidled uneasily towards the prompt entrance. He seemed aware that he was not a popular favourite.

"E 'as 'ad an unfortunate accident,' he declared, nervousness beginning to sweep away his aitches wholesale. 'On 'is way 'ere to this 'all 'e was unfortunately run into by a truck, sustaining bruises and contusions which render 'im unfortunately unable to appear before you tonight. I beg to announce that 'is place will be taken by Professor Devine, who will render 'is marvellous imitations of various birds and familiar animals. Ladies and gentlemen,' concluded the ambassador, stepping nimbly off the stage, 'I thank you one and all.'

The curtain rose and a dapper individual with a waxed moustache skipped on.

'Ladies and gentlemen, my first imitation will be of that well-known songster, the common thrush – better known to some of you per'aps as the throstle. And in connection with my performance I wish to state that I 'ave nothing whatsoever in my mouth. The effects which I produce —'

I withdrew, and two-thirds of the audience started to do the same. From behind us, dying away as the doors closed, came the plaintive note of the common thrush feebly competing with that other and sterner bird which haunts those places of entertainment where audiences are critical and swift to take offence.

Out in the street, a knot of Shoreditch's younger set were hanging on the lips of an excited orator in a battered hat and trousers which had been made for a larger man. Some stirring tale which he was telling held them spellbound. Words came raggedly through the noise of the traffic.

'— like this. Then 'e 'its 'im another like that. Then they start – on the side of the jor —'

'Pass along, there,' interrupted an official voice. 'Come on, there, pass along.'

The crowd thinned and resolved itself into its elements. I found myself moving down the street in company with the wearer of the battered hat. Though we had not been formally introduced, he seemed to consider me a suitable recipient for his tale. He enrolled me at once as a nucleus for a fresh audience.

"'E comes up, this bloke does, just as Tod is goin' in at the stage-door —'

'Tod?' I queried.

'Tod Bingham. 'E comes up just as 'e's goin' in at the stage-door, and 'e says "'Ere!" and Tod says "Yus?" and this bloke 'e says "Put 'em up!" and Tod says "Put wot up?" and this bloke says "Yer 'ands," and Tod says "Wot, me?" – sort of surprised. An' the next minute they're fightin' all over the shop.'

'But surely Tod Bingham was run over by a truck?'

The man in the battered hat surveyed me with the mingled scorn and resentment which the devout bestow on those of heretical views.

'Truck! 'E wasn't run over by no truck. Wot mikes yer fink 'e was run over by a truck? Wot 'ud 'e be doin' bein' run over by a truck? 'E 'ad it put across 'im by this red-'eaded bloke, same as I'm tellin' yer.'

A great light shone upon me.

'Red-headed?' I cried.

'Yus.'

'A big man?'

'Yus.'

'And he put it across Tod Bingham?'

'Put it across 'im proper. 'Ad to go 'ome in a keb, Tod did. Funny a bloke that could fight like that bloke could fight 'adn't the sense to go and do it on the stige and get some money for it. That's wot I think.'

Across the street an arc-lamp shed its cold rays. And into its glare there strode a man draped in a yellow mackintosh. The light gleamed on his pince-nez and lent a gruesome pallor to his set face. It was Ukridge retreating from Moscow.

'Others,' I said, 'are thinking the same.'

And I hurried across the road to administer what feeble consolation I might. There are moments when a fellow needs a friend.

October

The Metropolitan Touch

Nobody is more alive than I am to the fact that young Bingo Little is in many respects a sound old egg. In one way and another he has made life pretty interesting for me at intervals ever since we were at school. As a companion for a cheery hour I think I would choose him before anybody. On the other hand, I'm bound to say that there are things about him that could be improved. His habit of falling in love with every second girl he sees is one of them; and another is his way of letting the world in on the secrets of his heart. If you want shrinking reticence, don't go to Bingo, because he's got about as much of it as a soap advertisement.

I mean to say – well, here's the telegram I got from him one evening in November, about a month after I'd got back to town from my visit to Twing Hall:

I say Bertie old man I am in love at last. She is the most wonderful girl Bertie old man. This is the real thing at last Bertie. Come here at once and bring Jeeves. Oh I say you know that tobacco shop in Bond Street on the left side as you go up. Will you get me a hundred of their special cigarettes and send them to me here. I have run out. I know when you see her you will think she is the most wonderful girl. Mind you bring Jeeves. Don't forget the cigarettes. Bingo

It had been handed in at Twing Post Office. In other words, he had submitted that frightful rot to the goggling eye of a village postmistress who was probably the mainspring of local gossip and would have the place ringing with the news before nightfall. He couldn't have given himself away more completely if he had hired the town crier. When I was a kid, I used to read stories about knights and vikings and that species of chappie who would get up without a blush in the middle of a crowded banquet and loose off a song about how perfectly priceless they thought their best girl. I've often felt that those days would have suited young Bingo down to the ground.

Jeeves had brought the thing in with the evening drink, and I slung it over to him.

'It's about due, of course,' I said. 'Young Bingo hasn't been in love for at least a couple of months. I wonder who it is this time?'

'Miss Mary Burgess, sir,' said Jeeves, 'the niece of the Reverend Mr Heppenstall. She is staying at Twing Vicarage.'

'Great Scott!' I knew that Jeeves knew practically everything in the world, but this sounded like second sight. 'How do you know that?'

'When we were visiting Twing Hall in the summer, sir, I formed a somewhat close friendship with Mr Heppenstall's butler. He is good enough to keep me abreast of the local news from time to time. From his account, sir, the young lady appears to be a very estimable young lady. Of a somewhat serious nature, I understand. Mr Little is very *épris*, sir. Brookfield, my correspondent, writes that last week he observed him in the moonlight at an advanced hour gazing up at his window.'

'Whose window! Brookfield's?'

'Yes, sir. Presumably under the impression that it was the young lady's.'

'But what the deuce is he doing at Twing at all?'

'Mr Little was compelled to resume his old position as tutor to Lord Wickhammersley's son at Twing Hall, sir. Owing to having been unsuccessful in some speculations at Hurst Park at the end of October.'

'Good Lord, Jeeves! Is there anything you don't know?'

'I couldn't say, sir.'

I picked up the telegram.

'I suppose he wants us to go down and help him out a bit?'

'That would appear to be his motive in dispatching the message, sir.'

'Well, what shall we do? Go?'

'I would advocate it, sir. If I may say so, I think that Mr Little should be encouraged in this particular matter.'

'You think he's picked a winner this time?'

'I hear nothing but excellent reports of the young lady, sir. I think it is beyond question that she would be an admirable influence for Mr Little, should the affair come to a happy conclusion. Such a union would also, I fancy, go far to restore Mr Little to the good graces of his uncle, the young lady being well connected and possessing private means. In short, sir, I think that if there is anything that we can do we should do it.'

'Well, with you behind him,' I said, 'I don't see how he can fail to click.'

'You are very good, sir,' said Jeeves. 'The tribute is much appreciated.'

Bingo met us at Twing station next day, and insisted on my sending Jeeves on in the car with the bags while he and I walked. He started in about the female the moment we had begun to hoof it.

'She is very wonderful, Bertie. She is not one of these flippant, shallow-minded modern girls. She is sweetly grave and beautifully earnest. She reminds me of – what is the name I want?'

'Marie Lloyd?'

'Saint Cecilia,' said young Bingo, eyeing me with a good deal of loathing. 'She reminds me of Saint Cecilia. She makes me yearn to be a better, nobler, deeper, broader man.'

'What beats me,' I said, following up a train of thought, 'is what principle you pick them on. The girls you fall in love with, I mean. I mean to say, what's your system? As far as I can see, no two of them are alike. First it was Mabel the waitress, then Honoria Glossop, then that fearful blister Charlotte Corday Rowbotham—'

I own that Bingo had the decency to shudder. Thinking of Charlotte always made me shudder, too.

'You don't seriously mean, Bertie, that you are intending to compare the feeling I have for Mary Burgess, the holy devotion, the spiritual—'

'Oh, all right, let it go,' I said. 'I say, old lad, aren't we going rather a long way round?'

Considering that we were supposed to be heading for Twing Hall, it seemed to me that we were making a longish job of it. The Hall is about two miles from the station by the main road, and we had cut off down a lane, gone across country for a bit, climbed a stile or two, and were now working our way across a field that ended in another lane.

'She sometimes takes her little brother for a walk round this way,' explained Bingo. 'I thought we would meet her and bow, and you could see her, you know, and then we would walk on.'

'Of course,' I said, 'that's enough excitement for anyone, and undoubtedly a corking reward for tramping three miles out of one's way over ploughed fields with tight boots, but don't we do anything else? Don't we tack on to the girl and buzz along with her?'

'Good Lord!' said Bingo, honestly amazed. 'You don't suppose I've got nerve enough for that, do you? I just look at her from afar off and all that sort of thing. Quick! Here she comes! No, I'm wrong!'

It was like that song of Harry Lauder's where he's waiting for the girl and says 'This is her-r-r. No, it's a rabbut.' Young Bingo made me stand there in the teeth of a nor'-east half-gale for ten minutes, keeping me on my toes with a series of false alarms, and I was just thinking of suggesting that we should lay off and give the rest of the proceedings a miss, when round the corner there came a fox-terrier, and Bingo quivered like an aspen. Then there hove in sight a small boy, and he shook like a jelly. Finally, like a star whose entrance has been worked up by the *personnel* of the *ensemble*, a girl appeared, and his emotion was painful to witness. His face got so red that, what with his white collar and the fact that the wind had turned his nose blue, he looked more like a French flag than anything else.

He sagged from the waist upwards, as if he had been filleted.

He was just raising his fingers limply to his cap when he suddenly saw that the girl wasn't alone. A chappie in clerical costume was also among those present, and the sight of him didn't seem to do Bingo a bit of good. His face got redder and his nose bluer, and it wasn't till they had nearly passed that he managed to get hold of his cap.

The girl bowed, the curate said, 'Ah, Little. Rough weather,' the dog barked, and then they toddled on and the entertainment was over.

The curate was a new factor in the situation to me. I reported his movements to Jeeves when I got to the Hall. Of course, Jeeves knew all about it already.

'That is the Reverend Mr Wingham, Mr Heppenstall's new curate, sir. I gathered from Brookfield that he is Mr Little's rival, and at the moment the young lady appears to favour him. Mr Wingham has the advantage of being on the premises. He and the young lady play duets after dinner, which acts as a bond. Mr Little on these occasions, I understand, prowls about in the road, chafing visibly.'

'That seems to be all the poor fish is able to do, dash it. He can chafe all right, but there he stops. He's lost his pep. He's got no dash. Why, when we met her just now, he hadn't even the common manly courage to say "Good evening"!'

'I gather that Mr Little's affection is not unmingled with awe, sir.'

'Well, how are we to help a man when he's such a rabbit as that? Have you anything to suggest? I shall be seeing him after dinner, and he's sure to ask first thing what you advise.'

'In my opinion, sir, the most judicious course for Mr Little to pursue would be to concentrate on the young gentleman.'

'The small brother? How do you mean?'

'Make a friend of him, sir – take him for walks and so forth.'

'It doesn't sound one of your red-hottest ideas. I must say I expected something fruitier than that.'

'It would be a beginning, sir, and might lead to better things.'

'Well, I'll tell him. I liked the look of her, Jeeves.'

'A thoroughly estimable young lady, sir.'

I slipped Bingo the tip from the stable that night, and was glad to observe that it seemed to cheer him up.

'Jeeves is always right,' he said. 'I ought to have thought of it myself. I'll start in tomorrow.'

It was amazing how the chappie bucked up. Long before I left for town it had become a mere commonplace for him to speak to the girl. I mean he didn't simply look stuffed when they met. The brother was forming a bond that was a dashed sight stronger than the curate's duets. She and Bingo used to take him for walks together. I asked Bingo what they talked about on these occasions, and he said Wilfred's future. The girl hoped that Wilfred would one day become a curate, but Bingo said no, there was something about curates he didn't quite like.

The day we left, Bingo came to see us off with Wilfred frisking about him like an old college chum. The last I saw of them, Bingo was standing him chocolates out of the slot-machine. A scene of peace and cheery goodwill. Dashed promising, I thought.

Which made it all the more of a jar, about a fortnight later, when his telegram arrived. As follows:

> *Bertie old man I say Bertie could you possibly come down here at once. Everything gone wrong hang it all. Dash it Bertie you simply must come. I am in a state of absolute despair and heartbroken. Would you mind sending another hundred of those cigarettes. Bring Jeeves when you come Bertie. You simply must come Bertie. I rely on you. Don't forget to bring Jeeves. Bingo.*

For a chap who's perpetually hard-up, I must say that young Bingo is the most wasteful telegraphist I ever struck. He's got no notion of condensing. The silly ass simply pours out his wounded soul at twopence a word, or whatever it is, without a thought.

'How about it, Jeeves?' I said. 'I'm getting a bit fed. I can't go chucking all my engagements every second week in order to biff down to Twing and rally round young Bingo. Send him a wire telling him to end it all in the village pond.'

'If you could spare me for the night, sir, I should be glad to run down and investigate.'

'Oh, dash it! Well, I suppose there's nothing else to be done. After all, you're the fellow he wants. All right, carry on.'

Jeeves got back late the next day.

'Well?' I said.

Jeeves appeared perturbed. He allowed his left eyebrow to flicker upwards in a concerned sort of manner.

'I have done what I could, sir,' he said, 'but I fear Mr Little's chances do not appear bright. Since our last visit, sir, there has been a decidedly sinister and disquieting development.'

'Oh, what's that?'

'You may remember Mr Steggles, sir – the young gentleman who was studying for an examination with Mr Heppenstall at the Vicarage?'

'What's Steggles got to do with it?' I asked.

'I gather from Brookfield, sir, who chanced to overhear a conversation, that Mr Steggles is interesting himself in the affair.'

'Good Lord! What, making a book on it?'

'I understand that he is accepting wagers from those in his immediate circle, sir. Against Mr Little, whose chances he does not seem to fancy.'

'I don't like that, Jeeves.'

'No, sir. It is sinister.'

'From what I know of Steggles there will be dirty work.'

'It has already occurred, sir.'

'Already?'

'Yes, sir. It seems that, in pursuance of the policy which he had been good enough to allow me to suggest to him, Mr Little escorted Master Burgess to the church bazaar, and there met Mr Steggles, who was in the company of young Master Heppenstall, the Reverend Mr Heppenstall's second son, who is home from Rugby just now, having recently recovered from an attack of mumps. The encounter took place in the refreshment room, where Mr Steggles was at that moment entertaining Master Heppenstall. To cut a long story short, sir, the two gentlemen became extremely interested in the hearty manner in which the lads were fortifying themselves; and Mr Steggles offered to back his nominee in a weight-for-age eating contest against Master Burgess for a pound a side. Mr Little admitted to me that he was conscious of a certain hesitation as to what the upshot might be, should Miss Burgess get to hear of the matter, but his sporting blood was too much for him and he agreed to the contest. This was duly carried out, both lads exhibiting the utmost willingness and enthusiasm, and eventually Master Burgess justified Mr Little's confidence by winning, but only after a bitter struggle. Next day both contestants were in considerable pain; inquiries were made and confessions extorted, and Mr Little – I learn from Brookfield, who happened to be near the door of the drawing room at the moment – had an extremely unpleasant interview with the young lady, which ended in her desiring him never to speak to her again.'

There's no getting away from the fact that, if ever a man required watching, it's Steggles. Machiavelli could have taken his correspondence course.

'It was a put-up job, Jeeves!' I said. 'I mean, Steggles worked the whole thing on purpose. It's his old nobbling game.'

'There would seem to be no doubt about that, sir.'

'Well, he seems to have dished poor old Bingo all right.'

'That is the prevalent opinion, sir. Brookfield tells me that down in the village at the Cow and Horses seven to one is being freely offered on Mr Wingham and finding no takers.'

'Good Lord! Are they betting about it down in the village, too?'

'Yes, sir. And in adjoining hamlets also. The affair has caused widespread interest. I am told that there is a certain sporting reaction in even so distant a spot as Lower Bingley.'

'Well, I don't see what there is to do. If Bingo is such a chump—'

'One is fighting a losing battle, I fear, sir, but I did venture to indicate to Mr Little a course of action which might prove of advantage. I recommended him to busy himself with good works.'

'Good works?'

'About the village, sir. Reading to the bedridden – chatting with the sick – that sort of thing, sir. We can but trust that good results will ensue.'

'Yes, I suppose so,' I said doubtfully. 'But, by gosh, if I was a sick man I'd hate to have a loony like young Bingo coming and gibbering at my bedside.'

'There *is* that aspect of the matter, sir,' said Jeeves.

I didn't hear a word from Bingo for a couple of weeks, and I took it after a while that he had found the going too hard and had chucked in the towel. And then, one night not long before Christmas, I came back to the flat pretty latish, having been out dancing at the Embassy. I was fairly tired, having swung a practically non-stop shoe from shortly after dinner till two a.m., and bed seemed to be indicated. Judge of my chagrin and all that sort of thing, therefore, when, tottering to my room and switching on the light, I observed the foul features of young Bingo all over the pillow. The blighter had appeared from nowhere and was in my bed, sleeping like an infant with a sort of happy, dreamy smile on his map.

A bit thick I mean to say! We Woosters are all for the good old medieval hosp and all that, but when it comes to finding chappies collaring your bed, the thing becomes a trifle too mouldy. I hove a shoe, and Bingo sat up, gurgling.

' 's matter? 's matter?' said young Bingo.

'What the deuce are you doing in my bed?' I said.

'Oh, hallo, Bertie! So there you are!'

'Yes, here I am. What are you doing in my bed?'

'I came up to town for the night on business.'

'Yes, but what are you doing in my bed?'

'Dash it all, Bertie,' said young Bingo querulously, 'don't keep harping on your beastly bed. There's another made up in the spare room. I saw Jeeves make it with my own eyes. I believe he meant it for me, but I knew what a perfect host you were, so I just turned in here. I say, Bertie, old man,' said Bingo, apparently fed up with the discussion about sleeping quarters, 'I see daylight.'

'Well, it's getting on for three in the morning.'

'I was speaking figuratively, you ass. I meant that hope has begun to dawn. About Mary Burgess, you know. Sit down and I'll tell you all about it.'

'I won't. I'm going to sleep.'

'To begin with,' said young Bingo, settling himself comfortably against the pillows and helping himself to a cigarette from my private box, 'I must once again pay a marked tribute to good old Jeeves. A modern Solomon. I was badly up against it when I came to him for advice, but he rolled up with a tip which has put me – I use the term advisedly and in a conservative spirit – on velvet. He may have told you that he recommended me to win back the lost ground by busying myself with good works? Bertie, old man,' said young Bingo earnestly, 'for the last two weeks I've been comforting the sick to such an extent that, if I had a brother and you brought him to me on a sickbed at this moment, by Jove, old man, I'd heave a brick at him. However, though it took it out of me like the deuce, the scheme worked splendidly. She softened visibly before I'd been at it a week. Started to bow again when we met in the street, and so forth. About a couple of days ago she distinctly smiled – in a sort of faint, saint-like kind of way, you know – when I ran into her outside the Vicarage. And yesterday – I say, you remember that curate chap, Wingham? Fellow with a long nose.'

'Of course I remember him. Your rival.'

'Rival?' Bingo raised his eyebrows. 'Oh, well, I suppose you could have called him that at one time. Though it sounds a little far-fetched.'

'Does it?' I said, stung by the sickening complacency of the chump's manner. 'Well, let me tell you that the last I heard was that at the Cow and Horses in Twing village and all over the place as far as Lower Bingley they were offering seven to one on the curate and finding no takers.'

Bingo started violently and sprayed cigarette ash all over my bed.

'Betting!' he gargled. 'Betting! You don't mean that they're betting on this holy, sacred— Oh, I say, dash it all! Haven't people any sense of decency and reverence? Is nothing safe from their beastly, sordid graspingness? I wonder,' said young Bingo thoughtfully, 'if there's a chance of my getting any of that seven-to-one money? Seven to one! What a price! Who's offering it, do you know? Oh, well, I suppose it wouldn't do. No, I suppose it wouldn't be quite the thing.'

'You seem dashed confident,' I said. 'I'd always thought that Wingham—'

'Oh, I'm not worried about him,' said Bingo. 'I was just going to tell you. Wingham's got the mumps, and won't be out and about for weeks. And, jolly as that is in itself, it's not all. You see, he was producing the Village School Christmas Entertainment, and now I've taken over the job. I went to old Heppenstall last night and clinched the contract. Well, you see what that means. It means that I shall be absolutely the centre of the village life and thought for three solid weeks, with a terrific triumph to wind up with. Everybody looking up to me and fawning on me, don't you see, and all that. It's bound to have a powerful effect on Mary's mind. It will show her that I am capable of serious effort; that there is a solid foundation of worth in me; that, mere butterfly as she may once have thought me, I am in reality—'

'Oh, all right, let it go!'

'It's a big thing, you know, this Christmas Entertainment. Old Heppenstall is very much wrapped up in it. Nibs from all over the countryside rolling up. The Squire present, with family. A big chance for me, Bertie, my boy, and I mean to make the most of it. Of course, I'm handicapped a bit by not having been in on the thing from the start. Will you credit it that that uninspired doughnut of a curate wanted to give the public some rotten little fairy play out of a book for children published about fifty years ago without one good laugh or the semblance of a gag in it? It's too late to alter the thing entirely, but at least I can jazz it up. I'm going to write them in something zippy to brighten the thing up a bit.'

'You can't write.'

'Well, when I say write, I mean pinch. That's why I've popped up to town. I've been to see that revue, *Cuddle Up!* at the Palladium, tonight. Full of good stuff. Of course, it's rather hard to get anything in the nature of a big spectacular effect in the Twing Village Hall, with no scenery to speak of and a chorus of practically imbecile kids of ages ranging from nine to fourteen, but I think I see my way. Have you seen *Cuddle Up!?*'

'Yes. Twice.'

'Well, there's some good stuff in the first act, and I can lift practically all the numbers. Then there's that show at the Palace. I can see the *matinée* of that tomorrow before I leave. There's sure to be some decent bits in that. Don't you worry about my not being able to write a hit. Leave it to me, laddie, leave it to me. And now, my dear old chap,' said young Bingo, snuggling down cosily, 'you mustn't keep me up talking all night. It's all right for you fellows who have nothing to do, but I'm a busy man. Good night, old thing. Close the door quietly after you and switch out the light. Breakfast about ten tomorrow, I suppose, what? Right ho. Good night.'

For the next three weeks I didn't see Bingo. He became a sort of Voice Heard Off, developing a habit of ringing me up on long-distance and consulting me on various points arising at rehearsal, until the day when he got me out of bed at eight in the morning to ask whether I thought *Merry Christmas!* was a good title. I told him then that this nuisance must now cease, and after that he cheesed it, and practically passed out of my life, till one afternoon when I got back to the flat to dress for dinner and found Jeeves inspecting a whacking big poster sort of thing which he had draped over the back of an armchair.

'Good Lord, Jeeves!' I said. I was feeling rather weak that day, and the thing shook me. 'What on earth's that?'

'Mr Little sent it to me, sir, and desired me to bring it to your notice.'

'Well, you've certainly done it!'

I took another look at the object. There was no doubt about it, it caught the eye. It was about seven feet long, and most of the lettering in about as bright red ink as I ever struck.

This was how it ran:

TWING VILLAGE HALL,
Friday, December 23rd,
RICHARD LITTLE
presents
A New and Original Revue
Entitled
WHAT HO, TWING!!
Book by
RICHARD LITTLE
Lyrics by
RICHARD LITTLE

Music by
RICHARD LITTLE
With the Full Twing Juvenile
Company and Chorus
Scenic Effects by
RICHARD LITTLE
Produced by
RICHARD LITTLE

'What do you make of it, Jeeves?' I said.

'I confess I am a little doubtful, sir. I think Mr Little would have done better to follow my advice and confine himself to good works about the village.'

'You think the thing will be a frost?'

'I could not hazard a conjecture, sir. But my experience has been that what pleases the London public is not always so acceptable to the rural mind. The metropolitan touch sometimes proves a trifle too exotic for the provinces.'

'I suppose I ought to go down and see the dashed thing?'

'I think Mr Little would be wounded were you not present, sir.'

The Village Hall at Twing is a smallish building, smelling of apples. It was full when I turned up on the evening of the twenty-third, for I had purposely timed myself to arrive not long before the kick-off. I had had experience of one or two of these binges, and didn't want to run any risk of coming early and finding myself shoved into a seat in one of the front rows where I wouldn't be able to execute a quiet sneak into the open air halfway through the proceedings, if the occasion seemed to demand it. I secured a nice strategic position near the door at the back of the hall.

From where I stood I had a good view of the audience. As always on these occasions, the first few rows were occupied by the Nibs – consisting of the Squire, a fairly mauve old sportsman with white whiskers, his family, a platoon of local parsons and perhaps a couple of dozen of prominent pew-holders. Then came a dense squash of what you might call the lower middle classes. And at the back, where I was, we came down with a jerk in the social scale, this end of the hall being given up almost entirely to a collection of frankly Tough Eggs, who had rolled up not so much for any love of the drama as because there was a free tea after the show. Take it for all in all, a representative gathering of Twing life and thought. The Nibs were whispering in a pleased manner to each other, the Lower Middles were sitting up very straight, as if they'd been bleached, and the Tough Eggs whiled away the time by cracking nuts and exchanging low rustic wheezes. The girl, Mary Burgess, was at the piano playing a waltz. Beside her stood the curate, Wingham, apparently recovered. The temperature, I should think, was about a hundred and twenty-seven.

Somebody jabbed me heartily in the lower ribs, and I perceived the man Steggles.

'Hallo!' he said. 'I didn't know you were coming down.'

I didn't like the chap, but we Woosters can wear the mask. I beamed a bit.

'Oh, yes,' I said. 'Bingo wanted me to roll up and see his show.'

'I hear he's giving us something pretty ambitious,' said the man Steggles. 'Big effects and all that sort of thing.'

'I believe so.'

'Of course, it means a lot to him, doesn't it? He's told you about the girl, of course?'

'Yes. And I hear you're laying seven to one against him,' I said, eyeing the blighter a trifle austerely.

He didn't even quiver.

'Just a little flutter to relieve the monotony of country life,' he said. 'But you've got the facts a bit wrong. It's down in the village that they're laying seven to one. I can do you better than that, if you feel in a speculative mood. How about a tenner at a hundred to eight?'

'Good Lord! Are you giving that?'

'Yes. Somehow,' said Steggles meditatively, 'I have a sort of feeling, a kind of premonition that something's going to go wrong tonight. You know what Little is. A bungler, if ever there was one. Something tells me that this show of his is going to be a frost. And if it is, of course, I should think it would prejudice the girl against him pretty badly. His standing always was rather shaky.'

'Are you going to try and smash up the show?' I said sternly.

'Me!' said Steggles. 'Why, what could I do? Half a minute, I want to go and speak to a man.'

He buzzed off, leaving me distinctly disturbed. I could see from the fellow's eye that he was meditating some of his customary rough stuff, and I thought Bingo ought to be warned. But there wasn't time and I couldn't get at him. Almost immediately after Steggles had left me the curtain went up.

Except as a prompter, Bingo wasn't much in evidence in the early part of the performance. The thing at the outset was merely one of those weird dramas which you dig out of books published around Christmas time and entitled *Twelve Little Plays for the Tots,* or something like that. The kids drooled on in the usual manner, the booming voice of Bingo ringing out from time to time behind the scenes when the fatheads forgot their lines; and the audience was settling down into the sort of torpor usual on these occasions, when the first of Bingo's interpolated bits occurred. It was that number which What's-her-name sings in that revue at the Palace – you would recognise the tune if I hummed it, but I can never get hold of the dashed thing. It always got three encores at the Palace, and it went well now, even with a squeaky-voiced child jumping on and off the key like a chamois of the Alps leaping from crag to crag. Even the Tough Eggs liked it. At the end of the second refrain the entire house was shouting for an encore, and the kid with the voice like a slate-pencil took a deep breath and started to let it go once more.

At this point all the lights went out.

I don't know when I've had anything so sudden and devastating happen to me before. They didn't flicker. They just went out. The hall was in complete darkness.

Well, of course, that sort of broke the spell, as you might put it. People started to shout directions, and the Tough Eggs stamped their feet and settled down for a pleasant time. And, of course, young Bingo had to make an ass of himself. His voice suddenly shot at us out of the darkness.

'Ladies and gentlemen, something has gone wrong with the lights—'

The Tough Eggs were tickled by this bit of information straight from the stable. They took it up as a sort of battle-cry. Then, after about five minutes, the lights went up again, and the show was resumed.

It took ten minutes after that to get the audience back into its state of coma, but eventually they began to settle down, and everything was going nicely when a small boy with a face like a turbot edged out in front of the curtain, which had been lowered after a pretty painful scene about a wishing-ring or a fairy's curse or something of that sort, and started to sing that song of George Thingummy's out of *Cuddle Up!* You know the one I mean. 'Always Listen to Mother, Girls!' it's called, and he gets the audience to join in and sing the refrain. Quite a ripeish ballad, and one which I myself have frequently sung in my bath with not a little vim; but by no means – as anyone but a perfect sap-headed prune like young Bingo would have known – by no means the sort of thing for a children's Christmas entertainment in the old Village Hall. Right from the start of the first refrain the bulk of the audience had begun to stiffen in their seats and fan themselves, and the Burgess girl at the piano was accompanying in a stunned, mechanical sort of way, while the curate at her side averted his gaze in a pained manner. The Tough Eggs, however, were all for it.

At the end of the second refrain the kid stopped and began to sidle towards the wings. Upon which the following brief duologue took place:

YOUNG BINGO (*Voice heard off, ringing against the rafters*): 'Go on!'

THE KID (*coyly*): 'I don't like to.'

YOUNG BINGO (*still louder*): 'Go on, you little blighter, or I'll slay you!'

I suppose the kid thought it over swiftly and realised that Bingo, being in a position to get at him, had better be conciliated, whatever the harvest might be; for he shuffled down to the front and, having shut his eyes and giggled hysterically, said, 'Ladies and gentlemen, I will now call upon Squire Tressidder to oblige by singing the refrain!'

You know, with the most charitable feelings towards him, there are moments when you can't help thinking that young Bingo ought to be in some sort of a home. I suppose, poor fish, he had pictured this as the big punch of the evening. He had imagined, I take it, that the Squire would spring jovially to his feet, rip the song off his chest, and all would be gaiety and mirth. Well, what happened was simply that old Tressidder – and, mark you, I'm not blaming him – just sat where he was, swelling and turning a brighter purple every second. The lower middle classes remained in frozen silence, waiting for the roof to fall. The only section of the audience that really seemed to enjoy the idea was the Tough Eggs, who yelled with enthusiasm. It was jam for the Tough Eggs.

And then the lights went out again.

When they went up, some minutes later, they disclosed the Squire marching stiffly out at the head of his family, fed up to the eyebrows; the Burgess girl at the piano with a pale, set look; and the curate gazing at her with something in his expression that seemed to suggest that, although all this was no doubt deplorable, he had spotted the silver lining.

The show went on once more. There were great chunks of Plays-for-the-Tots dialogue, and then the girl at the piano struck up the prelude to that Orange-Girl number that's the big hit of the Palace revue. I took it that this was to be Bingo's smashing act one finale. The entire company was on the stage, and a clutching hand had appeared round the edge of the curtain, ready to pull at the right moment. It looked like the finale all right. It wasn't long before I realised that it was something more. It was the finish.

I take it you know that Orange number at the Palace? It goes:

Oh, won't you something something oranges,
  My something oranges,
  My something oranges;
Oh, won't you something something something I forget,
Something something something tumty tumty yet:
Oh—

or words to that effect. It's a dashed clever lyric, and the tune's good, too; but the thing that made the number was the business where the girls take oranges out of their baskets, you know, and toss them lightly to the audience. I don't know if you've ever noticed it, but it always seems to tickle an audience to bits when they get things thrown at them from the stage. Every time I've been to the Palace the customers have simply gone wild over this number.

But at the Palace, of course, the oranges are made of yellow wool, and the girls don't so much chuck them as drop them limply into the first and second rows. I began to gather that the business was going to be treated rather differently tonight when a dashed great chunk of pips and mildew sailed past my ear and burst on the wall behind me. Another landed with a squelch on the neck of one of the Nibs in the third row. And then a third took me right on the tip of the nose, and I kind of lost interest in the proceedings for a while.

When I had scrubbed my face and got my eye to stop watering for a moment, I saw that the evening's entertainment had begun to resemble one of Belfast's livelier nights. The air was thick with shrieks and fruit. The kids on the stage, with Bingo buzzing distractedly to and fro in their midst, were having the time of their lives. I suppose they realised that this couldn't go on for ever, and were making the most of their chances. The Tough Eggs had begun to pick up all the oranges that hadn't burst and were shooting them back, so that the audience got it both coming and going. In fact, take it all round, there was a certain amount of confusion; and, just as things had begun really to hot up, out went the lights again.

It seemed to me about my time for leaving, so I slid for the door. I was hardly outside when the audience began to stream out. They surged about me in twos and threes, and I've never seen a public body so dashed unanimous on any point. To a man – and to a woman – they were cursing poor old Bingo; and there was a large and rapidly growing school of thought which held that the best thing to do would be to waylay him as he emerged and splash him about in the village pond a bit.

There were such a dickens of a lot of these enthusiasts and they looked so jolly determined that it seemed to me that the only matey thing to do was to go behind and warn young Bingo to turn his coat-collar up and breeze off snakily by some side exit. I went behind, and found him sitting on a box in the wings, perspiring pretty freely and looking more or less like the spot marked with a cross where the accident happened. His hair was standing up and his ears were hanging down, and one harsh word would undoubtedly have made him burst into tears.

'Bertie,' he said hollowly, as he saw me, 'it was that blighter Steggles! I caught one of the kids before he could get away and got it all out of him. Steggles substituted real oranges for the balls of wool which with infinite sweat and at a cost of nearly a quid I had specially prepared. Well, I will now proceed to tear him limb from limb. It'll be something to do.'

I hated to spoil his daydreams, but it had to be.

'Good heavens, man,' I said, 'you haven't time for frivolous amusements now. You've got to get out. And quick!'

'Bertie,' said Bingo in a dull voice, 'she was here just now. She said it was all my fault and that she would never speak to me again. She said she had always suspected me of being a heartless practical joker, and now she knew. She said— Oh, well, she ticked me off properly.'

'That's the least of your troubles,' I said. It seemed impossible to rouse the poor zib to a sense of his position. 'Do you realise that about two hundred of Twing's heftiest are waiting for you outside to chuck you into the pond?'

'No!'

'Absolutely!'

For a moment the poor chap seemed crushed. But only

for a moment. There has always been something of the good old English bulldog breed about Bingo. A strange, sweet smile flickered for an instant over his face.

'It's all right,' he said. 'I can sneak out through the cellar and climb over the wall at the back. They can't intimidate *me*!'

It couldn't have been more than a week later when Jeeves, after he had brought me my tea, gently steered me away from the sporting page of the *Morning Post* and directed my attention to an announcement in the engagements and marriages column.

It was a brief statement that a marriage had been arranged and would shortly take place between the Hon. and Rev. Hubert Wingham, third son of the Right Hon. the Earl of Sturridge, and Mary, only daughter of the late Matthew Burgess, of Weatherly Court, Hants.

'Of course,' I said, after I had given it the east-to-west, 'I expected this, Jeeves.'

'Yes, sir.'

'She would never forgive him what happened that night.'

'No, sir.'

'Well,' I said, as I took a sip of the fragrant and steaming, 'I don't suppose it will take old Bingo long to get over it. It's about the hundred and eleventh time this sort of thing has happened to him. You're the man I'm sorry for.'

'Me, sir?'

'Well, dash it all, you can't have forgotten what a deuce of a lot of trouble you took to bring the thing off for Bingo. It's too bad that all your work should have been wasted.'

'Not entirely wasted, sir.'

'Eh?'

'It is true that my efforts to bring about the match between Mr Little and the young lady were not successful, but I still look back upon the matter with a certain satisfaction.'

'Because you did your best, you mean?'

'Not entirely, sir, though of course that thought also gives me pleasure. I was alluding more particularly to the fact that I found the affair financially remunerative.'

'Financially remunerative? What do you mean?'

'When I learned that Mr Steggles had interested himself in the contest, sir, I went shares with my friend Brookfield and bought the book which had been made on the issue by the landlord of the Cow and Horses. It has proved a highly profitable investment. Your breakfast will be ready almost immediately, sir. Kidneys on toast and mushrooms. I will bring it when you ring.'

November
The Magic Plus Fours

'After all,' said the young man, 'golf is only a game.'

He spoke bitterly and with the air of one who has been following a train of thought. He had come into the smoking room of the clubhouse in low spirits at the dusky close of a November evening, and for some minutes had been sitting, silent and moody, staring at the log fire.

'Merely a pastime,' said the young man.

The Oldest Member, nodding in his armchair, stiffened with horror, and glanced quickly over his shoulder to make sure that none of the waiters had heard these terrible words.

'Can this be George William Pennefather speaking!' he said, reproachfully. 'My boy, you are not yourself.'

The young man flushed a little beneath his tan: for he had had a good upbringing and was not bad at heart.

'Perhaps I ought not to have gone quite so far as that,' he admitted. 'I was only thinking that a fellow's got no right, just because he happens to have come on a bit in his form lately, to treat a fellow as if a fellow was a leper or something.'

The Oldest Member's face cleared, and he breathed a relieved sigh.

'Ah! I see,' he said. 'You spoke hastily and in a sudden

fit of pique because something upset you out on the links today. Tell me all. Let me see, you were playing with Nathaniel Frisby this afternoon, were you not? I gather that he beat you.'

'Yes, he did. Giving me a third. But it isn't being beaten that I mind. What I object to is having the blighter behave as if he were a sort of champion condescending to a mere mortal. Dash it, it seemed to bore him playing with me! Every time I sliced off the tee he looked at me as if I were a painful ordeal. Twice when I was having a bit of trouble in the bushes I caught him yawning. And after we had finished he started talking about what a good game croquet was, and he wondered more people didn't take it up. And it's only a month or so ago that I could play the man level!'

The Oldest Member shook his snowy head sadly.

'There is nothing to be done about it,' he said. 'We can only hope that the poison will in time work its way out of the man's system. Sudden success at golf is like the sudden acquisition of wealth. It is apt to unsettle and deteriorate the character. And, as it comes almost miraculously, so only a miracle can effect a cure. The best advice I can give you is to refrain from playing with Nathaniel Frisby till you can keep your tee-shots straight.'

'Oh, but don't run away with the idea that I wasn't pretty good off the tee this afternoon!' said the young man. 'I should like to describe to you the shot I did on the—'

'Meanwhile,' proceeded the Oldest Member, 'I will relate to you a little story which bears on what I have been saying.'

'From the very moment I addressed the ball—'

'It is the story of two loving hearts temporarily estranged owing to the sudden and unforeseen proficiency of one of the couple—'

'I waggled quickly and strongly, like Duncan. Then, swinging smoothly back, rather in the Vardon manner—'

'But as I see,' said the Oldest Member, 'that you are all impatience for me to begin, I will do so without further preamble.'

To the philosophical student of golf like myself (said the Oldest Member) perhaps the most outstanding virtue of this noble pursuit is the fact that it is a medicine for the soul. Its great service to humanity is that it teaches human beings that, whatever petty triumphs they may have achieved in other walks of life, they are after all merely human. It acts as a corrective against sinful pride. I attribute the insane arrogance of the later Roman emperors almost entirely to the fact that, never having played golf, they never knew that strange chastening humility which is engendered by a topped chip-shot. If Cleopatra had been outed in the first round of the Ladies' Singles, we should have heard a lot less of her proud imperiousness. And, coming down to modern times, it was undoubtedly his rotten golf that kept Wallace Chesney the nice unspoiled fellow he was. For in every other respect he had everything in the world calculated to make a man conceited and arrogant. He was the best-looking man for miles around; his health was perfect; and, in addition to this, he was rich; danced, rode, played bridge and polo with equal skill; and was engaged to be married to Charlotte Dix. And when you saw Charlotte Dix you realised that being engaged to her would by itself have been quite enough luck for any one man.

But Wallace, as I say, despite all his advantages, was a thoroughly nice, modest young fellow. And I attribute this to the fact that, while one of the keenest golfers in the club, he was also one of the worst players. Indeed, Charlotte Dix used to say to me in his presence that she could not understand why people paid money to go to the circus when by merely walking over the brow of a hill they could watch Wallace Chesney trying to get out of the bunker by the eleventh green. And Wallace took the gibe with perfect good humour, for there was a delightful camaraderie between them which robbed it of any sting. Often at lunch in the clubhouse I used to hear him and Charlotte planning the handicapping details of a proposed match between Wallace and a non-existent cripple whom Charlotte claimed to have discovered in the village – it being agreed finally that he should accept seven bisques from the cripple, but that, if the latter ever recovered the use of his arms, Wallace should get a stroke a hole.

In short, a thoroughly happy and united young couple. Two hearts, if I may coin an expression, that beat as one.

I would not have you misjudge Wallace Chesney. I may have given you the impression that his attitude towards golf was light and frivolous, but such was not the case. As I have said, he was one of the keenest members of the club. Love made him receive the joshing of his *fiancée* in the kindly spirit in which it was meant, but at heart he was as earnest as you could wish, he practised early and late; he bought golf books; and the mere sight of a patent club of any description acted on him like catnip on a cat.

I remember remonstrating with him on the occasion of his purchasing a wooden-faced driving-mashie which weighed about two pounds, and was, taking it for all in all, as foul an instrument as ever came out of the workshop of a clubmaker who had been dropped on the head by his nurse when a baby.

'I know, I know,' he said, when I had finished indicating some of the weapon's more obvious defects. 'But the point is, I believe in it. It gives me confidence. I don't believe you could slice with a thing like that if you tried.'

Confidence! That was what Wallace Chesney lacked, and that, as he saw it, was the prime grand secret of golf. Like an alchemist on the track of the Philosopher's Stone, he was for ever seeking for something which would really give him confidence. I recollect that he even tried repeating to himself fifty times every morning the words, 'Every day in every way I grow better and better.' This, however, proved such a black lie that he gave it up. The fact is, the man was a visionary, and it is to auto-hypnosis of some kind that I attribute the extraordinary change that came over him at the beginning of his third season.

You may have noticed in your perambulations about the City a shop bearing above its door and upon its windows the legend:

COHEN BROS.,
Second-hand Clothiers,

a statement which is borne out by endless vistas seen through the door of every variety of what is technically known as Gents' Wear. But the Brothers Cohen, though their main stock-in-trade is garments which have been rejected by their owners for one reason or another, do not confine their dealings to Gents' Wear. The place is a museum of derelict goods of every description. You can get a second-hand revolver there, or a second-hand sword, or a second-hand umbrella. You can do a cheap deal in field glasses, trunks, dog collars, canes, photograph frames, attaché cases, and bowls for goldfish. And on the bright spring morning when Wallace Chesney happened to pass by there was exhibited in the window a putter of such pre-eminently lunatic design that he stopped dead as if he had run into an invisible wall, and then, panting like an overwrought fish, charged in through the door.

The shop was full of the Cohen family, sombre-eyed, smileless men with purposeful expressions; and two of these, instantly descending upon Wallace Chesney like leopards, began in swift silence to thrust him into a suit of yellow tweed. Having worked the coat over his shoulders with a shoehorn, they stood back to watch the effect.

'A beautiful fit,' announced Isidore Cohen.

'A little snug under the arms,' said his brother Irving. 'But that'll give.'

'The warmth of the body will make it give,' said Isidore.

'Or maybe you'll lose weight in the summer,' said Irving.

Wallace, when he had struggled out of the coat and was able to breathe, said that he had come in to buy a putter. Isidore thereupon sold him the putter, a dog collar, and a set of studs, and Irving sold him a fireman's helmet: and he was about to leave when their elder brother Lou, who had just finished fitting out another customer, who had come in to buy a cap, with two pairs of trousers and a miniature aquarium for keeping newts in, saw that business was in progress and strolled up. His fathomless eye rested on Wallace, who was toying feebly with the putter.

'You play golf?' asked Lou. 'Then looka here!'

He dived into an alleyway of dead clothing, dug for a moment, and emerged with something at the sight of which Wallace Chesney, hardened golfer that he was, blenched and threw up an arm defensively.

'No, no!' he cried.

The object which Lou Cohen was waving insinuatingly before his eyes was a pair of those golfing breeches which are technically known as Plus Fours. A player of two years' standing, Wallace Chesney was not unfamiliar with Plus Fours – all the club cracks wore them – but he had never seen Plus Fours like these. What might be termed the main *motif* of the fabric was a curious vivid pink, and with this to work on the architect had let his imagination run free, and had produced so much variety in the way of chessboard squares of white, yellow, violet, and green that the eye swam as it looked upon them.

'These were made to measure for Sandy McHoots, the Open Champion,' said Lou, stroking the left leg lovingly. 'But he sent 'em back for some reason or other.'

'Perhaps they frightened the children,' said Wallace, recollecting having heard that Mr McHoots was a married man.

'They'll fit you nice,' said Lou.

'Sure they'll fit him nice,' said Isidore, warmly.

'Why, just take a look at yourself in the glass,' said Irving, 'and see if they don't fit you nice.'

And, as one who wakes from a trance, Wallace discovered that his lower limbs were now encased in the prismatic garment. At what point in the proceedings the brethren had slipped them on him, he could not have said. But he was undeniably in.

Wallace looked in the glass. For a moment, as he eyed his reflection, sheer horror gripped him. Then suddenly, as he gazed, he became aware that his first feelings were changing. The initial shock over, he was becoming calmer. He waggled his right leg with a certain sangfroid.

There is a certain passage in the works of the poet Pope with which you may be familiar. It runs as follows:

> Vice is a monster of so frightful mien
> As to be hated needs but to be seen:
> Yet seen too oft, familiar with her face,
> We first endure, then pity, then embrace.

Even so was it with Wallace Chesney and these Plus Fours. At first he had recoiled from them as any decent-minded man would have done. Then, after a while, almost abruptly he found himself in the grip of a new emotion. After an unsuccessful attempt to analyse this, he suddenly got it. Amazing as it may seem, it was pleasure that he felt. He caught his eye in the mirror, and it was smirking. Now that the things were actually on, by Hutchinson, they didn't look half bad. By Braid, they didn't. There was a sort of something about them. Take away that expanse of bare leg with its unsightly sock-suspender and substitute a woolly stocking, and you would have the lower section of a golfer. For the first time in his life, he thought, he looked like a man who could play golf.

There came to him an odd sensation of masterfulness. He was still holding the putter, and now he swung it up above his shoulder. A fine swing, all lissomness and supple grace, quite different from any swing he had ever done before.

Wallace Chesney gasped. He knew that at last he had discovered that prime grand secret of golf for which he had searched so long. It was the costume that did it. All you had to do was wear Plus Fours. He had always hitherto played in grey flannel trousers. Naturally he had not been able to do himself justice. Golf required an easy dash, and how could you be easily dashing in concertina-shaped trousers with a patch on the knee? He saw now – what he had never seen before – that it was not because they were crack players that crack players wore Plus Fours: it was because they wore Plus Fours that they were crack players. And these Plus Fours had been the property of an Open Champion. Wallace Chesney's bosom swelled, and he was filled, as by some strange gas, with joy – with excitement – with confidence. Yes, for the first time in his golfing life, he felt really confident.

True, the things might have been a shade less gaudy: they might perhaps have hit the eye with a slightly less violent punch: but what of that? True, again, he could scarcely hope to avoid the censure of his club-mates when he appeared like this on the links: but what of *that*? His club-mates must set their teeth and learn to bear these Plus Fours like men. That was what Wallace Chesney thought about it. If they did not like his Plus Fours, let them go and play golf somewhere else.

'How much?' he muttered, thickly. And the Brothers Cohen clustered grimly round with notebooks and pencils.

In predicting a stormy reception for his new apparel, Wallace Chesney had not been unduly pessimistic. The moment he entered the clubhouse Disaffection reared its ugly head. Friends of years' standing called loudly for the committee, and there was a small and vehement party of the left wing, headed by Raymond Gandle, who was an artist by profession, and consequently had a sensitive eye, which advocated the tearing off and public burial of the obnoxious garment. But, prepared as he had been for some such demonstration on the part of the coarser-minded, Wallace had hoped for better things when he should meet Charlotte Dix, the girl who loved him. Charlotte, he had supposed, would understand and sympathise.

Instead of which, she uttered a piercing cry and staggered to a bench, whence a moment later she delivered her ultimatum.

'Quick!' she said. 'Before I have to look again.'

'What do you mean?'

'Pop straight back into the changing room while I've got my eyes shut, and remove the fancy-dress.'

'What's wrong with them?'

'Darling,' said Charlotte, 'I think it's sweet and patriotic of you to be proud of your cycling club colours or whatever they are, but you mustn't wear them on the links. It will unsettle the caddies.'

'They *are* a trifle on the bright side,' admitted Wallace.

'But it helps my game, wearing them. I was trying a few practice-shots just now, and I couldn't go wrong. Slammed the ball on the meat every time. They inspire me, if you know what I mean. Come on, let's be starting.'

Charlotte opened her eyes incredulously. 'You can't seriously mean that you're really going to *play* in – those? It's against the rules. There must be a rule somewhere in the book against coming out looking like a sunset. Won't you go and burn them for my sake?'

'But I tell you they give me confidence. I sort of squint down at them when I'm addressing the ball, and I feel like a pro.'

'Then the only thing to do is for me to play you for them. Come on, Wally, be a sportsman. I'll give you a half and play you for the whole outfit – the breeches, the red jacket, the little cap, and the belt with the snake's-head buckle. I'm sure all those things must have gone with the breeches. Is it a bargain?'

Strolling on the clubhouse terrace some two hours later, Raymond Gandle encountered Charlotte and Wallace coming up from the eighteenth green.

'Just the girl I wanted to see,' said Raymond. 'Miss Dix, I represent a select committee of my fellow-members, and I have come to ask you on their behalf to use the influence of a good woman to induce Wally to destroy those Plus Fours of his, which we all consider nothing short of Bolshevik propaganda and a menace to the public weal. May I rely on you?'

'You may not,' retorted Charlotte. 'They are the poor boy's mascot. You've no idea how they have improved his game. He has just beaten me hollow. I am going to try to learn to bear them, so you must. Really, you've no notion how he has come on. My cripple won't be able to give him more than a couple of bisques if he keeps up this form.'

'It's something about the things,' said Wallace. 'They give me confidence.'

'They give *me* a pain in the neck,' said Raymond Gandle.

To the thinking man nothing is more remarkable in this life than the way in which Humanity adjusts itself to conditions which at their outset might well have appeared intolerable. Some great cataclysm occurs, some storm or earthquake, shaking the community to its foundations; and after the first pardonable consternation one finds the sufferers resuming their ordinary pursuits as if nothing had happened. There have been few more striking examples of this adaptability than the behaviour of the members of our golf-club under the impact of Wallace Chesney's Plus Fours. For the first few days it is not too much to say that they were stunned. Nervous players sent their caddies on in front of them at blind holes, so that they might be warned in time of Wallace's presence ahead and not have him happening to them all of a sudden. And even the pro was not unaffected. Brought up in Scotland in an atmosphere of tartan kilts, he nevertheless winced, and a startled 'Hoots!' was forced from his lips when Wallace Chesney suddenly appeared in the valley as he was about to drive from the fifth tee.

But in about a week conditions were back to normal. Within ten days the Plus Fours became a familiar feature of the landscape, and were accepted as such without comment. They were pointed out to strangers together with the waterfall, the Lovers' Leap, and the view from the eighth green as things you ought not to miss when visiting the course; but apart from that one might almost say they were ignored. And meanwhile Wallace Chesney continued day by day to make the most extraordinary progress in his play.

As I said before, and I think you will agree with me when I have told you what happened subsequently, it was probably a case of auto-hypnosis. There is no other sphere in which a belief in oneself has such immediate effects as it has in golf. And Wallace, having acquired self-confidence, went on from strength to strength. In under a week he had ploughed his way through the Unfortunate Incidents – of which class Peter Willard was the best example – and was challenging the fellows who kept three shots in five somewhere on the fairway. A month later he was holding his own with ten-handicap men. And by the middle of the summer he was so far advanced that his name occasionally cropped up in speculative talks on the subject of the July medal. One might have been excused for supposing that, as far as Wallace Chesney was concerned, all was for the best in the best of all possible worlds.

And yet—

The first inkling I received that anything was wrong came through a chance meeting with Raymond Gandle, who happened to pass my gate on his way back from the links just as I drove up in my taxi; for I had been away from home for many weeks on a protracted business tour. I welcomed Gandle's advent and invited him in to smoke a pipe and put me abreast of local gossip. He came readily enough – and seemed, indeed, to have something on his mind and to be glad of the opportunity of revealing it to a sympathetic auditor.

'And how,' I asked him, when we were comfortably settled, 'did your game this afternoon come out?'

'Oh, he beat me,' said Gandle, and it seemed to me that there was a note of bitterness in his voice.

'Then He, whoever he was, must have been an extremely competent performer,' I replied, courteously, for Gandle was one of the finest players in the club. 'Unless, of course, you were giving him some impossible handicap?'

'No; we played level.'

'Indeed! Who was your opponent?'

'Chesney.'

'Wallace Chesney! And he beat you, playing level! This is the most amazing thing I have ever heard.'

'He's improved out of all knowledge.'

'He must have done. Do you think he would ever beat you again?'

'No. Because he won't have the chance.'

'You surely do not mean that you will not play him because you are afraid of being beaten?'

'It isn't being beaten I mind—'

And if I omit to report the remainder of his speech it is not merely because it contained expressions with which I am reluctant to sully my lips, but because, omitting these expletives, what he said was almost word for word what you were saying to me just now about Nathaniel Frisby. It was, it seemed, Wallace Chesney's manner, his arrogance, his attitude of belonging to some superior order of being that had so wounded Raymond Gandle. Wallace Chesney had, it appeared, criticised Gandle's mashie-play in no friendly spirit; had hung up the game on the fourteenth tee in order to show him how to place his feet; and on the way back to the clubhouse had said that the beauty of golf was that the best player could enjoy a round even with a dud, because, though there might be no interest in the match, he could always amuse himself by playing for his medal score.

I was profoundly shaken.

'Wallace Chesney!' I exclaimed. 'Was it really Wallace Chesney who behaved in the manner you describe?'

'Unless he's got a twin brother of the same name, it was.'

'Wallace Chesney a victim to swelled head! I can hardly credit it.'

'Well, you needn't take my word for it unless you want to. Ask anybody. It isn't often he can get anyone to play with him now.'

'You horrify me!'

Raymond Gandle smoked awhile in brooding silence.

'You've heard about his engagement?' he said at length.

'I have heard nothing, nothing. What about his engagement?'

'Charlotte Dix has broken it off.'

'No!'

'Yes. Couldn't stand him any longer.'

I got rid of Gandle as soon as I could. I made my way as quickly as possible to the house where Charlotte lived with her aunt. I was determined to sift this matter to the bottom and to do all that lay in my power to heal the breach between two young people for whom I had a great affection.

'I have just heard the news,' I said, when the aunt had retired to some secret lair, as aunts do, and Charlotte and I were alone.

'What news?' said Charlotte, dully. I thought she looked pale and ill, and she had certainly grown thinner.

'This dreadful news about your engagement to Wallace Chesney. Tell me, why did you do this thing? Is there no hope of a reconciliation?'

'Not unless Wally becomes his old self again.'

'But I had always regarded you two as ideally suited to one another.'

'Wally has completely changed in the last few weeks. Haven't you heard?'

'Only sketchily, from Raymond Gandle.'

'I refuse,' said Charlotte, proudly, all the woman in her leaping to her eyes, 'to marry a man who treats me as if I were a kronen at the present rate of exchange, merely because I slice an occasional tee-shot. The afternoon I broke off the engagement' – her voice shook, and I could see that her indifference was but a mask – 'the afternoon I broke off the en-gug-gug-gagement, he t-told me I ought to use an iron off the tee instead of a dud-dud-driver.'

And the stricken girl burst into an uncontrollable fit of sobbing. And realising that, if matters had gone as far as that, there was little I could do, I pressed her hand silently and left her.

But though it seemed hopeless I decided to persevere. I turned my steps towards Wallace Chesney's bungalow, resolved to make one appeal to the man's better feelings. He was in his sitting room when I arrived, polishing a putter; and it seemed significant to me, even in that tense moment, that the putter was quite an ordinary one, such as any capable player might use. In the brave old happy days of his dudhood, the only putters you ever found in the society of Wallace Chesney were patent self-adjusting things that looked like croquet mallets that had taken the wrong turning in childhood.

'Well, Wallace, my boy,' I said.

'Hallo!' said Wallace Chesney. 'So you're back?'

We fell into conversation, and I had not been in the room two minutes before I realised that what I had been told about the change in him was nothing more than the truth. The man's bearing and his every remark were insufferably bumptious. He spoke of his prospects in the July medal competition as if the issue were already settled. He scoffed at his rivals.

I had some little difficulty in bringing the talk round to the matter which I had come to discuss.

'My boy,' I said at length, 'I have just heard the sad news.'

'What sad news?'

'I have been talking to Charlotte—'

'Oh, that!' said Wallace Chesney.

'She was telling me—'

'Perhaps it's all for the best.'

'All for the best? What do you mean?'

'Well,' said Wallace, 'one doesn't wish, of course, to say anything ungallant, but, after all, poor Charlotte's handicap *is* fourteen and wouldn't appear to have much chance of getting any lower. I mean, there's such a thing as a fellow throwing himself away.'

Was I revolted at these callous words? For a moment, yes. Then it struck me that, though he had uttered them with a light laugh, that laugh had had in it more than a touch of bravado. I looked at him keenly. There was a bored, discontented expression in his eyes, a line of pain about his mouth.

'My boy,' I said, gravely, 'you are not happy.'

For an instant I think he would have denied the imputation. But my visit had coincided with one of those twilight moods in which a man requires, above all else, sympathy. He uttered a weary sigh.

'I'm fed up,' he admitted. 'It's a funny thing. When I was a dud, I used to think how perfect it must be to be scratch. I used to watch the cracks buzzing round the course and envy them. It's all a fraud. The only time when you enjoy golf is when an occasional decent shot is enough to make you happy for the day. I'm plus two, and I'm bored to death. I'm too good. And what's the result? Everybody's jealous of me. Everybody's got it in for me. Nobody loves me.'

His voice rose in a note of anguish, and at the sound his terrier, which had been sleeping on the rug, crept forward and licked his hand.

'The dog loves you,' I said, gently, for I was touched.

'Yes, but I don't love the dog,' said Wallace Chesney.

'Now come, Wallace,' I said. 'Be reasonable, my boy. It is only your unfortunate manner on the links which has made you perhaps a little unpopular at the moment. Why not pull yourself up? Why ruin your whole life with this arrogance? All that you need is a little tact, a little forbearance. Charlotte, I am sure, is just as fond of you as ever, but you have wounded her pride. Why must you be unkind about her tee-shots?'

Wallace Chesney shook his head despondently.

'I can't help it,' he said. 'It exasperates me to see anyone foozling, and I have to say so.'

'Then there is nothing to be done,' I said, sadly.

All the medal competitions at our club are, as you know, important events; but, as you are also aware, none of them is looked forward to so keenly or contested so hotly as the one in July. At the beginning of the year of which I am speaking, Raymond Gandle had been considered the probable winner of the fixture; but as the season progressed and Wallace Chesney's skill developed to such a remarkable extent most of us were reluctantly inclined to put our money on the latter. Reluctantly, because Wallace's unpopularity was now so general that the thought of his winning was distasteful to all. It grieved me to see how cold his fellow-members were towards him. He drove off from the first tee without a solitary handclap; and, though the drive was of admirable quality and nearly carried the green, there was not a single cheer. I noticed Charlotte Dix among the spectators. The poor girl was looking sad and wan.

In the draw for partners Wallace had had Peter Willard allotted to him; and he muttered to me in a quite audible voice that it was as bad as handicapping him half a dozen strokes to make him play with such a hopeless performer. I do not think Peter heard, but it would not have made much difference to him if he had, for I doubt if anything could have had much effect for the worse on his game. Peter Willard always entered for the medal competition, because he said that competition-play was good for the nerves.

On this occasion he topped his ball badly, and Wallace lit his pipe with the exaggeratedly patient air of an irritated man. When Peter topped his second also, Wallace was moved to speech.

'For goodness' sake,' he snapped, 'what's the good of playing at all if you insist on lifting your head? Keep it down, man, keep it down. You don't need to watch to see where the ball is going. It isn't likely to go as far as all that. Make up your mind to count three before you look up.'

'Thanks,' said Peter, meekly. There was no pride in Peter to be wounded. He knew the sort of player he was.

The couples were now moving off with smooth rapidity, and the course was dotted with the figures of players and their accompanying spectators. A fair proportion of these latter had decided to follow the fortunes of Raymond Gandle, but by far the larger number were sticking to Wallace, who right from the start showed that Gandle or anyone else would have to return a very fine card to beat him. He was out in thirty-seven, two above bogey, and with the assistance of a superb second, which landed the ball within a foot of the pin, got a three on the tenth, where a four is considered good. I mention this to show that by the time he arrived at the short lake-hole Wallace Chesney was at the top of his form. Not even the fact that he had been obliged to let the next couple through owing to Peter Willard losing his ball had been enough to upset him.

*

The course has been rearranged since, but at that time the lake-hole, which is now the second, was the eleventh, and was generally looked on as the crucial hole in a medal round. Wallace no doubt realised this, but the knowledge did not seem to affect him. He lit his pipe with the utmost coolness: and, having replaced the matchbox in his hip-pocket, stood smoking nonchalantly as he waited for the couple in front to get off the green.

They holed out eventually, and Wallace walked to the tee. As he did so, he was startled to receive a resounding smack.

'Sorry,' said Peter Willard, apologetically. 'Hope I didn't hurt you. A wasp.'

And he pointed to the corpse, which was lying in a used-up attitude on the ground.

'Afraid it would sting you,' said Peter.

'Oh, thanks,' said Wallace.

He spoke a little stiffly, for Peter Willard had a large, hard, flat hand, the impact of which had shaken him up considerably. Also, there had been laughter in the crowd. He was fuming as he bent to address his ball, and his annoyance became acute when, just as he reached the top of his swing, Peter Willard suddenly spoke.

'Just a second, old man,' said Peter. Wallace spun round, outraged.

'What *is* it? I do wish you would wait till I've made my shot.'

'Just as you like,' said Peter, humbly.

'There is no greater crime that a man can commit on the links than to speak to a fellow when he's making his stroke.'

'Of course, of course,' acquiesced Peter, crushed.

Wallace turned to his ball once more. He was vaguely conscious of a discomfort to which he could not at the moment give a name. At first he thought that he was having a spasm of lumbago, and this surprised him, for he had never in his life been subject to even a suspicion of that malady. A moment later he realised that this diagnosis had been wrong.

'Good heavens!' he cried, leaping nimbly some two feet into the air. 'I'm on fire!'

'Yes,' said Peter, delighted at his ready grasp of the situation. 'That's what I wanted to mention just now.'

Wallace slapped vigorously at the seat of his Plus Fours.

'It must have been when I killed that wasp,' said Peter, beginning to see clearly into the matter. 'You had a match-box in your pocket.'

Wallace was in no mood to stop and discuss first causes. He was springing up and down on his pyre, beating at the flames.

'Do you know what I should do if I were you?' said Peter Willard. 'I should jump into the lake.'

One of the cardinal rules of golf is that a player shall accept no advice from anyone but his own caddie; but the warmth about his lower limbs had now become so generous that Wallace was prepared to stretch a point. He took three rapid strides and entered the water with a splash.

The lake, though muddy, is not deep, and presently Wallace was to be observed standing up to his waist some few feet from the shore.

'That ought to have put it out,' said Peter Willard. 'It was a bit of luck that it happened at this hole.' He stretched out a hand to the bather. 'Catch hold, old man, and I'll pull you out.'

'No!' said Wallace Chesney.

'Why not?'

'Never mind!' said Wallace, austerely. He bent as near to Peter as he was able.

'Send a caddie up to the clubhouse to fetch my grey flannel trousers from my locker,' he whispered, tensely.

'Oh, ah!' said Peter.

It was some little time before Wallace, encircled by a group of male spectators, was enabled to change his costume; and during the interval he continued to stand waist-deep in the water, to the chagrin of various couples who came to the tee in the course of their round and complained with not a little bitterness that his presence there added a mental hazard to an already difficult hole. Eventually, however, he found himself back ashore, his ball before him, his mashie in his hand.

'Carry on,' said Peter Willard, as the couple in front left the green. 'All clear now.'

Wallace Chesney addressed his ball. And, even as he did so, he was suddenly aware that an odd psychological change had taken place in himself. He was aware of a strange weakness. The charred remains of the Plus Fours were lying under an adjacent bush; and, clad in the old grey flannels of his early golfing days, Wallace felt diffident, feeble, uncertain of himself. It was as though virtue had gone out of him, as if some indispensable adjunct to good play had been removed. His corrugated trouser-leg caught his eye as he waggled, and all at once he became acutely alive to the fact that many eyes were watching him. The audience seemed to press on him like a blanket. He felt as he had been wont to feel in the old days when he had had to drive off the first tee in front of a terraceful of scoffing critics.

The next moment his ball had bounded weakly over the intervening patch of turf and was in the water.

'Hard luck!' said Peter Willard, ever a generous foe. And the words seemed to touch some almost atrophied chord in Wallace's breast. A sudden love for his species flooded over him. Dashed decent of Peter, he thought, to sympathise. Peter was a good chap. So were the spectators good chaps. So was everybody, even his caddie.

Peter Willard, as if resolved to make his sympathy practical, also rolled his ball into the lake.

'Hard luck!' said Wallace Chesney, and started as he said it; for many weeks had passed since he had commiserated with an opponent. He felt a changed man. A better, sweeter, kindlier man. It was as if a curse had fallen from him.

He teed up another ball, and swung.

'Hard luck!' said Peter.

'Hard luck!' said Wallace, a moment later.

'Hard luck!' said Peter, a moment after that.

Wallace Chesney stood on the tee watching the spot in the water where his third ball had fallen. The crowd was now openly amused, and, as he listened to their happy laughter, it was borne in upon Wallace that he, too, was amused and happy. A weird, almost effervescent exhilaration filled him. He turned and beamed upon the spectators. He waved his mashie cheerily at them. This, he felt, was something like golf. This was golf as it should be – not the dull, mechanical thing which had bored him during all these past weeks of his perfection, but a gay, rollicking adventure. That was the soul of golf, the thing that made it the wonderful pursuit it was – that speculativeness, that not knowing where the dickens your ball was going when you hit it, that eternal hoping for the best, that never-failing chanciness. It is better to travel hopefully than to arrive, and at last this great truth had come home to Wallace Chesney. He realised now why pros were all grave, silent men who seemed to struggle manfully against some secret sorrow. It was because they were too darned good. Golf had no surprises for them, no gallant spirit of adventure.

'I'm going to get a ball over if I stay here all night,' cried Wallace Chesney, gaily, and the crowd echoed his mirth. On the face of Charlotte Dix was the look of a mother whose prodigal son has rolled into the old home once more. She caught Wallace's eye and gesticulated to him blithely.

'The cripple says he'll give you a stroke a hole, Wally!' she shouted.

'I'm ready for him!' bellowed Wallace.

'Hard *luck*!' said Peter Willard.

Under their bush the Plus Fours, charred and dripping, lurked unnoticed. But Wallace Chesney saw them. They caught his eye as he sliced his eleventh into the marshes on the right. It seemed to him that they looked sullen. Disappointed. Baffled.

Wallace Chesney was himself again.

December

The Knightly Quest of Mervyn

Some sort of smoking concert seemed to be in progress in the large room across the passage from the bar-parlour of the Angler's Rest, and a music-loving Stout and Mild had left the door open, the better to enjoy the entertainment. By this means we had been privileged to hear Kipling's 'Mandalay', 'I'll Sing Thee Songs of Araby', 'The Midshipmite', and 'Ho, Jolly Jenkin!': and now the piano began to tinkle again and a voice broke into a less familiar number.

The words came to us faintly, but clearly:

'The days of Chivalry are dead,
Of which in stories I have read,
When knights were bold and acted kind of scrappy;
They used to take a lot of pains
And fight all day to please the Janes,
And if their dame was tickled they was happy.
But now the men are mild and meek:
They seem to have a yellow streak:
They never lay for other guys, to flatten 'em:
They think they've done a darned fine thing
If they just buy the girl a ring
Of imitation diamonds and platinum.

> 'Oh, it makes me sort of sad
> To think about Sir Galahad
> And all the knights of that romantic day:
> To amuse a girl and charm her
> They would climb into their armour
> And jump into the fray:
> They called her "Lady love",
> They used to wear her little glove,
> And everything that she said went:
> For those were the days when a lady was a lady
> And a gent was a perfect gent.'

A Ninepennyworth of Sherry sighed.
'True,' he murmured. 'Very true.'
The singer continued:

> 'Some night when they sat down to dine,
> Sir Claude would say: "That girl of mine
> Makes every woman jealous when she sees her."
> Then someone else would shout: "Behave,
> Thou malapert and scurvy knave,
> Or I will smite thee one upon the beezer!"
> And then next morning in the lists
> They'd take their lances in their fists
> And mount a pair of chargers, highly mettled:
> And when Sir Claude, so fair and young,
> Got punctured in the leg or lung,
> They looked upon the argument as settled.'

The Ninepennyworth of Sherry sighed again.
'He's right,' he said. 'We live in degenerate days, gentle-

men. Where now is the fine old tradition of derring-do? Where,' demanded the Ninepennyworth of Sherry with modest fervour, 'shall we find in these prosaic modern times the spirit that made the knights of old go through perilous adventures and brave dreadful dangers to do their lady's behest?'

'In the Mulliner family,' said Mr Mulliner, pausing for a moment from the sipping of his hot Scotch and lemon, 'in the clan to which I have the honour to belong, the spirit to which you allude still flourishes in all its pristine vigour. I can scarcely exemplify this better than by relating the story of my cousin's son, Mervyn, and the strawberries.'

'But I want to listen to the concert,' pleaded a Rum and Milk. 'I just heard the curate clear his throat. That always means "Dangerous Dan McGrew".'

'The story,' repeated Mr Mulliner with quiet firmness, as he closed the door, 'of my cousin's son, Mervyn, and the strawberries.'

In the circles in which the two moved (said Mr Mulliner) it had often been debated whether my cousin's son, Mervyn, was a bigger chump than my nephew Archibald – the one who, if you recall, was so good at imitating a hen laying an egg. Some took one side, some the other; but, though the point still lies open, there is no doubt that young Mervyn was quite a big enough chump for everyday use. And it was this quality in him that deterred Clarice Mallaby from consenting to become his bride.

He discovered this one night when, as they were dancing at the Restless Cheese, he put the thing squarely up to her, not mincing his words.

'Tell me, Clarice,' he said, 'why is it that you spurn a fellow's suit? I can't for the life of me see why you won't consent to marry a chap. It isn't as if I hadn't asked you often enough. Playing fast and loose with a good man's love is the way I look at it.'

And he gazed at her in a way that was partly melting and partly suggestive of the dominant male. And Clarice Mallaby gave one of those light, tinkling laughs and replied:

'Well, if you really want to know, you're such an ass.'

Mervyn could make nothing of this.

'An ass? How do you mean an ass? Do you mean a silly ass?'

'I mean a goof,' said the girl. 'A gump. A poop. A nitwit and a returned empty. Your name came up the other day in the course of conversation at home, and Mother said you were a vapid and irreflective guffin, totally lacking in character and purpose.'

'Oh?' said Mervyn. 'She did, did she?'

'She did. And while it isn't often that I think along the same lines as Mother, there – for once – I consider her to have hit the bull's-eye, rung the bell, and to be entitled to a cigar or coconut, according to choice. It seemed to me what they call the *mot juste*.'

'Indeed?' said Mervyn, nettled. 'Well, let me tell you something. When it comes to discussing brains, your mother, in my opinion, would do better to recede modestly into the background and not try to set herself up as an authority. I strongly suspect her of being the woman who was seen in Charing Cross Station the other day, asking a porter if he could direct her to Charing Cross

Station. And, in the second place,' said Mervyn, 'I'll show you if I haven't got character and purpose. Set me some quest, like the knights of old, and see how quick I'll deliver the goods as per esteemed order.'

'How do you mean – a quest?'

'Why, bid me do something for you, or get something for you, or biff somebody in the eye for you. You know the procedure.'

Clarice thought for a moment. Then she said: 'All my life I've wanted to eat strawberries in the middle of winter. Get me a basket of strawberries before the end of the month and we'll take up this matrimonial proposition of yours in a spirit of serious research.'

'Strawberries?' said Mervyn.

'Strawberries.'

Mervyn gulped a little.

'Strawberries?'

'But, I say, dash it! *Strawberries?*'

'Strawberries,' said Clarice.

And then at last Mervyn, reading between the lines, saw that what she wanted was strawberries. And how he was to get any in December was more than he could have told you.

'I could do you oranges,' he said.

'Strawberries.'

'Or nuts. You wouldn't prefer a nice nut?'

'Strawberries,' said the girl firmly. 'And you're jolly lucky, my lad, not to be sent off after the Holy Grail or something, or told to pluck me a sprig of edelweiss from the top of the Alps. Mind you, I'm not saying yes and I'm not saying no, but this I will say – that if you bring me that basket of strawberries in the stated time, I shall know that there's more in you than sawdust – which the casual observer wouldn't believe – and I will reopen your case and examine it thoroughly in the light of the fresh evidence. Whereas, if you fail to deliver the fruit, I shall know that Mother was right, and you can jolly well make up your mind to doing without my society from now on.'

Here she stopped to take in breath, and Mervyn, after a lengthy pause, braced himself up and managed to utter a brave laugh. It was a little roopy, if not actually hacking, but he did it.

'Right ho,' he said. 'Right ho. If that's the way you feel, well, to put it in a nutshell, right ho.'

My cousin's son Mervyn passed a restless night that night, tossing on the pillow not a little, and feverishly at that. If this girl had been a shade less attractive, he told himself, he would have sent her a telegram telling her to go to the dickens. But, as it so happened, she was not; so the only thing that remained for him to do was to pull up the old socks and take a stab at the programme, as outlined. And he was sipping his morning cup of tea, when something more or less resembling an idea came to him.

He reasoned thus. The wise man, finding himself in a dilemma, consults an expert. If, for example, some knotty point of the law has arisen, he will proceed immediately in search of a legal expert, bring out his eight-and-six, and put the problem up to him. If it is a crossword puzzle and he is stuck for the word in three letters, beginning with E and ending with U and meaning 'large Australian bird', he places the matter in the hands of the editor of the *Encyclopoedia Britannica*.

And, similarly, when the question confronting him is how to collect strawberries in December, the best plan is obviously to seek out that one of his acquaintances who has the most established reputation for giving expensive parties.

This, Mervyn considered, was beyond a doubt Oofy Prosser. Thinking back, he could recall a dozen occasions when he had met chorus-girls groping their way along the street with a dazed look in their eyes, and when he had asked them what the matter was they had explained that they were merely living over again the exotic delights of the party Oofy Prosser had given last night. If anybody knew how to get strawberries in December, it would be Oofy.

He called, accordingly, at the latter's apartment, and found him in bed, staring at the ceiling and moaning in an undertone.

'Hullo!' said Mervyn. 'You look a bit red-eyed, old corpse.'

'I feel red-eyed,' said Oofy. 'And I wish, if it isn't absolutely necessary, that you wouldn't come charging in here early in the morning like this. By about ten o'clock tonight, I imagine, if I take great care of myself and keep quite quiet, I shall once more be in a position to look at gargoyles without wincing; but at the moment the mere sight of your horrible face gives me an indefinable shuddering feeling.'

'Did you have a party last night?'

'I did.'

'I wonder if by any chance you had strawberries?'

Oofy Prosser gave a sort of quiver and shut his eyes.

He seemed to be wrestling with some powerful emotion. Then the spasm passed, and he spoke.

'Don't talk about the beastly things,' he said. 'I never want to see strawberries again in my life. Nor lobster, caviare, pâté de fois gras, prawns in aspic, or anything remotely resembling Bronx cocktails, Martinis, Side-Cars, Lizard's Breaths, All Quiet on the Western Fronts, and any variety of champagne, whisky, brandy, chartreuse, benedictine, and curaçao.'

Mervyn nodded sympathetically.

'I know just how you feel, old man,' he said. 'And I hate to have to press the point. But I happen – for purposes which I will not reveal – to require about a dozen strawberries.'

'Then go and buy them, blast you,' said Oofy, turning his face to the wall.

'*Can* you buy strawberries in December?'

'Certainly. Bellamy's in Piccadilly have them.'

'Are they frightfully expensive?' asked Mervyn, feeling in his pocket and fingering the one pound, two shillings and threepence which had got to last him to the end of the quarter when his allowance came in. 'Do they cost a fearful lot?'

'Of course not. They're dirt cheap.'

Mervyn heaved a relieved sigh.

'I don't suppose I pay more than a pound apiece – or at most, thirty shillings – for mine,' said Oofy. 'You can get quite a lot for fifty quid.'

Mervyn uttered a hollow groan.

'Don't gargle,' said Oofy. 'Or, if you must gargle, gargle outside.'

'Fifty quid?' said Mervyn.

'Fifty or a hundred, I forget which. My man attends to these things.'

Mervyn looked at him in silence. He was trying to decide whether the moment had arrived to put Oofy into circulation.

In the matter of borrowing money, my cousin's son, Mervyn, was shrewd and level-headed. He had vision. At an early date he had come to the conclusion that it would be foolish to fritter away a fellow like Oofy in a series of ten bobs and quids. The prudent man, he felt, when he has an Oofy Prosser on his list, nurses him along till he feels the time is ripe for one of those quick Send-me-two-hundred-by-messenger-old-man-or-my-head-goes-in-the-gas-oven touches. For years accordingly, he had been saving Oofy up for some really big emergency.

And the point he had to decide was: Would there ever be a bigger emergency than this? That was what he asked himself.

Then it came home to him that Oofy was not in the mood. The way it seemed to Mervyn was that, if Oofy's mother had crept to Oofy's bedside at this moment and tried to mace him for as much as five bob, Oofy would have risen and struck her with the bromo-seltzer bottle.

With a soft sigh, therefore, he gave up the idea and oozed out of the room and downstairs into Piccadilly.

Piccadilly looked pretty mouldy to Mervyn. It was full, he tells me, of people and other foul things. He wandered along for a while in a distrait way, and then suddenly out of the corner of his eye he became aware that he was in the presence of fruit. A shop on the starboard side was full of it, and he discovered that he was standing outside Bellamy's.

And what is more, there, nestling in a basket in the middle of a lot of cotton-wool and blue paper, was a platoon of strawberries.

And, as he gazed at them, Mervyn began to see how this thing could be worked with the minimum of discomfort and the maximum of profit to all concerned. He had just remembered that his maternal Uncle Joseph had an account at Bellamy's.

The next moment he had bounded through the door and was in conference with one of the reduced duchesses who do the fruit-selling at this particular emporium. This one, Mervyn tells me, was about six feet high and looked down at him with large, haughty eyes in a derogatory manner – being, among other things, dressed from stem to stern in black satin. He was conscious of a slight chill, but he carried on according to plan.

'Good morning,' he said, switching on a smile and then switching it off again as he caught her eye. 'Do you sell fruit?'

If she had answered 'No,' he would, of course, have been nonplussed. But she did not. She inclined her head proudly.

'Quate,' she said.

'That's fine,' said Mervyn heartily. 'Because fruit happens to be just what I'm after.'

'Quate.'

'I want that basket of strawberries in the window.'

'Quate.'

She reached for them and started to wrap them up. She did not seem to enjoy doing it. As she tied the string, her brooding look deepened. Mervyn thinks she may have had some great love tragedy in her life.

'Send them to the Earl of Blotsam, 66A, Berkeley Square,' said Mervyn, alluding to his maternal Uncle Joseph.

'Quate.'

'On second thoughts,' said Mervyn, 'no. I'll take them with me. Save trouble. Hand them over, and send the bill to Lord Blotsam.'

This, naturally, was the crux or nub of the whole enterprise. And to Mervyn's concern, his suggestion did not seem to have met with the ready acceptance for which he had hoped. He had looked for the bright smile, the courteous inclination of the head. Instead of which, the girl looked doubtful.

'You desi-ah to remove them in person?'

'Quate,' said Mervyn.

'Podden me,' said the girl, suddenly disappearing.

She was not away long. In fact, Mervyn, roaming hither and thither about the shop, had barely had time to eat three or four dates and a custard apple, when she was with him once more. And now she was wearing a look of definite disapproval, like a duchess who has found half a caterpillar in the castle salad.

'His lordship informs me that he desi-ahs no strawberries.'

'Eh?'

'I have been in telephonic communication with his lordship and he states explicitly that he does not desi-ah strawberries.'

Mervyn gave a little at the knees, but he came back stoutly.

'Don't you listen to what he says,' he urged. 'He's always kidding. That's the sort of fellow he is. Just a great big happy schoolboy. Of course he desi-ahs strawberries. He told me so himself. I'm his nephew.'

Good stuff, he felt, but it did not seem to be getting over. He caught a glimpse of the girl's face, and it was definitely cold and hard and proud. However, he gave a careless laugh, just to show that his heart was in the right place, and seized the basket.

'Ha, ha!' he tittered lightly, and started for the street at something midway between a saunter and a gallop.

And he had not more than reached the open spaces when he heard the girl give tongue behind him.

'EEEE – EEEE – EEEE – EEEE – EEEEEE-EEEEE!' she said, in substance.

Now, you must remember that all this took place round about the hour of noon, when every young fellow is at his lowest and weakest and the need for the twelve o'clock bracer has begun to sap his morale pretty considerably. With a couple of quick cold ones under his vest, Mervyn would, no doubt, have faced the situation and carried it off with an air. He would have raised his eyebrows. He would have been nonchalant and lit a Murad. But, coming on him in his reduced condition, this fearful screech unnerved him completely.

The duchess had now begun to cry 'Stop thief!' and Mervyn, most injudiciously, instead of keeping his head and leaping carelessly into a passing taxi, made the grave strategic error of picking up his feet with a jerk and starting to run along Piccadilly.

Well, naturally, that did him no good at all. Eight

hundred people appeared from nowhere, willing hands gripped his collar and the seat of his trousers, and the next thing he knew he was cooling off in Vine Street Police Station.

After that, everything was more or less of a blur. The scene seemed suddenly to change to a police court, in which he was confronted by a magistrate who looked like an owl with a dash of weasel blood in him.

A dialogue then took place, of which all he recalls is this:

POLICEMAN: 'Earing cries of 'Stop thief!' your worship, and observing the accused running very 'earty, I apprehended 'im.
MAGISTRATE: How did he appear, when apprehended?
POLICEMAN: Very apprehensive, your worship.
MAGISTRATE: You mean he had a sort of pinched look?
(*Laughter in court.*)
POLICEMAN: It then transpired that 'e 'ad been attempting to purloin strawberries.
MAGISTRATE: He seems to have got the raspberry.
(*Laughter in court.*)
Well, what have you to say, young man?
MERVYN: Oh, ah!
MAGISTRATE: More 'owe' than 'ah', I fear.
(*Laughter in court, in which his worship joined.*)
Ten pounds or fourteen days.

Well, you can see how extremely unpleasant this must have been for my cousin's son. Considered purely from the dramatic angle, the magistrate had played him right off the stage, hogging all the comedy and getting the sympathy of the audience from the start; and, apart from that, here he was, nearing the end of the quarter, with all his allowance spent except one pound, two and threepence, suddenly called upon to pay ten pounds or go to durance vile for a matter of two weeks.

There was only one course before him. His sensitive soul revolted at the thought of languishing in a dungeon for a solid fortnight, so it was imperative that he raise the cash somewhere. And the only way of raising it that he could think of was to apply to his uncle, Lord Blotsam.

So he sent a messenger round to Berkeley Square, explaining that he was in jail and hoping his uncle was the same, and presently a letter was brought back by the butler, containing ten pounds in postal orders, the Curse of the Blotsams, a third-class ticket to Blotsam Regis in Shropshire and instructions that, as soon as they smote the fetters from his wrists, he was to take the first train there and go and stay at Blotsam Castle till further notice.

Because at the castle, his uncle said in a powerful passage, even a blasted pimply pop-eyed good-for-nothing scallywag and nincompoop like his nephew couldn't get into mischief and disgrace the family name.

And in this, Mervyn tells me, there was a good deal of rugged sense. Blotsam Castle, a noble pile, is situated at least half a dozen miles from anywhere, and the only time anybody ever succeeded in disgracing the family name, while in residence, was back in the reign of Edward the Confessor, when the then Earl of Blotsam, having lured a number of neighbouring landowners into the banqueting hall on the specious pretence of standing them mulled sack, had proceeded to murder one and all with a battle-axe – subsequently cutting their heads off and – in rather loud taste – sticking them on spikes along the outer battlements.

So Mervyn went down to Blotsam Regis and started to camp at the castle, and it was not long, he tells me, before he began to find the time hanging a little heavy on his hands. For a couple of days he managed to endure the monotony, occupying himself in carving the girl's initials on the immemorial elms with a heart round them. But on the third morning, having broken his Boy Scout pocket knife, he was at something of a loose end. And to fill in the time he started on a moody stroll through the messuages and pleasances, feeling a good deal cast down.

After pacing hither and thither for a while, thinking of the girl Clarice, he came to a series of hothouses. And, it being extremely cold, with an east wind that went through his plus fours like a javelin, he thought it would make an agreeable change if he were to go inside where it was warm and smoke two or perhaps three cigarettes.

And, scarcely had he got past the door, when he found he was almost entirely surrounded by strawberries. There they were, scores of them, all hot and juicy.

For a moment, he tells me, Mervyn had a sort of idea that a miracle had occurred. He seemed to remember a similar thing having happened to the Israelites in the desert – that time, he reminded me, when they were all saying to each other how well a spot of manna would go down and what a dashed shame it was they hadn't any manna and that was the slipshod way the commissariat department ran things and they wouldn't be surprised if it wasn't a case of graft in high places, and then suddenly out of a blue sky all the manna they could do with and enough over for breakfast next day.

Well, to be brief, that was the view which Mervyn took of the matter in the first flush of his astonishment.

Then he remembered that his uncle always opened the castle for the Christmas festivities, and these strawberries were, no doubt, intended for Exhibit A at some forthcoming rout or merrymaking.

Well, after that, of course, everything was simple. A child would have known what to do. Hastening back to the house, Mervyn returned with a cardboard box and, keeping a keen eye out for the head gardener, hurried in, selected about two dozen of the finest specimens, placed them in the box, ran back to the house again, reached for the railway guide, found that there was a train leaving for London in an hour, changed into town clothes, seized his top hat, borrowed the stable-boy's bicycle, pedalled to the station, and about four hours later was mounting the front-door steps of Clarice Mallaby's house in Eaton Square with the box tucked under his arm.

No, that is wrong. The box was not actually tucked under his arm, because he had left it in the train. Except for that, he had carried the thing through without a hitch.

Sturdy common sense is always a quality of the Mulliners, even of the less mentally gifted of the family. It was obvious to Mervyn that no useful end was to be gained by ringing the bell and rushing into the girl's presence, shouting 'See what I've brought you!'

On the other hand, what to do? He was feeling somewhat unequal to the swirl of events.

Once, he tells me, some years ago, he got involved in some amateur theatricals, to play the role of a butler: and his part consisted of the following lines and business:

(*Enter* JORKINS, *carrying telegram on salver.*)
JORKINS: A TELEGRAM, M'LADY.
(*Exit* JORKINS)

and on the night in he came, full of confidence, and, having said: 'A telegram, m'lady,' extended an empty salver towards the heroine, who, having been expecting on the strength of the telegram to clutch at her heart and say, 'My God!' and tear open the envelope and crush it in nervous fingers and fall over in a swoon, was considerably taken aback, not to say perturbed.

He felt now as he had felt then.

Still, he had enough sense left to see the way out. After a couple of turns up and down the south side of Eaton Square, he came – rather shrewdly, I must confess – to the conclusion that the only person who could help him in this emergency was Oofy Prosser.

The way Mervyn sketched out the scenario in the rough, it all looked pretty plain sailing. He would go to Oofy, whom, as I told you, he had been saving up for years, and with one single impressive gesture get into his ribs for about twenty quid.

He would be losing money on the deal, of course, because he had always had Oofy scheduled for at least fifty. But that could not be helped.

Then off to Bellamy's and buy strawberries. He did not exactly relish the prospect of meeting the black satin girl again, but when love is calling these things have to be done.

He found Oofy at home, and plunged into the agenda without delay.

'Hullo, Oofy, old man!' he said. 'How are you, Oofy, old man? I say, Oofy, old man, I do like that tie you're wearing. What I call something like a tie. Quite the snappiest thing I've seen for years and years and years and years. I wish I could get ties like that. But then, of course, I haven't your exquisite taste. What I've always said about you, Oofy, old man, and what I always will say, is that you have the most extraordinary *flair* – it amounts to genius – in the selection of ties. But, then, one must bear in mind that anything would look well on you, because you have such a clean-cut, virile profile. I met a man the other day who said to me, "I didn't know Ronald Colman was in England." And I said, "He isn't." And he said, "But I saw you talking to him outside the Blotto Kitten." And I said, "That wasn't Ronald Colman. That was my old pal – the best pal any man ever had – Oofy Prosser." And he said, "Well, I never saw such a remarkable resemblance." And I said, "Yes, there is a great resemblance, only, of course, Oofy is much the better-looking." And this fellow said, "Oofy Prosser? Is that *the* Oofy Prosser, the man whose name you hear everywhere?" And I said, "Yes, and I'm proud to call him my friend. I don't suppose," I said, "there's another fellow in London in such demand. Duchesses clamour for him, and, if you ask a princess to dinner, you have to add, 'To meet Oofy Prosser,' or she won't come. This," I explained, "is because, in addition to being the handsomest and best-dressed man in Mayfair, he is famous for his sparkling wit and keen – but always kindly – repartee. And yet, in spite of all, he remains simple, unspoilt, unaffected." Will you lend me twenty quid, Oofy, old man?'

'No,' said Oofy Prosser.

Mervyn paled.

'What did you say?'

'I said No.'

'No?'

'N – ruddy – o!' said Oofy firmly.

Mervyn clutched at the mantelpiece.

'But, Oofy, old man, I need the money – need it sorely.'

'I don't care.'

It seemed to Mervyn that the only thing to do was to tell all. Clearing his throat, he started in at the beginning. He sketched the course of his great love in burning words, and brought the story up to the point where the girl had placed her order for strawberries.

'She must be cuckoo,' said Oofy Prosser.

Mervyn was respectful, but firm.

'She isn't cuckoo,' he said. 'I have felt all along that the incident showed what a spiritual nature she has. I mean to say, reaching out yearningly for the unattainable and all that sort of thing, if you know what I mean. Anyway, the broad, basic point is that she wants strawberries, and I've got to collect enough money to get her them.'

'Who is this halfwit?' asked Oofy.

Mervyn told him, and Oofy seemed rather impressed.

'I know her.' He mused awhile. 'Dashed pretty girl.'

'Lovely,' said Mervyn. 'What eyes!'

'Yes.'

'What hair!'

'Yes.'

'What a figure!'

'Yes,' said Oofy. 'I always think she's one of the prettiest girls in London.'

'Absolutely,' said Mervyn. 'Then, on second thoughts, old pal, you will lend me twenty quid to buy her strawberries?'

'No,' said Oofy.

And Mervyn could not shift him. In the end he gave it up.

'Very well,' he said. 'Oh, very well. If you won't, you won't. But, Alexander Prosser,' proceeded Mervyn, with a good deal of dignity, 'just let me tell you this. I wouldn't be seen dead in a tie like that beastly thing you're wearing. I don't like your profile. Your hair is getting thin on the top. And I heard a certain prominent society hostess say the other day that the great drawback to living in London was that a woman couldn't give so much as the simplest luncheon party without suddenly finding that that appalling man Prosser – I quote her words – had wriggled out of the woodwork and was in her midst. Prosser, I wish you a very good afternoon!'

Brave words, of course, but, when you came right down to it, they could not be said to have got him anywhere. After the first thrill of telling Oofy what he thought of him had died away, Mervyn realised that his quandary was now greater than ever. Where was he to look for aid and comfort? He had friends, of course, but the best of them wasn't good for more than an occasional drink or possibly a couple of quid, and what use was that to a man who needed at least a dozen strawberries at a pound apiece?

Extremely bleak the world looked to my cousin's unfortunate son, and he was in sombre mood as he wandered along Piccadilly. As he surveyed the passing populace, he suddenly realised, he tells me, what these Bolshevist blokes were driving at. They had spotted – as he had spotted now – that what was wrong with the world was that all the cash seemed to be centred in the wrong hands and needed a lot of broad-minded redistribution.

Where money was concerned, he perceived, merit counted for nothing. Money was too apt to be collared by some rotten bounder or bounders, while the good and deserving man was left standing on the outside, looking in. The sight of all those expensive cars rolling along, crammed to the bulwarks with overfed males and females with fur coats and double chins, made him feel, he tells me, that he wanted to buy a red tie and a couple of bombs and start the Social Revolution. If Stalin had come along at that moment, Mervyn would have shaken him by the hand.

Well, there is, of course, only one thing for a young man to do when he feels like that. Mervyn hurried along to the club and in rapid succession drank three Martini cocktails.

The treatment was effective, as it always is. Gradually the stern, censorious mood passed, and he began to feel an optimistic glow. As the revivers slid over the larynx, he saw that all was not lost. He perceived that he had been leaving out of his reckoning that sweet, angelic pity which is such a characteristic of woman.

Take the case of a knight of old, he meant to say. Was anyone going to tell him that if a knight of old had been sent off by a damsel on some fearfully tricky quest and had gone through all sorts of perils and privations for her sake, facing dragons in black satin and risking going to chokey and what not, the girl would have given him the bird when he got back, simply because – looking at the matter from a severely technical standpoint – he had failed to bring home the gravy?

Absolutely not, Mervyn considered. She would have been most awfully braced with him for putting up such a good show and would have comforted and cosseted him.

This girl Clarice, he felt, was bound to do the same, so obviously the move now was to toddle along to Eaton Square again and explain matters to her. So he gave his hat a brush, flicked a spot of dust from his coat-sleeve, and shot off in a taxi.

All during the drive he was rehearsing what he would say to her, and it sounded pretty good to him. In his mind's eye he could see the tears coming into her gentle eyes as he told her about the Arm of the Law gripping his trouser-seat. But, when he arrived, a hitch occurred. There was a stage wait. The butler at Eaton Square told him the girl was dressing.

'Say that Mr Mulliner has called,' said Mervyn.

So the butler went upstairs, and presently from aloft there came the clear penetrating voice of his loved one telling the butler to bung Mr Mulliner into the drawing room and lock up all the silver.

And Mervyn went into the drawing room and settled down to wait.

It was one of those drawing rooms where there is not a great deal to entertain and amuse the visitor. Mervyn tells me that he got a good laugh out of a photograph of the girl's late father on the mantelpiece – a heavily whiskered old gentleman who reminded him of a burst horsehair sofa – but the rest of the appointments were on the dull side. They consisted of an album of views of Italy and a copy of Indian Love Lyrics bound in limp cloth: and it was not long before he began to feel a touch of ennui.

He polished his shoes with one of the sofa-cushions, and took his hat from the table where he had placed it and gave it another brush: but after that there seemed to be nothing in the way of intellectual occupation offering itself, so he just leaned back in a chair and unhinged his lower jaw and let it droop, and sank into a sort of coma. And it was while he was still in this trance that he was delighted to hear a dogfight in progress in the street. He went to the window and looked out, but the thing was apparently taking place somewhere near the front door, and the top of the porch hid it from him.

Now, Mervyn hated to miss a dogfight. Many of his happiest hours had been spent at dogfights. And this one appeared from the sound of it to be on a more or less major scale. He ran down the stairs and opened the front door.

As his trained senses had told him, the encounter was being staged at the foot of the steps. He stood in the open doorway and drank it in. He had always maintained that you got the best dogfights down in the Eaton Square neighbourhood, because there tough animals from the King's Road, Chelsea, district, were apt to wander in – dogs who had trained on gin and flat irons at the local public houses and could be relied on to give of their best.

The present encounter bore out this view. It was between a sort of *consommé* of mastiff and Irish terrier, on the one hand, and, on the other, a long-haired *macédoine* of about seven breeds of dog who had an indescribable raffish look, as if he had been mixing with the artist colony down by the river. For about five minutes it was as inspiring a contest as you could have wished to see; but at the end of that time it stopped suddenly, both principals simultaneously observing a cat at an area gate down the road and shaking hands hastily and woofing after her.

Mervyn was not a little disappointed at this abrupt conclusion to the entertainment, but it was no use repining. He started to go back into the house and was just closing the front door, when a messenger boy appeared, carrying a parcel.

'Sign, please,' said the messenger boy.

The lad's mistake was a natural one. Finding Mervyn standing in the doorway without a hat, he had assumed him to be the butler. He pushed the parcel into his hand, made him sign a yellow paper, and went off, leaving Mervyn with the parcel.

And Mervyn, glancing at it, saw that it was addressed to the girl – Clarice.

But it was not this that made him reel where he stood. What made him reel where he stood was the fact that on the paper outside the thing was a label with 'Bellamy &

Co., Bespoke Fruitists' on it. And he was convinced, prodding it, that there was some squashy substance inside which certainly was not apples, oranges, nuts, bananas, or anything of that nature.

Mervyn lowered his shapely nose and gave a good hard sniff at the parcel. And, having done so, he reeled where he stood once more.

A frightful suspicion had shot through him.

It was not that my cousin's son was gifted beyond the ordinary in the qualities that go to make a successful detective. You would not have found him deducing anything much from footprints or cigar ash. In fact, if this parcel had contained cigar ash, it would have meant nothing to him. But in the circumstances anybody with his special knowledge would have been suspicious.

For consider the facts. His sniff had told him that beneath the outward wrapping of paper lay strawberries. And the only person beside himself who knew that the girl wanted strawberries was Oofy Prosser. About the only man in London able to buy strawberries at that time of year was Oofy. And Oofy's manner, he recalled, when they were talking about the girl's beauty and physique generally, had been furtive and sinister.

To rip open the paper, therefore, and take a look at the enclosed card was with Mervyn Mulliner the work of a moment.

And, sure enough, it was as he had foreseen. 'Alexander C. Prosser' was the name on the card, and Mervyn tells me he wouldn't be a bit surprised if the C. didn't stand for 'Clarence'.

His first feeling, he tells me, as he stood there staring at that card, was one of righteous indignation at the thought that any such treacherous, double-crossing hound as Oofy Prosser should have been permitted to pollute the air of London, W1, all these years. To refuse a fellow twenty quid with one hand, and then to go and send his girl strawberries with the other, struck Mervyn as about as lowdown a bit of hornswoggling as you could want.

He burned with honest wrath. And he was still burning when the last cocktail he had had at the club, which had been lying low inside him all this while, suddenly came to life and got action. Quite unexpectedly, he tells me, it began to frisk about like a young lamb, until it leaped into his head and gave him the idea of a lifetime.

What, he asked himself, was the matter with suppressing this card, freezing on to the berries, and presenting them to the girl with a modest flourish as coming from M. Mulliner, Esq? And, he answered himself, there was abso-bally-nothing the matter with it. It was a jolly sound scheme and showed what three medium-dry Martinis could do.

He quivered all over with joy and elation. Standing there in the hall, he felt that there was a Providence, after all, which kept an eye on good men and saw to it that they came out on top in the end. In fact, he felt so extremely elated that he burst into song. And he had not got much beyond the first high note when he heard Clarice Mallaby giving tongue from upstairs.

'Stop it!'

'What did you say?' said Mervyn.

'I said "Stop it!" The cat's downstairs with a headache, trying to rest.'

'I say,' said Mervyn, 'are you going to be long?'

'How do you mean – long?'

'Long dressing. Because I've something I want to show you.'

'What?'

'Oh, nothing much,' said Mervyn carelessly. 'Nothing particular. Just a few assorted strawberries.'

'Eek!' said the girl. 'You don't mean you've really got them?'

'Got them?' said Mervyn. 'Didn't I say I would?'

'I'll be down in just one minute,' said the girl.

Well, you know what girls are. The minute stretched into five minutes, and the five minutes into a quarter of an hour, and Mervyn made the tour of the drawing room, and looked at the photograph of her late father, and picked up the album of Views of Italy, and opened Indian Love Lyrics at page forty-three and shut it again, and took up the cushion and gave his shoes another rub, and brushed his hat once more, and still she didn't come.

And so, by way of something else to do, he started brooding on the strawberries for a space.

Considered purely as strawberries, he tells me, they were a pretty rickety collection, not to say spavined. They were an unhealthy whitish-pink in colour and looked as if they had just come through a lingering illness which had involved a good deal of bloodletting by means of leeches.

'They don't look much,' said Mervyn to himself.

Not that it really mattered, of course, because all the girl had told him to do was to get her strawberries, and nobody could deny that these were strawberries. C_3, though they might be, they were genuine strawberries, and from that fact there was no getting away.

Still, he did not want the dear little soul to be disappointed.

'I wonder if they have any flavour at all?' said Mervyn to himself.

Well, the first one had not. Nor had the second. The third was rather better. And the fourth was quite juicy. And the best of all, oddly enough, was the last one in the basket.

He was just finishing it when Clarice Mallaby came running in.

Well, Mervyn tried to pass it off, of course. But his efforts were not rewarded with any great measure of success. In fact, he tells me that he did not get beyond a tentative 'Oh, I say ...' And the upshot of the whole matter was that the girl threw him out into the winter evening without so much as giving him a chance to take his hat.

Nor had he the courage to go back and fetch it later, for Clarice Mallaby stated specifically that if he dared to show his ugly face at the house again the butler had instructions to knock him down and skin him, and the butler was looking forward to it, as he had never liked Mervyn.

So there the matter rests. The whole thing has been a great blow to my cousin's son, for he considers – and rightly, I suppose – that, if you really come down to it, he failed in his quest. Nevertheless, I think that we must give him credit for the possession of the old knightly spirit to which our friend here was alluding just now.

He meant well. He did his best. And even of a Mulliner more cannot be said than that.

DIVE INTO THE HILARIOUS WORLD OF WODEHOUSE

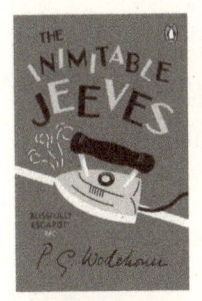

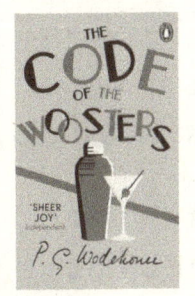

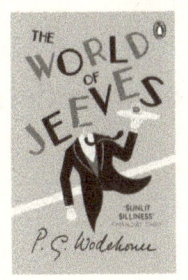

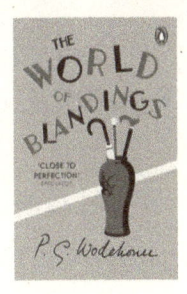

'The purest kind of comedy'

Independent

WHAT HO!

For more gloriously witty goings on,
join the P. G. Wodehouse community.

Visit the official website
www.wodehouse.co.uk

Follow on Twitter
@wodehouseoffice

Become a fan on Facebook
facebook.com/wodehousepage

Revel with fellow aficionados as a
member of the P. G. Wodehouse society
www.pgwodehousesociety.org.uk